Rules of Pretend

Maya Timbery

Contents

Chapter 1

The stairs creaked as footsteps echoed through the slightly rowdy home of the Arthurs in a rushed manner. Millicent was the first to appear down to the living room. Her thick black hair, unlike her other friends', was long, shiny and looked healthy and her flawless dark bronze skin sang with brightened delight in the rays of the setting sun. Her usually bright and open doe-eyes were now squinted not to the unwelcomed rays of light that her brother had caused to shine through their home but to support the little crease that marred her forehead now. She held up the long dress that she wore as the last stair proved a nuisance almost tripping her in her escape. Before she could successfully grab her bag and dash out of her childhood home though, she heard her mother's voice which she had yet again unsuccessfully tried to escape since she arrived home at 1pm.

She rushed down behind her daughter speaking in a hurried tone and an eagerness that always displayed her affection toward the matter at hand.

"Aba, I'm telling you, there are not many decent men today. You have to hurry up before they are taken up by the raging women. A woman is a flower in a garden; her husband is the fence around it." Regina lifted her hands up to readjust her skirt while giving her daughter a meaningful look as if that was enough to cut her message across to her obstinate daughter. The latter's mouth had almost opened up in surprise to her mother's statement. With a click of her tongue which she managed to discreetly hide so that the older woman did not excessively berate her, she frowned even harder.

"Ma, you are the same person that also said that marriage is like a groundnut which you have to crack open in order to see what is inside. So, allow me to enjoy life and not rush into some petty things." She was glad her mother did not have a fancy for blind dates as that was not culture otherwise, she would have run from the city to another location. Millicent being coerced into marriage was not something that was always existent in her life. It started after a year after her graduation from the university, when her mother had seen her pose as a bridesmaid for almost half of her friends.

"The market would give out on you if you also do not take action to secure yours," Regina had said to her daughter in those early stages.

"Ha! Kwabena, listen to your sister eh. Petty! She called marriage a petty affair." The heated conversation was directed to the young man who had his legs propped up into the couch with a plate of fried yam in hand while watching his favorite show pretending as if nothing was ensuing next to him. His cropped black hair, which was lightly shaved at his sides with a little more mass in the mid-section evening down at the sides, gave him a mix of a gentle and handsomely deviant look. He slowly cast his smoky eyes shadowed by his long lashes on the two who stood their ground each and grinned with his teeth displayed to his mother, a way of acknowledging that he indeed had chuckled. His soul-name that had been given to represent the day he was born was rarely used, especially as he had also moved out like his sister, so it took him a while to fully focus on the direction that his name was called out from.

"Please don't mention my name. I'm a ghost." Before Regina could address him again, Millicent turned an expectant gaze to her brother who had resumed focus on the television. He had contemplated whether to move out of his current placement already fearing the impending launch of a slipper at his face for the words he had cast to his mother.

"Maxwell."

"I told you my name has changed Aba. Listen and repeat. Max!" Their challenging gazes met, and their mother had lost complete focus as her children spoke.

"Wasn't Maxwell the name you were given..." Her argument was cut short when she realized that she had to be the compliant little sister if she wanted her brother to speak in her favor.

"Max, don't you think you need to get married? Ma, ask this old man, who is two years older than me and does nothing but lounge in his father's house, why don't you ask him to get married." Max glowered at her as their mother's attention fell on him.

"No, no. If it's moving that way, then ask my brother who is three years older than me." Millicent took that as an opportunity to slip her feet into her shoes and dash out of the house.

"Bye people. See you never!"

"Hey Aba, we want to see a change the next time you enter this house." She heard someone's voice drift out as she rushed through her escape. Halting the first bus that passed her street after getting to the stop, she hopped on and let out a deep breath of relief and adjusted her head to relax on the side of the bus. Her thoughts which had regained calmness after her successful escape went into another turmoil when she saw her mother's name appear on the screen of her phone.

"You forgot the food I prepared for you in your haste." Millicent almost let out a cuss. She might dislike her mother's opinions on marriage, but she looked forward to the food she prepared as this would mean she did not have to struggle to purchase ingredients or be in the kitchen after long hours of working just to prepare food.

"Come for it tomorrow." The said day would be a Saturday and she wasn't looking forward to starving, so she heartily agreed with her mother's options. Food was probably a major reason why she and her siblings returned home away from their busy schedules often.

The next day, Milicent made it again to her family's residence in white top paired with blue jeans. She had forfeited breakfast, while anticipating the taste of her mother's food and getting more food home. The early morning sun accentuated her bronze skin and added a glow that could not be rendered by a mere person or product. As soon as she opened the door to their home, she was met with Max, who grinned mischievously as soon as he set his eyes on his sister. He made it obvious that he was privy to knowledge that she had been kept from.

"Are you ready, Mimi?" She lifted her brows in question but became distracted when she saw the deliciously packed sandwich her brother held in his hand. It was then that she noticed his appearance - his blue Lacoste shirt made him seem like a fancy person going to play golf and he had a pair of jean pants on with the kind of shoes she knew he only walked out to good places with.

"What? Is there more of that? I'm starving. Are you going back to your house now?" She took a step forward and stretched out her hand to reach for the meal, but he was quick to retract it while sending a quick swatting slap to Milicent's approaching hand.

"Go get your own. Be prepared. Bye, I'm going home." As soon as he heard the descending footsteps from the stairs, he made his way out after flicking his sister's nose.

"Aba, you've come. Good, get something to eat and escort me to the market. Where's that brother of yours called Kwabena? He better leave the money for making me cook for him without providing any ingredients." Millicent chuckled and followed her mother to the kitchen. So that was why he dashed out like a dog whose tail had caught fire. Her brother was indeed a little miser. She thought of the good he had done the world by refraining to torture another person's daughter with his attitude. But did one ever know what love could do to a man? Only time would tell.

It was after breakfast and Millicent trekked along with her mother in an unknown territory which did not look like the market she had spoken of.

"Ma, what place is this? Does a market exist on this lonely and isolated path? The only human beings I saw were two people who looked like they were running away from hot water." She twisted around uncomfortably looking around at the tall trees that surrounded the path where she walked with her mother.

"Oh shush! What do you know? What I'm going to get is for your own benefit." The daughter was debating whether to turn back to the civilization she had seen ten minutes earlier, but she also feared her mom endangering herself. But the woman walked as if she had walked the path a thousand times. Trying to calm her beating heart, she stuck close to her mother and tried to listen to the song of the birds in the afternoon heat.

Finally, after another ten minutes she caught sight of an isolated building at the center of a large landscape. The houses around it were some good miles away from it. The white house looked like it loved its solitude. Her mother had turned silent after humming for a while as soon as the white building became visible. There was a cross on it. Millicent tried to check her phone for the location but of course the poor system of geographic acknowledgement in Accra never helped anyone.

"Mama, there's no market. I'm going back home." Knowing her mother's unpredictable nature put her on tenterhooks. Before she could turn however, Regina grabbed the hand of her daughter and dragged her to the front of what looked like a church.

A young man dressed in a white flowing dress with a long staff in his right hand approached them. He didn't smile. He just looked at Regina straight in the eyes and spoke in a chilling voice.

Millicent looked at his pale and thin face with wide eyes before stepping back behind her mother for protection. But there was no escape from the danger game her mother had brought her to.

Chapter 2

"Did Ruth direct you here?" Ruth? Millicent frowned at the name catching on to the weird friend her mother had made a year ago. She pulled at her mother's hand making the latter's eyes turn to eyes that could shoot daggers.

"You're still around that woman? Ma, how many times have we told you to stop listening to her advice. What's this place that she has recommended huh? Don't you care about your children anymore and didn't you say you were Christian. What are we doing at a place that looks like a chanting home?" A loud scream which erupted from the building startled both women, and it caused Millicent to take a fearful step back. It was a woman's voice, and it sounded so shrill like that of a wounded animal. She saw fleetingly, the fear on her mother's face.

The young man spoke in a severe tone before any of them could react.

"Woman, are you coming or not? We don't have time." Millicent stared in anger as her mother took a step forward.

"Aba, this is for your own good. They can help you get a good husband easily. Maybe something is blocking your path." Her mother had never seemed any more crazier than at the moment. She had changed a lot after her father passed away. Now she was struggling to get out of the hold of her mother.

"Regina Bruce Arthur! And how are they going to get me a man? Have they ever created one before?" This might have been the only time she had been rattled enough to rudely challenge her mother and she regretted it immediately after she had done it, and at this moment, it was probably the guilt that made her comply with her mother's wishes. Max had definitely been in the same situation and that is probably why he ran out at the first instance.

"Mimi, please." Now she was persuading her and all Millicent could do was grunt and follow the man and her mother into the dark room, already planning her escape.

Once they entered, she couldn't help but stare at how clean and opulent the interior of the building with the rusty exterior looked. There was a great chair that looked like the semblance of a royal throne at the top of the raised dais and a young man who looked to be in his forties clothed in a golden wear sat on it watching as other men and women dressed in a similar attire as the one who ushered them in stood between the aisles beside the seat where many people sat waiting for their turn to go to the man on the throne.

"What is he? A pastor or a king?" Millicent muttered spitefully to her mother.

"Let the two women who just entered come first." Again she was startled by how chilling their voices sounded and she turned back to see if anyone entered behind them.

"He's not talking about us is he?" But Regina, who was delighted to be able to cut the long queue and be attended to first, ignored her daughter's comments and dragged her to the podium where the request had sounded from.

"How may I help you?" Millicent refrained from visibly looking appalled when she cast her eyes on the weird look that the man threw to her. She distracted herself looking around wanting the meeting to be over so she could escape the nightmare her mother had thrown her into. Another shrill scream sounded from a room like an animal or this time a woman being tortured. Where was this place and did the government even know about it? She questioned herself. Her legs crossed and uncrossed themselves several times in her anxiety and she could hardly sit comfortably.

"She needs to get married." At this point she had no reason to fight her mother. It was evident that whoever the man was, he was a scam for a pastor or whatever cult it was. She had tuned them out and was utterly surprised when her mother pulled her up and pushed her toward the man. He was indeed handsome but he was also old. She wanted to ask what was going on but the man had already grabbed her hand and was taking her into a door.

"Hey, leave me alone." But he only tightened his hand and so with a fearful gaze she turned her head to her mother who stood anxiously watching but Regina shook her head as if she was reassuring herself that her daughter would be fine. Millicent could not imagine but question the woman's sanity as she watched her daughter struggle to get out of the hold of a weird stranger. She should have called her brothers. They would flip if they knew where their mother had taken her or that she was now being coerced by a man who wanted to force himself on her to take her dignity, the one she had worked hard to preserve. She wouldn't let a stranger rape her.

Picking up the vase on the side of the lone bed in the dark room, she struck him, hard, on the joint between his neck and back.

"Is this how you get men for women? Sleeping with them and taking their money, and giving them pregnancies they never asked for? Did you think I was an easy target? I have a video right here so don't even try to get back up to attempt anything. I already called the police so you better run." His golden dress trailed behind him as he run out of the room when she showed her phone.

A weird croak of laughter bubbled up from the depth of Millicent's bowels and not long afterwards, after the adrenaline had washed down, the cries that caused her knees to buckle and fall, after collapsing and holding down to the side table in the creepily dark room, fell out louder than the ominous laughter she had initially released and that reminded her of the cries of the women who sounded like they were being tortured. She felt a warm hand curl around her figure, and she couldn't tell if she was the one shaking or the person holding her was. That was the scariest experience she had ever faced, and it broke her heart to think that her loving mother was the one who put her there. Through her teary gaze, she saw the group of people huddled at the door and she heard faint whispers of how the fake pastor had run away.

Struggling to hold up herself as she stood she heard her mother's cries as she held up her daughter but she shrugged out of her hold, still miserably crying, she dialed Max's number. His tone told how serious and disappointed he was.

"What happened? Send me your location, I'm driving there. Give the phone to mom." She quietly passed the phone to her mother,

Regina who ashamedly took it and listened to the passionate scolding of his son. They had become fathers to their sister, no matter how many times they bickered, after their father passed when Max was eighteen.

The phone was returned back to Millicent who stayed on while waiting for her brother.

"I just told Josh. He's the lawyer and he'll deal with the police." Joshua Arthur, the oldest child of the Arthurs was bound to be furious if he heard of what transpired. Indeed, the mother was going to be miserable for a while but in Regina's heart all she could cry for was a man to protect her child and for society to leave her be because those women she had as neighbors would mock her behind her back as well as her children if they did not settle down with marriage. She was someone who cared too much about the external voices. The society always thirsts for more: from schooling with excellence, they look next at the job you secure and after that is done, they look forward to pressing you down with marriage and the next thing you know, they're looking for a baby. She thought to herself how she had approached the entire situation wrong as she heartbreakingly tried to hold her daughter who had yet to calm down from the trauma. It didn't take much to tell what the pastor had tried to do. Regina's hand suddenly flew to her chest as she tried to beat down the pain enveloping her heart at the situation, she put her daughter in.

Max entered the strange premises with an air of semi-controlled anger. As soon as he noticed both his sister and mother solemnly resting on the ground, he rushed to them, helped both of them stand and allowed Millicent to lean entirely on him. He barely spoke to his mother as they entered the car.

Millicent sat quietly in the backseat. Her tears had barely dried up when her brother appeared, but the presence of his extremely concerned face broke him down. The apology she looked for in her mother was probably the tears that had been shed. It was difficult to ever get her Ghanaian mother to render apologies.

"Max, I want to go to Manuela's." She couldn't bear to be in the stressful atmosphere of her family so she would rather be with her best friend who met at the university. When she saw her brother ready to protest she sent a small plea with her eyes to the mirror.

"Please, I already called and she is expecting me." Even if she wasn't, Millicent would have gone all the same and both Max and Regina who had become like a silent mouse could attest.

Max held his chastisement for his mother being extremely concerned about his sister.

When Millicent got down from her brother's car, her friend Manuela was already stationed at the door waiting patiently. Max alighted and went around to his sister and lightly brought her in for a hug.

"You know Josh and I are always here for you." With a stifled cry Millicent meekly nodded her head on her brother's chest. "I'll come check up on you tomorrow. Try to forgive her. She's scared of us facing the wrath of society- she's forgotten we are now old enough to cater for ourselves with dad." At the mention of her dad, her shoulders shook with her cries wanting ever more that he was present. With another light squeeze, Max acknowledged Manuela who came for her friend.

"I was so scared, Elle." Millicent laid in her friend's arm on the couch as she recounted the horrendous experience. With Manuela's comforting hug she had relaxed greatly.

"I could have been raped today!" Millicent's hoarse voice from crying whispered fiercely, partly in fear and in anger.

"Your mom really did go far but I'm glad you're fine. You scared the heck out of me when I heard you crying like that." She hugged her friend again hoping that she was okay. She met Millicent when they were freshly moving to college and that period had been difficult for her friend who had just lost her father. She had come out of that only to be met with her mother's marriage demands that stressed her out even more.

"Manuela, why didn't you wake me. Now I'm going to be late." The two girls sat up in fright on the couch as the hoarse and deep male voice sounded through the hallway.

"You have a man in here?" Millicent asked her friend in wonder. Before a reply could come through, the said man appeared in the archway to the living room while gently yawning and rubbing his eyes like a baby. Millicent, who caught his appearance first, felt her heart skyrocket through its beats. He was handsome and in her books extremely handsome. His hair was slightly curly and unnatural for a pure African and he was lighter in terms of skin tone by just a fraction to her bronze tone. He wore no shirt and the pants he was wearing were resting dangerously low on his hips.

Millicent turned a questioning gaze to Manuela who just smiled and winked at her.

"You're still here? I thought you had left." That was when the young man lifted his seductive eyes and timely caught Millicent's. He just stared like she was the most interesting thing he had seen the entire day. His mouth was slightly parted as if he needed to breathe through his mouth like his nostrils weren't working. Manuela cleared her throat.

"This is Millicent. Millicent, Jace but he likes to go by Kwaku, my cousin." Millicent stared at the lashes that had captivated her once she saw his face entirely. None of them spoke a work until Millicent said the craziest words.

"Marry me."

CHAPTER 3

"Huh?"

"What?" Both Manuela and Kwaku turned to Millicent with a confused look at her abrupt or what Kwaku then thought as a ridiculous request. He was the first to come out of the moment of surprise the remark had cast on them.

"Are you sure you want to marry me? Cause I'm down little M." Millicent drew a sharp breath in when she saw that the mischievous look he was giving her looked to be mingled with a serious air.

"What in the name of God does that mean and why are you still in my house?" The glare that Manuela was giving her cousin would have been enough to send any other person running for the hills, but Kwaku was already used to it. Millicent's vigilant eyes were continuously darting to the new open chest that was not her brother's and that had begun to set aflame all the desires of her teenage years that her mother and her church had helped to bottle up. Her eyes were a little watery and that heartbeat of hers had ceased to be normal. She cast her gaze quickly to her friend beside her to alleviate her of the sudden onset of unwarranted feelings that were flowing desperately through her veins.

"Don't I help you pay for most of the food you eat in here?" Kwaku caught Millicent's eyes in his hold and he felt his breath hitch in the base of his throat. How could a girl be that beautiful? Her skin was calling out to him but he knew that this was his sister's friend. If he didn't want to get into any other trouble, he had to rush out of there and that too quickly. But her flustered look right now as she looked at him from those fluffy lashes set his skin on fire. He had had a lot of expeditions with the opposite sex after staying abroad in his teens but nothing had taken him out of his element as he had been upon setting eyes on Millicent.

"Okay, I get that but don't call my friend little M. What weird nickname is that?" Manuela's fiery tone called out, making Millicent smile at their bickering. They were behaving like actual siblings that her heart called out to hers right now. The entire meeting had let her forget the heartaches from the past few hours. It was still haunting her.

"What? Millicent reminds me of M&Ms like her name starts with an M." Millicent turned to her friend giggling and shaking her head to her friend to indicate that her cousin was something else.

"Believe me. I didn't know he was that dumb until today."

"Hey, that's uncalled for! Stop trying to make me look bad in front of all of your friends. Well you try but it never works." The two friends were now full-heartedly laughing at the flustered man still standing by the door looking at them. Or particularly at one woman whose skin looked so soft that his fingers were itching to touch them, and the sound of her laugh made him want to laugh and joy in her happiness. He thought he was going crazy when he noticed his own lips were quirked up in a smile.

"I thought the lines from the sibling association was 'why are you always dumb?'" Millicent spoke again in playful sass peeking to look at the man who stood with a little smile and a bit of a wounded ego as the laugh of the two women on the couch was quietening down. But the new words threw them into another fit of laughter with Manuela nodding her head eagerly to the statement her friend made and Millicent was slapping her friend's thigh amidst laughter as was her habit.

"And they say we are the dumb ones." With a scowl on his face Kwaku turned away from the laughing women to the kitchen where he fetched a bowl of cereal for his late afternoon meal.

"By the way, my name also starts with an M. Why don't you call me little M too." It seemed like the fit of laughter that the two girls were in did not want to stop. So, picking up his bowl with a little bit of grumbling and a confused mind, Kwaku made way to the guest room where he slept in his cousin's home. He did not know why he thought of the cute little m&ms he liked to snack upon when he saw Millicent but he had undoubtedly wanted to devour her on their first meeting. With a groan of despair and images of the pretty lady still in his mind, he shut his eyes tightly as if to rid him of the foul thoughts. He was already done with his puberty or was he?

In the living room, Millicent's head laid on her friend's shoulder, trying to sort out her mixed feelings of trauma and attraction for the cousin of her friend when the said man came out all dressed looking ready to go out.

"Ladies, gotta go. Are you leaving now, Millicent? I could drive you." His eyes found Millicent and he was momentarily struck by the bright beauty they held in those doe shapes. It was like every part of her was unintentionally screaming for the attention of the opposite sex like they were singing a song, a siren that wants the other person to answer to it.

"Oh, no. Thank you for the offer though. I am spending the night here." At the response, Millicent saw his face brighten with a smile as Kwaku turned to his cousin with a mischievous look.

"Thank you for your incredible hospitality shortie." Millicent could sense Elle fuming before the fumes came out of her at the way her cousin had addressed her but he had long dashed out of the room with a quick wave and wink at Millicent.

"Make sure never to step into this house, Jace because I swear that I would kill you." The outburst of her friend almost made her chortle but she held it in with a cough. Honestly, it was Jace who was just ridiculously tall because Elle was anything but short. As Manuela continued to ramble how she was going to probably murder her cousin, Millicent's phone rang. She sat up when she saw her brother's name on it which made Manuela lift a brow in question at the sudden change in atmosphere.

"Josh." She called out with affection and emotions from the offense her mother had committed.

"Hey kk." And at the low affectionate nickname her brother responded with the dam broke and she started to cry again. He was one of the few people she could be completely vulnerable with.

She felt Manuela's warm hand moving in a circular soothing motion while her brother's soft breathing filled the device she had held to her ears.

After a while the tears subsided leaving her sniffles behind and when Josh realized she had released a bit of the pain down, he began to speak.

"I would have thought you'd leave the crying to be done in person, kk. Come on, get dressed. I'm ten minutes away from your friend's." She shot up from the couch and mouthed to Ella that her brother was on his way. With a nod of understanding from the latter she went into her friend's room where she had kept multiple of her clothes and she changed. True to his word, Joshua made it to her in ten minutes just as she stepped out from the compound of her friend's home.

Millicent watched as her brother who she had not seen in some months now elegantly unwounded himself from the driver's seat. Adorned in a white Reiss shirt and dark pants, he walked over to where his sister had stopped by his Hyundai car and opened his arms so she could walk into his familiar arms and smell. He rubbed her hair affectionately before pulling back to arms length.

"Now, what do you think about some street waakye with kelewele (spiced fried plantain)?" Hearing the two delicacies that were her comfort food, Millicent beamed up at her brother and he knew he had made the right choice.

They parked close to an eatery called Amelia's Food. It was their favorite spot in Accra to eat those foods. As she gobbled the food that had been brought, the flavors that burst in her mouth had temporarily eased her worries again and her brother sat with a fond smile at the way she was eating. Josh had passed by home to see his mother before coming to his sister. He was as angry as Max had been when they realized they had failed to protect the little girl dear to their late father and themselves. With a heavy chastisement to his mother he was able to leave with a little less burden than he initially had. And now watching his sister, he hoped that that was the last urging to marriage his mother had for them. He knew to get the attention of their sister, he had to be the one to get married but even he had yet to find the right woman and he was a very picky man.

"Ah, I'm so full. I feel pregnant." He chuckled as Millicent stretched back in her seat and patted her stomach. "With food of course."

She watched her brother whose hair was a little longer than Max's and whose eyes were as dark as her father's and in that instant she felt safe.

"You know we are so sorry that that happened to you kk, right? I'm so sorry that I didn't protect you as you deserve." Millicent felt the tears pool up at the corners of her eyes. Indeed her brothers had become her knights.

"I'm going to do a better job at that- at protecting you- no matter how far away I may be from you." She watched as he looked at her earnestly.

"I know JJ." She blinked down the tears in her eyes and wiped them from her face with her forearm.

"And mom is looking for grandchildren to continue dad's lineage. That's what this is all about."

"If that's so, you have more power than I do." Josh looked at her sister as he was lost at sea and she tipped her head to his lap making his eyes widen in horror.

"Get out!" Where's my innocent kk?" They both fell into a fit of laughter at her innuendo.

"But there is no pressure if you are not ready to get married, you know. I'm not allowing any guy five feet from you." She almost thought he was joking till she saw the contours of his face pressed in deep lines and his lips set thinly.

"You're joking, aren't you JJ? I'm twenty-six for goodness sake." Millicent's eyes probed him till he sulked in his seat admitting that his sister was no more the small child he was used to.

"And there's no pressure for you as well, you know that? Both from Max and me. We respect the fact that you respect yourself enough to find a good sister-in-law for yourself." She smiled warmly at her brother whose heart felt lighter at her words.

It was well past 10 pm when Josh brought his sister back to Manuela's abode. He stepped out with her and drew her in for a hug before placing a tender kiss on her temple.

"Be good. I'll be home tomorrow. Max too." Millicent wrapped her arms tightly about her brother before stepping back and allowing him to drive out of the curve. They had gone about to a mall, walking all around and ridding themselves of the energy that they had built up from eating. She was exhausted as she tried to tacitly open the front door knowing Manuela was asleep by then.

Instead of making her way to her room to sleep, her grumbling stomach lead her to the kitchen. She had some pizza slices in the kitchen but she wanted to place them in the oven to heat them up instead of the microwave. She was searching for the sheets to place them in when she found them in a very high spot of the top cabinets.

"Who even places those in there at the top? Aren't they normally at the bottom?" She found a stool beneath the counter at the center of the kitchen as she whispered to herself in bewilderment. Picking up the stool she placed it down favorably and climbed onto it to get the sheet. Millicent had a little difficulty in picking up the sheet even with her great height in addition to the height the stool added and had to step up on her toes to reach for it. Finally, after finding the best angle to tiptoe on, the tip of her finger was able to grab unto the sheet.

As she pulled it out and got ready to place her feet down, the stool tipped and swayed causing her arms to flail about looking for a surface to grab onto for balance. However, the action caused the instability of the stool to increase, toppling her over while her mouth formed an oval shape and her heart to race while she waited for her impending fall.

Instead, she was met with flesh - a part soft and a part of the flesh hard. It took her a moment to register that her lips were on another person's lips while both of their wide eyes comically stared into each others'.

CHAPTER 4

For a moment, the lips of the two remained locked in a more surprising than sensual embrace. Millicent, who was the first to regain her senses and realize her blunder, quickly understood the abuse that she had placed her virgin lips through. Placing both of her palms on the chest of Jace, who was still lost in the moment of the accident, she pushed him with a bit of strength, allowing their lips to separate with a smooching sound. The stool wobbled again but Jace whose hands were unconsciously holding her secured her in place.

Millicent's hands flew up to her lips in fear of the feeling that was lingering on them and she looked at the man who had been tempting her mind since she met him in confusion.

"What the hell is this Korean drama?" Jace regained his complete senses when he heard the sweet tone of the woman, who he couldn't keep his hands from, exclaim. Her wide doe eyes were roaming his face in disbelief and he concluded that this might have been her first kiss with a man. Dragging her body closer to his with a sense of mischievousness as he couldn't help himself, he heard a rather loud gasp fall from her lips.

"Wha..What are you doing?" The feeling of her hand lightly being placed on his chest as if to stop him spurred him to continue his actions. His mind was clouded without a lot of his judgment now, especially with the glass of alcohol that had soothed his system when he had seen her hug another man in front of the house just before she stepped in.

"Tell me, is this the first time you have been this close to a man?" Millicent froze every action of hers as she feared this sexually open atmosphere that Jace was creating. Her heart beat crazily in her chest when she reckoned the truth in the question that the man holding her dangerously close to himself had asked. This was, in fact, the first time that a man had even placed his lips this close to her neck as he was doing now. Thinking of a way to diffuse the situation, she lightly tapped his chest in the dark lit kitchen where they were still standing with her still holding the sheet in her hand up above their heads while two muscular arms circled her waist and two of the lightest brown eyes moved to look at her in question.

"Uh, you can let me go now, Jace. Thank you for catching me." With a light smile, she brought down her arms when the said man looked even more confused than before. Taking pride in how she could render people befuddled with their thoughts, she jumped down from the stool with half a smile as she pushed away his hands and slowly disentangled herself from the man who was still not responding to any of her actions. Moving towards the counter, she placed the baking pan down only to see a pair of similar muscular arms with light skin trap her in. Millicent in surprise, turned around sharply with her arm open to catch Jace staring at her with some misplaced emotions in his eyes.

"You. What did you call me?" Her mind went through the last few minutes before she responded.

"Uh, Jace?" She spoke unsurely, still trying to understand why he was staring at her with those creamy eyes as if he was trying to make something of her. She watched as his throat bobbed lightly and he shuffled a little closer to her with his arms moving in to form a tight cage around her. He swallowed thickly before speaking.

"I think you should be the only one that calls me thar from now on." Millicent was again muddled by his statement when she remembered something Manuela had said this afternoon when they were in the living room being introduced. He liked to go by the name Kwaku.

"So, you don't mind me calling you Jace?" She questioned in a low tone making sure not to arouse her sleeping friend and trying to keep any offense at bay for using a name that the person refusing to let her go right now may have. But he shook his head in confirmation to let her know that he did not mind it. Heaving out a breath of relief, she stared into his watchful gaze and some tendrils of his hair had her looking at those light curls that fell loosely from his hair. It did not look like a chemical had been used to relax them, so the only explanation that she could offer was that he was a mulatto.

"You did not answer my previous question, little M." Jace's gaze traveled along the sharp edges of Millicent's bronze skin and he felt his hands clench on the counter. She was definitely one of the most beautiful women he had seen yet. When those bright eyes of hers found his eyes, he had to stop himself from grabbing her. He was wanting to kiss her again and that was the reason for stalling her presence in the kitchen. Up in his mind, he was thinking of ways to make it possible, knowing that if she was anything like his cousin, she avoided intimacy with men and was going to deny him.

"What question?" Millicent asked in mock forgetfulness, smiling and looking at him while in her chest her heart was beating a mile per second. She drew in a heated breath when she felt one hand now move to her hips and the other now move to trace the skin of her neck with his fingers. She looked at Jace like he was out of his mind but she couldn't find the will and resistance to push him away because in her treacherous mind, this was one of her teen fantasies come to life.

"Will you let me kiss you?" Jace's heated gaze moved from her supple skin, where his finger moved up to the nape of her head to play with her hair, to look into her once bright eyes that were now clouded. His hand was now pushing her head closer to his. He could feel the heat of each breath she released sensually mixed with his and he felt no resistance from her. However, as soon as his bottom lip touched hers, he felt her release one last breath while pushing him away with resolution and quickly dashing past him in urgency. Jace chuckled quietly, still looking in her direction before the guilt set in. That was his sister's friend and normally he respected all of them. Millicent, on the other hand, brought out the recklessness of his youth. He just wanted to be reckless with her. Treating her as another woman who would pass through his life and leave though, he wiped his lips with the back of his right hand, immediately smelling her perfume. With one last shaking of his head he left the kitchen in a haste.

Millicent silently closed the door to the room she shared with her friend and placed her right hand on her chest that was heaving as if she had just run a marathon. Her eyes closed and all she could see was Jace's face close to hers, the feel of his breath on her skin and the light touch of his hand on her skin. She was not appalled by it, on the contrary, she had enjoyed being close to her friend's cousin a little too much. Her eyes flew open at the thought of Manuela. Seeing her asleep she debated whether to let her know about what passed between her cousin and her, but Millicent thought of it as a preposterous romantic moment that could not mean anything. She was searching for the purest and truest form of love and if what Manuela told about her cousin was correct, Jace was certainly not the one. It was by some grace that she had escaped him, she sighed in though as she got into bed. She even forgot all about her cookies.

The next morning, Millicent was the first to wake up and she got ready to escape the clutches of the budding temptations of her heart for the man in the next room. She had been sleep deprived as all she could think about was a man with beautiful light skin, lightly curled hair and muscular arms. Nevertheless, unbeknownst to her that was the exact dilemma of the said man next door as she lightly roused her friend to say goodbye before dashing out of the house like she was being chased. She climbed into the awaiting car outside to be met by the questioning gaze of Max.

"Why are you sweating Mimi? It's just like five steps coming out of that house." He spoke amusedly to his sister to see her frown at herself it seemed, dusting the jeans she wore and looking at herself worriedly.

"Nothing! Nothing!" Millicent rushed out the words, urging her brother to drive out and go.

After Jace had confirmed her departure, he slowly made himself comfortable in bed trying to rid himself of her thoughts but hardly succeeding before throwing his covers over his head and getting the sleep he couldn't have the night before.

The siblings arrived home to the sun brilliantly giving off its shine to the city of Accra in the Tema area. They were met with the breakfast made by the oldest of the Arthurs and Millicent squealed in the realization that her brother had indeed remained home after their time together yesterday.

"I'm so glad to be eating your food and not the one made by a mouse." She spoke condescendingly, directing her gaze to Max as they sat on the ground in the living room.

"Wait, JJ, do they even cook?" She smiled innocently to her brother who was on the couch behind them, lifting her gaze to meet him. Josh smiled at her display of sassy naughtiness but he played along nonetheless.

"No. Actually, they come out of hiding at night to devour the food prepared by others." The two roared out in laughter when Max, who believed he was being abused, grumbled out some intelligible words with his food in his mouth. The laughter and squabbles died down when they heard the footsteps indicative of their mother's arrival.

"Oh, Aba, my child." She spoke in a regretful voice when she saw her daughter. The latter getting some understanding of her mother's behavior had some forgiveness spawning out in her heart. But it seemed Josh had some thoughts of his own.

"Ma, can we speak to you please?" The room's playful air quickly dissolved when Regina took the seat opposite her children with a solemn look.

"I understand where you are coming from with the entire marriage shenanigans, but Millicent is your only daughter and our only sister. How would you have felt if she isn't as bold as she is and was not able to come out of the situation you placed her in unscathed? If she was indeed raped do you know how you would have felt, how we as her brothers would have felt and how she first and foremost would have felt struggling with that abuse?"

Joshua's words were clear and enunciated as if he was in the courtroom doing his life's calling and with the reflective look that his mother had taken and the couple of tears running down her face, they knew that his diplomatically calm speech had taken effect on her.

"I know Kojo, trust me I know. I am regretful for putting my dear daughter in that situation without verifying the sources. But my intention has never been to hurt any of you. It's the opposite really. Ever since we lost your father, I have been thinking of ways to make sure that our darling girl is protected." Regina smiled as she momentarily stopped to look at Millicent and then looked at her boys.

"The world is lenient with you men but not exactly so with women. Even when she has a good job and all the financial securities in the world, she is still subject to the social strata abuse of society which is why I was imploring her to get married. Because once you do my boys and she hasn't, she wouldn't be having this full protection you are giving right now. Your wives would be demanding it." The room was silent as everyone was lost in thoughts of the truth in their mother's words when Millicent moved to hug her mother acknowledging that the woman had her best thoughts in mind. So, she cried with her in her embrace.

"So, my friend Esther is coming to visit today and her son is driving her. It would be good if you could say hi." Millicent drifted back from the hug in surprise while the brothers were no more surprised with their mothers antics. The fire in her smoke caught quickly and there was nothing that they could do about it.

"Are you serious?" At her mother's nod she took a deep breath.

"Okay. When are they coming?"

"In about thirty minutes?" Millicent did not utter a word and turned to her brothers to which Max stretched out his hand with his car key. She grabbed it in appreciation and dashed out of the house before her mother could protest.

Phoning Manuela in the car she spoke of the next level of challenge she had to overcome.

"At this rate, I'd say find a fake husband and let her accept him." Millicent thought of her friend's words as she drove to the said friend's apartment in East Legon. She had no one to have that fake feud with and with their customs she might as well be disowned if she got married without her elders approval.

"You know that would be difficult and which man would I use?"

"We have a bunch of loyal male friends, Mimi. But you're right about customs." A pair of light brown eyes flashed through her eyes and she was asking before she could think.

"Is your cousin home?"

"He is and he is the reason I'm in town searching for a pair of sunglasses. The nerve of the guy. But why what's up?" Manuela questioned suspiciously.

"Oh it's nothing." But there was a very funky plan running through her mind and she only hoped that her friend could forgive her. "I'm here. Do your thing and I'll see you when you come."

Millicent rushed in and opened the door to come face to face with the glorious naked torso of Jace with his hair moistened. With an air of fluid confidence she marched over to Jace who was throwing her a confused look as she walked to him without stopping. Reaching him, she grabbed him like she had seen in many shows.

"Wha.. He couldn't finish his question as she also spoke.

"Can I kiss you?" There was no response before Millicent crashed their lips together in a searing kiss. She had no idea what she was doing and Jace was stupefied into just standing as his hands dangled. When Millicent stepped back he gained his senses when he saw that the dreams that plagued him last night had become his reality in the moment. He crashed her into him for a demanding kiss that went on for more than a minute before they separated panting, each looking at the other with a new desperation.

"What was that for?" Jace's deep voice questioned her. Millicent searched his eyes and hoped that she did not regret who she had asked this question to. After a minute of contemplating, she asked him, once again, the most disturbing question.

"Marry me."

CHAPTER 5

J ace retracted his body from Millicent's in surprise when he felt that the statement that she made was one based on sincerity. He searched her eyes and found an earnest look in them as she watched him with a plea that he could not understand. She was not the kind of person who seemed eager to get married as the customs of the country had tied many down to.

"Hey, hey, hey. This must be a joke." He jumped back even more as if to place more distance between the woman and him. He was torn between giving into his carnal and primal temptations after the kiss they shared and just throwing her out for the absurd remark she had made just a moment ago.

"No. I'm very serious." Millicent looked as he began to pace all about the room in the available space that was not occupied by couches and decors. He stopped and looked at her with a seriousness that she had yet to notice in him.

"Look! I don't do marriages." Millicent grinned and Jace was taken aback by the look she had. She should have been disheartened but the look of hope that she was giving him right now made him think that he had met a crazy person. He had yet to analyze but it seemed that the people who lingered near close proximity to his cousin shared almost the same features with her- they were all sort of other worldly with their thoughts and demands.

"That works even better. Let's get married then."

"Did you turn deaf after you entered this place or am I dumb? I said I don't do marriages!" He all but shouted, stepping back a bit further from the woman whose curly and long silky hair had been tied at the back of her head, leaving the frame of her face visible and her bright face almost had him walking closer to hold her. But he resisted when he saw her mouth opening up to give a counter remark to what he had said.

"No, say no more. I'm leaving." He shook his head in frustration and turned to go to his room. But Millicent was fast enough to move to block his entry.

"Wait! Hear me out. What I mean is let's form a fake marriage alliance. It's not going to be real. I just need to get my mother's attention off me." She panted out after rushing out the words to Jace, who had stopped in his tracks when she had grabbed his upper arms in her rant. He squinted his eyes down at her in question.

"Why do you want to escape your mother?" Millicent sighed in relief and proceeded to explain matters to him. She saw the way he frowned when she spoke about the most recent incident in the unknown market land which gave her the confidence to add the dramatic effects she had learned in story telling from her mother.

"She's pressing me to get married and at this rate I think she'll force me into a marriage that is not of my choice."

"So, you want to plan a fake marriage?" At the question, Millicent bit her lip in anticipation of a rejection of her plan to Jace but she nodded regardless.

"Even though I know little about the culture here, I know something like that will not be easily approved." Jace frowned at the lady who was increasingly getting excited about an idea that seemed almost inconceivable. He was definitely not in agreement with the way her mother was treating her and the strange situation she had placed her daughter in was not what he would think a mother would do. But he was Jace and he avoided delving into family issues as much as possible.

"Who says she needs to witness the marriage? If we show her a certificate, all she can do is accept the marriage. They'll only want to force us into a traditional marriage to accept the validity of the marriage. We can delay that and never do it till I get a man I want and tell the truth." She paused to sit on one of the couches with a thoughtful look and a despondent heart at how absurd the story she was conjuring seemed even to her.

"If I'm not dead by then." She muttered half-heartedly. If her mother did not get to her first, her brothers without a doubt would have done the job by then. That was how fiercely protective their love for her was despite the usual sibling bickers.

Jace, who had been following her thoughts, continued to frown when he heard her gloomy tone. He moved to squat in front of her grabbing onto the sides of the couch and smiling up gently at her. To a certain degree, he had an understanding about how demanding the Ghanaian culture could be. The only reason why he wasn't so restrained was because he could escape out to the US where his father was from anytime but even that did not do much. Feeling his heart go out to hers, he grabbed her face gently with his hand to feel something akin to a teardrop fall on his hand.

"I'm sorry. I'm just frustrated about the entire thing." Millicent sniffed and wiped her face. She felt that she could withstand the pressure and figure her life out on her own without people trying to interfere at every second. She could not even date as the men would try to make her as submissive as possible. Come to my place and cook for me. Come and do my laundry. I want to assess if you are wife material. The last guy who expressed interest in her said these 'stupid' words to get her to be the maid he needed without even asking her to be his girlfriend. She was snot showing any loyalty to a fool and especially not when he had such little respect for her. They wanted a woman who would do their bidding everytime not supporting the fact that she could provide for herself fair and square.

"Hey, are you sure that is the only way to stop your mom?" Millicent stopped herself from being intrigued with the accent that Jace had in speaking English. She had yet to hear him speak Twi, their local language.

"I think so." She said lightly while changing her gaze now that his face was close, so that she could persuade him. Jace grinned at her and stood up with a bounce in his step. The action made Millicent wary.

"Okay. But what is in it for me?" She pried her eyes from his rippling back muscles and thought of a payment that she could give a man, who was a stranger and who was doing her a big and unwarranted favor.

"Anything?" She asked in an uncertain manner. She disputed her choice of words when Jace turned to her with a brightened face.

"Anything huh?" He held out his hand to her. The house was too quiet for her sanity as she placed her hand in his smooth palm only to be roughly pulled toward him. Her hand naturally pressed on his chest which was covered by the light material of his shirt. She could feel all the muscle beneath and her breath turned hotter when her right hand slid down a little. She raised her head to meet Jace's cunning eyes. She felt his hands move around her waist so slyly that she was unknowingly held in place while his other hand moved up to grip her neck.

Jace was a man after all and in this moment, he was roused by that hooded lost look Millicent had in her eyes. She was looking at him like he had yielded control of her body to him. He hadn't even needed to speak like he had done with the others. As he brought her face toward him, angling her head as he towered a good foot and inches over her, he felt no restrain, and so he did not hold himself back from leaning down to bring their lips in a slow and sweet kiss.

This kiss had Millicent hands gripping onto the shirt Jace wore for support. She experienced the curling of toes she had read about when Jace tilted her head. She had no idea what she was doing with her lips so she allowed him to do the work. She knew she was going to die of regret for touching him in this way when she had promised all these experiences only for the man she would love and get married to. She felt her eyes flutter when Jace softly pulled back from the kiss with shining eyes but at the same time they seemed confused.

"This is a bonus. You have yet to pay me for my services little M." Millicent's eyes went wide. For Jace this was the first time he had embraced a girl as softly as this and it had unsettled him.

They heard the gate outside clang which let them jump apart in a haste and recollect their memories of the outside world. With their gazes still on each other, they heard Manuella screaming Millicent's name which made them separate even more awkwardly before the door to the house was thrown open.

"Mimi! Mimi! Mimi, where are you?" Millicent chuckled uncomfortably and walked to the door to meet her rowdy friend. Manuela threw a dark object toward Jace and pulled Millicent by her arm toward her room.

"Kwaku you have to pay me. Now, Mimi, follow me for some hot gossip I heard outside." She looked at her cousin who still stood in the middle of the room with a dazed look with his eyes unwittingly attached to the moving body of Millicent. Meanwhile the said woman timidly looked at her friend as if waiting for her chastening so that she set her thoughts right, so that she could flee from her provocative thoughts as she saw him from her peripheral view.

"What? You want me to pay for this small thing?"

"I never said it was a gift. So pay. Otherwise you'll have nothing in your wallet and room by tomorrow morning." He looked at his cousin with a jarring and incredulous look at her pettiness which he had as well.

"Can't you be kinder, Manu?" Jace finally focused his stare on his cousin who was scrolling through her phone. "This couldn't be more than 10 cedis." He explained his reasoning.

"Ha! Says the one who told me to give him back his biscuit that had already chewed and swallowed. Tell me to be kind when you become kinder." Millicent laughed when their argument reminded her of the ones she had with her siblings. She followed her friend's steps when Manuela turned to go to her room, ignoring the ramblings of Jace. Manuela slammed the door to her room shut before another reply could filter in and directed Millicent to the bed.

"Ella, you know I don't gossip." Millicent replied as she tried to stop herself from moving but her friend was strong enough to drag them both. They heard Jace also reply to her statement.

"Christabel is getting married!" Millicent watched as her friend bounced on the bed, sitting across her. With her mind still lingering on this friend's cousin, she did not hear what she said clearly.

"Christabel who?"

"Christabel Achiah. The girl who was in the next room to us in school who came to fight with you for just speaking to her boyfriend in our first year." She bounced on the bed looking forward to sharing the news that she had gathered from her time out.

"The crazy..." Manuela bobbed her head with a conniving smile. "And you said what was happening?"

"My gosh, where's your brain? She's getting married! And guess who to?" Now Millicent though she did not like listening to the life stories of others as she did not like to be in the situation herself could not help herself from becoming intrigued with the way Manuela described the issue. She sat up on the bed and wriggled her eyes at her friend to keep the story telling going.

"Her older sister's ex-boyfriend!" Manuela exclaimed while Millicent could not keep down her surprised gasp, holding onto her friend who was acting as surprised as her as if she was not the one sharing the news.

"No way! The very same one that was rumored to cheat on her sister?" The shocked tone of Millicent urged the other woman to enthusiastically sit up and indulge in giving out more information.

"The very same!" Millicent's wide eyes looked at her friend who was almost grinning and she couldn't help herself. The two of them were the crazy peas of their friend group when they wanted to be.

"Where did you hear this from?" She almost apologized when she saw the close to offended look that took over Manuela's face. There was a reason she was called the gist queen.

"From Rita, her best friend and her chosen maid-of-honor. I heard there's a raging war in their home. Her sister swore not to go to the wedding. She even rejected being a bridesmaid." No kidding. Millicent's thoughts conceded.

"Oh, but if they found love, shouldn't she support them?"

"Stop being like that Mimi! The man cheated on her. He slept with one of the friends of Christabel's sister." Manuela sneered as she stared into her friend's eye. She was always trying to be the bigger person and sometimes Manuela had to look bad to protect her.

"If anyone cheated me in any way, they better keep their eyes open as they sleep."

Millicent gulped at her friend's statement and swallowed thickly in fear when she remembered the deal she had made with her cousin. How was she going to explain it to her? She contemplated on telling the truth but with the raging look on Manuela's face, she decided to flee from her.

"Uh, Elle. I have to go. I have some work to do before going to work tomorrow. Love you." She quickly hugged Manuela and got off the bed.

"What? But I'm not done with the story. Let me walk you out." Millicent paused by the door and peeked in to see Manuela trying to get up.

"No, no. You just got back. I'm like just three streets down so you know we'll see each other. I'm off. Take care." With that she rushed out only to be caught in the hand of another person she was also escaping.

CHAPTER 6

Millicent felt herself being dragged to another room but she could not protest out loud in fear of Manuela hearing her from her room. When Jace finally pulled her into the room he was using and shut the door she spoke in a harsh whisper.

"What are you doing?"

"Well, if you care to know babe, we need to plan out the entire rambling you did earlier." He lifted a daring brow at her when she moved to protest. Millicent fell silent when she realized that he was right.

"Okay, but it cannot be here. I already told Manuela that I was leaving." Her feet commenced in a tapping motion on the tiled floor of the guest bedroom where they stood with her back to the door and Jace a couple of steps in front of her. Second guessing why he was so eager to ask her, she questioned his intentions.

"Are you sure that you are fine with pretending? I mean I know you also have a family, and this could be a huge mess. I don't want to be one to sabotage anything." Millicent spoke patiently and laid out her thoughts in a non-intrusive manner so that she could better assess the feelings of the man who stood in front of her. However, in the instant he was difficult to read, and she watched in worry as a crease settled in the contours of his forehead. She thought that she was already destroying whatever plans he had for himself by entering this ruse she was planning.

"Trust me. This is anything but ruining anything. You're actually doing me a favor. After I thought it through, I ended up figuring a bit of my own life out." She stared at him for a bit longer and he did the same. After she saw the frown easing into a smile she nodded. She did not want to force a family's prized member into her new found fantasies of naughtiness.

"Good. Then let's meet at 10 pm at the kebab joint at the end of atomic. Do you know the place?"

"I don't and I do not have a car right now so do the honors of driving me."

"Why, how polite of you." They both grinned at each other at the little moment of folly before Millicent cleared her throat again being caught in the light color of Jace's eyes. "How don't you even know where the place is? It's popular and right under your nose." He just shrugged with a coy smile.

"That cousin of mine likes hoarding me." Millicent smiled in a knowing way. Since she had met him, she had heard him going out almost every time she came to visit her friend, and that has been for a short while. Her eyes gauged him, and her voice drawled out skeptically, "is that so?" only to see him grin ruefully in reply.

"I'll be here at 9:50 to pick you up. Do you want Manuela to know about this?"

"No. It'll be our little secret." A breath Millicent was unaware of hitched in her throat when she felt the smooth palm of Jace lay on the skin of her cheek. And to save herself from doing something stupid, she gripped the handle of his door, turned to him and bid him farewell before peeking through the hallway and making her way to Max's car. But then she got to her car and thought about how stupid they were thinking because Manuela was the one who introduced them and she would be foolish if she was going to believe the web of fibs they were starting to spin.

Yet, at 9: 50 pm she found herself parked in front of her friend's house with Jace slyly coming out and opening the passenger's door to get in.

"Hi!" He breathed out with a grin when he got in. Millicent responded with a smile of hers.

"Hi! Ready?" She turned in the spot that was only illuminated with the street light before driving off.

"You're the only guy I know that my mother doesn't personally know. Don't ask me why but she found a way to pry into my life to know all the men I know."

"You're kidding!" Millicent looked up as she picked one spiced meat from the stick she held into her mouth. She looked at Jace and saw the breeze of the night pick his hair up. They had just sat after getting their order and from their spot behind the man grilling the meat, just a bit of smoke wafted across them as compared to the couple on their right who seemed to be bathing in the smoky cloud formed from the grill. This was the time when all the authorized and forbidden love rendezvous took place.

"I wish. But she actually used to pass by my old place which was close to home every weekend."

"You must be popular." Jace lifted a suggestive eyebrow at her while she chuckled at how funny the gesture seemed to her.

"Nope! So, what plan are you thinking of?" Taking the space between them and thinking of the secret plan they were going to be formulating, Millicent slid closer to keep their words just behind a whisper.

"I'm thinking of stealing you away to a foreign country, forging some papers, having fun and returning." He said in one breath. Millicent reeled back in surprise and also to check if he was serious about the words he spoke. But Jace sat there with an air of resolution and shrugged as if it was the easiest agenda to carry out.

"Really?"

"Yeah. What did you think?" He stopped to chew the goat meat he had picked and drank the coke he had gotten from the stall next to the grill. He however spoke again before she could place in a response. "Did you think we could do the things here in Ghana and not get caught? Trust me, these folks are smarter than they let on."

Millicent deliberated as she drank her own coke. The man was smart, that much she had gotten from their conversation, but she did not miss the impish tenacities he carried along with that faux gentleman persona.

"True. But I have some ground rules." Again, Jace lifted a brow as he regarded her. She seems to be smart after all. He thought to himself. She was offering herself like a sacrifice to an unknown god and she was going head in with her trust, quite senselessly. He leaned his elbow on the table they shared and supported his chin with his hand while leaning back to fully get a view of how the moonlight had cast its glow over her skin. At his hum of prompting, she spoke out her thoughts.

"Don't touch me if I haven't asked."

"So I can when you do?" Millicent did not like the way he put the question as if he was insinuating that she was definitely going to ask.

"And what if I ask and you agree." The smug look on Jace's face after she remained silent for more than a moment before responding infuriated her so much that she wanted to slap off the smile he had on.

She hit her empty can on the table in contempt when a groan of satisfaction fell from her lips unconsciously.

"I'm so full."

"Care for a walk?" Her eyes found Jace already on his feet with his hand stretched out. Seeing no harm in a walk, she held his hand for support and stood up leading the way.

As they strolled in the midst of people, they had an easy air about them with none of them delving too deep into their personal matters. Millicent thought it might have been a trait of Africans in general, but everyone held onto their personal issues safeguarding it as if it was a trophy which it indeed was if she thought carefully through people's betrayals. They were moving through the night market open with people shopping when Jace exclaimed weirdly.

"It's not here."

"Jace, what is wrong?" He stopped walking and turned to face her with an anxious look. His hands were tapping the back of his pants.

"My phone. It's gone."

"Are you sure? You didn't leave it in the car or at the kebab spot we were at?" He was shaking his head before she could continue with the questions she was spewing, still tapping his back pocket. Millicent looked at where his hands were searching and apologetically succumbed to the laughter that struck the depth of her tummy.

"This is not funny, little M."

"Don't tell me. Don't tell me you put it in your back pocket." Her eyes teared up while he nodded with a lost look.

"Hasn't anyone warned you never to hold out your valuables in the streets these days?" Millicent straightened up and wiped her eyes looking at the mass of people walking by with some waiting for buses.

"I do not think we can find it in this sea of people." She started laughing again at his expense when he seemed not to know what to do.

"I can search for the location." Millicent laughed even harder and Jace groaned out in annoyance.

"Little M, stop laughing." He pulled her closer by the arm when someone walked between them.

"Sorry, sorry. It's just it's like you said. They are smart enough to switch it off but you can try. Let's go to a quiet spot."

They tried for a while, but it was as Millicent said because all their attempts proved futile. A couple of strangers stopped by to try to help but they found nothing. In the end, Millicent drove home the man who seemed to be in high spirits even making jokes, as if he was not bothered that he no longer had a phone.

"Do you have a passport?" Jace asked leaning over Millicent's window after he alighted the car. Millicent's eyes overlooked him in a tired and lazy way before she bent her neck and raised it to nod her yes.

"A US visa?" She lifted her head with a questioning look but nodded all the same to the man who had his frame leaned over her. She could smell him from how close he was.

"Perfect! Take a week off next week." She could not even say a word in protest at the commanding tone he had used as he had already stood and walked away with a wave of his hand. She sat watching his strong figure walk through the gates and she giggled at the entire night's progress. Millicent knew she had begun to tread dangerous waters but it was still better than her mother's nagging. With one last look at the bleak midnight darkness of the neighborhood illuminated by the streetlight, she shook her head in wonder with a smile lingering on her face before driving off to her home.

Her brothers were going to be the first to kill her.

Chapter 7

The glaring sunlight hit her body with a different intensity than she was used to. Her face scrunched up with unusual distaste at the smell of cigarette smoke that lingered in the air and surrounded her. Millicent was intrigued at how casual Jace looked and how relaxed he felt in the midst of the multitude of people that surrounded them. She wanted nothing more than to hide from them. This place was truly his home.

Jace who was walking ahead of her after they exited the terminal at LAX, stopped when she was not walking next to him. The airport shielded a little bit of the light in the shaded spot where they stood. He turned around to see the woman who kept dragging on slowly. There was a frown on her face, and her eyes were squinted as they moved closer to the sunlight and to the to cross the street to the car park. With a smile he halted his steps to wait for her, and with her reaching him he spoke, "I bet you thought Ghana was hot. California puts that heat to shame."

Millicent would have glared at the scorching sun if she could, but the circumstance prevented her from doing so. Instead she focused on the fair man in front of her as the commotion of people dragging suitcases and getting into buses almost drowned her. Jace was rummaging through his backpack, the only belonging along with his tiny carry-on he brought from the coast of Africa, when she murmured, "Tell me about it."

She saw him turn after getting what he wanted, and he watched her with a triumphant look, his eyes now being obscured by dark sunglasses while his soft curly hair flew over and flopped down his forehead. Millicent felt her hand tighten on the dress she wore - an attempt to try to prevent it from creeping to the hair she was curious to touch.

"Here, you can wear this." Her heart thumped in surprise as his fingers brushed the side of her face when he slid the new pair of sunglasses on her face. Seeing his work done, he gestured for her own carry-on suitcase that she held beside her and grabbing onto that he gestured for them to cross the street when the pedestrian crossing turned on.

"It's normally really nice but since it is the summer, it's crazily hot but the swimming pools and beaches make up for it. Ready to have fun?" Again, Millicent found herself being enticed into all the activities that he was planning. It was exhilarating to be in a new place and she wanted to experience it all.

"How did you even convince your family?" Jace questioned once they moved through the parking where the car he rented was.

"Oh, I told them it was for work purposes. I got the visa after I started working after all, so it made sense." She looked to find him giving her an appreciative nod and felt herself begin to gloat in the approval the man was giving her.

"And you? How did you tell Ella? This was supposed to be your vacation I believe." They had reached the car. It was a shiny blue model of a car that she had never seen before. He unlocked it as he responded to her question.

"Well, if my dad wants me back, who can question?" Millicent was enraptured by his strength as he lifted even the little luggage into the booth of the car. She was feeling so weirdly about a man she had just met, and she had no use denying the attraction she had to both his features and his light-hearted attitude.

She cleared her throat a bit as he opened the door for her, but she turned to ask, "and they just believed you?" She slid into the low car and immediately felt how intimate the interior felt. She had never been in one where the seat felt this comfortable and were so close to each other. It resembled a sports car but it was not. As she continued to admire the car, Jace rounded the car and sat in the driver's seat speaking as he shut the door.

"I mean he was sad he couldn't go down with us for the holidays. He was held by work for a while and has no one else to keep him company." She caught onto the deepening of his voice and emphasized accent once they got to the US. She had to strain her ears more to hear him.

Jace strapped himself and turned to look at Millicent who was still darting her eyes to every item that was in the car in a wild curiosity. He was captivated by her naivety, and could do nothing but stare at her in wonder. She was truly beautiful. In her inquisitiveness, she had forgotten about the safety belt. His voice slowly dispelled her magical moment.

"Babe, your seatbelt." At her sudden jerk and questioning gaze, he grinned and pulled on his own belt before leaning back and drawing in a deep breath.

"Don't call me that!"

"What babe? Does it make your heart flutter?" She stared out of the window to avoid his face. "Well, little M, how do people believe us without my endearments for you?" As they zoomed through the streets, they spoke and engaged in anything but the pending plans they had.

After a long drive he brought her to the place he had gotten.

"Welcome to my home in LA!" Her eyes could barely take in all the opulence and splendor of the condo they had entered.

"You mean to tell me that you stay here?" Her mind was boggled when he nodded, casually dropping onto the seat that faced the opened window wall. "All alone."

"I like the quiet when I'm alone. There is so much that my social tolerance can take." Millicent hummed and turned around to finally notice all the artwork that filled the space of his home. They looked so real.

"Did you buy these?" But he only looked at the paintings unbothered by her awe and shut his eyes taking in the calmness his large home provided him.

"Do you have anywhere you want to go?" His voice called out the question just as Millicent carefully lowered herself onto the plush seat. She was suddenly scared about the kind of person she was plotting her ploy with. It was evident from the wealth that only his home screamed that he was not a simple man. Her attention was sought again when he called her name in the endearment he had created, and she hummed in question when she failed to hear him.

"I was asking if you had anywhere you wanted to see. We have three days more here before we catch the flight to the next city." He was upright on the seat with gleaming eyes as he parroted the ideas to her.

"Give me your best." Millicent slyly spoke watching as his entire countenance brightened with playful eagerness. She knew they had this in common - they loved challenges.

"Rest up then."

The next day Millicent found herself laughing and bouncing around Jace whose smile could not be wiped off his face at seeing her humbled to be a child at Disneyland. Her eyes were wider, if possible, and shining with mirth. It was almost time for the night show and they had bundled closer to the water fountain. Another person walked between the two making them stumble apart, and Jace who had been alarmed in the darkness of the lit park, edged closer to her and grabbed her hand in a hold, knowing the exact moment when he broke one of her rules.

"My favorite one was the one where we fell and went up in the sky. What's it called again?" She turned her body to face Jace and walked with her side profile. He grinned, unable to contain how happy he felt to be sharing the experience with a genuine person who really seemed to be enjoying where he brought her. Jace was full of a satisfaction that he could not describe in words as he turned to face the gorgeous lady next to him.

"Guardians of the galaxy?" He questioned and was pleased enough to chuckle at the little bounce in her step after his question. He was doing something he never did with other women who weren't his family and that was just enjoying their company. His heart squeezed when he thought of his life if they went their separate ways again, making his hand squeeze hers. She was like a bright star that accidentally fell into his hand. But he respected his cousin enough to know to respect all her friends especially this one who seemed to have a deeper connection with her.

Millicent contained her delight at being held by the man next to her and pretended to see anything but him. The pants she wore brushed against his own, when kids rushed past them to take their spot on the railing. They looked like a couple in matching clothes with their black tops and their light blue denim jeans which was purely coincidental, something they realized once they exited the house in the morning.

"Why are there so many people all of a sudden?" She frowned toward the number of people cascading toward the venue.

Jace watched them as well and smiled in nostalgic recognition before he replied, "It's for a show, the nighttime show. We're going to the spot I reserved so that we can watch."

"What do you do for a living?" Millicent found herself asking before she thought of what she said. Shaking her head while berating herself, she quickly added, "I'm sorry. You don't have to answer." She only saw him grin mischievously as they halted at an area with less people and closer to the fountain.

"It's a surprise. Don't worry, I'm not broke for your mother to reject me." She only watched him speculatively, forgetting that their hands were still locked in an embrace till he rubbed his thumb on her hand. Millicent snatched her hand back when her heart pitter pattered. Her head quickly looked straight ahead of her, yet again trying to avoid his deep, intense gaze on her. It always looked like he was trying to figure her out while she was trying to prevent herself from falling for his charms.

She felt him rub her head affectionately.

"It's true, little M. She'll be more than happy with me." He's so full of himself. She thought but could no longer speak as the excitement bubbled up in her when the show set in motion.

"That's so cool!" Her voice heaved with her eyes and phone glued to the water works.

Jace bent down to her ear and whispered, "we'll go and see the fireworks at the castle too." Her head bobbed quickly in agreement making the handsome man beside her chuckle as the colors spilled around them.

After another day of wandering in Los Angeles and responding to calls from family and Manuela, her mood deflated after lying so much. Jace, who had realized this, ordered them ice cream and had the joy of seeing her happier again.

Before Millicent could reconsider the mess of a proposition that she had made, she found her feet in the boisterous city of Las Vegas. Propping up her sunglasses, to take a good look at the place where they were, she saw the tall and broad body of Jace step in front of her. Like most of the Americans as compared to Africans, he towered well over her. Straining her neck to see his set lip which lifted at the corner as he arranged her glasses on her head- one would really think they were the perfect match- she asked, "So we're really doing this?"

Jace searched her eyes to see if she wanted to stop what they were doing, but he only saw a little doubt. So, setting his hands firmly on her shoulders with his smirk, without knowing what the future held, he spoke, "we're doing this."

"Now, are you ready to go see Elvis?"

Chapter 8

A bright orange car came to a stop in front of them after they crossed the street. The window to the side of the driver rolled down to reveal a blonde haired man who was grinning with his white teeth on display glinting in the brightness of the sun. Jace who was still holding onto their bags grinned in the same bright manner at the blond who exited the car.

"Yo Jace! I thought you'd been swallowed by the sea." He spoke as he bumped into Jace for a manly hug. The latter tipped his head up in a smug way.

"You wish, Sean. Back in the flesh."

When they pulled back the blond turned to look at Millicent in awe and then back at Jace in question. The young man and his long time friend next to him had never been seen with an African or African American woman beyond business, so he was intrigued, especially after he had received a bizarre request from Jace.

"Sean, this is Millicent. Millicent, Sean." Jace quickly dismissed the look of interest Sean had thrown to him when he had finally realized the woman's presence. Sean slowly released his hand from his khaki pants and extended it to the woman whose dark curly hair beautifully flowed down her back, and Millicent's big doe eyes took in his tall form before gently putting her hand in his.

"Hello Millicent. It's a pleasure to meet you." Millicent shifted on her feet, taking a moment to make out the words from his slur and feeling shy of the curious glance that Jace's friend was giving her.

"It's nice to meet you too." Her voice came out meeker than she would have liked. She felt intimidated by his tall form. This was the first time she was seeing someone with such light blue eyes and she could finally understand the charm behind the sandy blond hair and blue-eyed people and why it was revered. She felt Jace's hand drape around her shoulders and he pulled her in closer to his body warmth to which she glared up at him.

"You do remember the rule, don't you?" She questioned to which he only shrugged and stared at her with a mischievous glint.

"Rule? What rule?"

"Don't get cheeky with me Jace." They heard Sean bark out an abrupt laugh that caused their heads to turn to find him with his head thrown back to accommodate his weirdly loud laughter.

"Dude, we don't need to make a detour to the hospital right?" Millicent felt the immediate loss of the additional heat of Jace's body when he moved to grip the right shoulder of his friend, bringing him down back to sanity. The two battled in their height with Sean only an inch higher than Jace.

"Oh, I like her." Sean grinned in appreciation at the woman who seemed to be able to stand her ground around the almost always demanding Jace. He seemed to be extremely different around Millicent for whatever reason.

"And I like you!" She bounced up in an attempt to catch his gaze. She had taken a liking to the man after she saw his round of spontaneous laughter. He looked like a very laid-back person and she always looked forward to meeting people like that because in her line of work she has seen that they help to eliminate stress wherever they are. Millicent heard Jace clear his throat and shoot her a very strange look almost as if he was chastising her. Before she could understand the gesture, he sharply turned to face Sean who was grinning and pressed his hand into his fluffy and curly hair messing up its arrangement.

"Did you get what I asked you?" He asked Sean in a thick voice and proceeded to put the bags in the trunk that had been opened by Sean. They had stayed down for quite a while chatting and angry drivers who were looking for spaces to park were glaring in quite an obvious way at them.

"Oh! Is this her? Does she know?" But Jace quickly stopped his friend from speaking any further while pushing him into the driver's seat after he opened it for him.

Millicent watched as Jace lowered himself to speak through the open window to Sean. They whispered in harsh sentences. That was the first time since he met Sean that he looked serious. She was wondering what the meaning of the earlier statement was and the many glances that he shot her as the two men spoke made her even more mystified. They were definitely discussing something about her. She stood by the side with people walking past her while waiting to get the signal to get into the car. After about what looked like a minute, Jace stepped back, his back muscles flexing, carefully studying the suddenly surly expression Sean wore.

Jace turned to face Millicent with a little reassuring smile. He opened the backseat for her and gestured for her to slip in. She looked toward the blue-eyed man who was going to be driving them. He gave her a smirk as if he was not just looking angry. She tentatively lifted the corner of her lip at their weird behavior and entered the car, offering Jace her thanks. The latter entered after her only to hear Sean comment, "Bro, if you needed an uber, you should have just said it."

Jace raised a brow and spoke, stuck in his position of readying himself to sit down. "You want her to sit in the back all alone?" Millicent was admiring the interior of the flashy car as inconspicuous as she could and was not focusing on what was ensuing between her two companions.

Sean looked back for a while through the view mirror to see the pleasant smile on Millicent's face as she settled into the seat. He smiled when he caught Jace who had hardly been able to keep his eyes off of her. The man was treading on murky waters by doing what he was planning to do with the beautiful lady. He sulked puckishly and gestured for gaze to sit next to her.

Millicent enjoyed the ride with the jovial tales of Sean, laughing to the squinting of her eyes in addition to Sean's snorts.

"Your friend is so hilarious." She said to Jace once they alighted from the car. She was stopped in her walk by the dazzling building in front of them as Jace replied, "His jokes are overrated."

"He lives in a hotel?" She shuffled closer to Jace and on her tiptoes her voice tickled the skin of her ear drawing him to bend lower to bask in her whisper. She found Sean exiting the car with a sleek shut to the door.

"Yeah. He owns a penthouse in their suite." Millicent puffed her lips in surprise and felt her heart thump. She knew Manuela was well to do but Jace and his friend seemed to be the extravagantly wealthy socialites of the country.

"Are all your friends this rich?" She was baffled as he just shrugged. Her shoulders felt heavy under the weight of Sean's arms. His jolly personality was ever radiant.

"Trust me sweetheart, your guy here tops the charts." She was urged into the luxurious apartments with his shoulders around her.

"What is it with you guys here and all these pet names?" Jace knew Sean called every girl that and barely worried when he called her that but it seemed that Millicent was not used to affectionate names from strangers.

"Do you prefer dear?" Sean startled in a roistering laughter. "What? Mom calls dad that every time. Damn cringy but he loves it."

"Who uses that anymore in Gen Z?" Sean chuckled, opening the door to his penthouse after they exited the elevator.

"I think I'll stick to the sweet nothings you call me." Millicent shuddered from the term. It sounded like her uncle or a respected person in her family was calling her. Dear? Like my grandfather affectionately calling me. She giggled at her thoughts avoiding the opulence of the penthouse as much as she could while following Sean to the seats.

Jace who caught onto her silent giggle smiled softly at the sound when he guessed the stream of her thoughts. "I'll drop these in the room."

"Want anything, Millicent?" She heard Sean call from his fridge when she turned to search for him after Jace disappeared into one of the hallways.

"Water please and you can call me Mimi."

"Mimi. I like that." She smiled teasingly. "You like everything."

"Don't tease me too." She giggled and heard a door shut as Sean gave a bottle of water.

"What's got you excited?" Jace asked in a deep voice, He held a file in his hand as he sat next to Millicent. He grabbed the water from her hand when she finished the portion she needed and without hesitation brought the rim to his lips and covered it with his mouth, chugging the rest. Millicent, who was taken aback at the action, watched him silently.

"What?" She pointed to the empty bottle and then back at her lip. Jace only leaned forward till his face was in her view, making her draw back instantly.

"Hate to break it but we need to get to matters." Sean's baritone voice called, goading the tempting look his friend had when he drew closer to Millicent.

"What?"

"Sean here is talented in a few departments. Hm like authenticating false documents." Jace answered her question and Millicent looked at Sean who lowered himself to the seat in front of them with a very proud look.

"Fraudulence?" She asked incredulously.

"No. I like to call it authenticity in the eye of the beholder." Millicent ducked her head to hide her smile. He was not wrong. It becomes fake only when it is discovered.

"So what did you make?" Jace dropped the marriage certificate that had been forged by his very capable friend on her hand so that she could see it. "Oh my gosh! It looks so real." She lifted the sheet to have a careful look before turning a wondrous look at Sean who was awaiting them.

"Your surname is Elrod?" Millicent just acknowledged the fact that Jace was still a stranger and they basically knew nothing about each other. She wondered if the plan was going to survive for even a day.

"Wait! How much do you even know about each other?" Sean questioned the two disbelievingly.

"I know she had black hair."

"He has fair skin and a cousin who is my best friend." Sean watched them for some seconds, shook his head and leaned back, finding the entire situation hilarious. If they could pass Mr. Elrod's interrogations, it would be possible for them to deceive anyone but he doubted his young friend had any plans of seeing his father.

"Play twenty questions." He simply stated.

"No time. Perfect." Jace finally responded after analyzing the document again. Sean nodded and grinned.

"Dude it's me after all." Jace just shook his head and placed the fake certificate into the file.

"Now what next?"

"To Sin City and the dunes!" Sean's excited voice betrayed the seriousness his visage displayed.

"You have a city named sin?" Millicent could not comprehend the thoughts that run through Americans.

"Three days of fun, babe. You ready?" She could only stare at the two excited faces with hesitation.

The next few days, she found herself going in and out of sites with the two men - the sphere, grand canyon, Area15, emerald cave and every other spot they could think of. She did stop them from going into a casino at one instant but found herself being dragged into one ' for the experience' like Sean had persuaded. Albeit, she was never going to disclose that experience to any family member.

Before long, she stood at the airport yet again with Jace and Sean. Millicent was locked in Sean's embrace, saddened by her departure from the young man.

"I'm going to miss you, Mimi. Stay in touch." They had only known each other for as little as three days but Sean had managed to grow on her with his good humor. She hummed and patted him one last time, releasing herself from his hold to catch the scandalized look on Jace's face. He schooled his features playfully when he held her eyes.

"Ready to go back?"

"To the lion's den? As ready as I could ever be." Her false excitement drew out chuckles from them and soon, they were in the air.

CHAPTER 9

"Jace Kwaku Asante Elrod! Your legs are too long. Hold up." Millicent only grinned when the said man turned to her with a frown coating the area between his eyebrows. He looked displeased as he had told her more than he could count since she found it interesting to call out his full name. His entire name was only ever used when his mother was aggrieved at his naughty tendencies. So, whenever Millicent called him that way, he felt instantly on edge. Millicent, whose strides had finally caught up with him after they stepped out of the aircraft, smiled to herself when she again noticed the lines of aggravation on his face were yet to dematerialize.

"Little M, what can I do to make you stop?" He groaned out again. Millicent only held onto his right hand that was dragging her luggage yet again to get him to walk while chuckling.

"What can I say? Your name is so pretty." She beamed at him, walking by his side in the vast space of the Kotoka International Airport which was teeming with a lot of people.

"Who did you say was picking you up?" Jace proceeded to question when he realized that the stubborn woman beside him was not going to cease being dreadful to him after the knowledge of his full name. Yet, he was not fully peeved because he enjoyed hearing it from her just as much. He angled his neck lower so he could watch her play with the sides of her top, frowning at the number of people that walked in the airport.

"My brother Max. He's probably going to be here soon. Is Elle picking you up?" Millicent heard Jace hum to confirm the question. She got silent thinking about the various scenarios that could make everything they went up to the states to do go wrong. First, which African parent was going to believe that their child just got married without the consent of their family? Would I even be able to utter the complete sentence. My tongue would have fallen out of my mouth by then! She let out a heavy sigh before stopping in her tracks from the apprehension that was building up in her.

"What's wrong?" Jace also stopped walking in worry when she just casually stopped in their rambunctious environment.

"How are we going to disclose this Jace?" Jace watched the woman with an indecipherable look. He truthfully did not even know how he was going to handle his own mother let alone an entire family. He had hatched a few plans on the long plane ride.

Placing the bags in front of him, he crossed both hands across his chest and puffed up his stance before replying, "I thought of a few ideas. Hm, we could tell them that we were signing business documents but got the documents mixed up with the marriage certificate?"

Millicent sighed against his thoughtlessness. "Did you ever stop to think that we were the ones that made the certificate?"

"Oops." Jace simply stated, widening his eyes for the effect.

"Oh, I got it. We could say the office got our names on the document, but it had been printed on the marriage certificate of our manager who messed up himself instead of the business documents." Millicent shuffled closer to the carry-ons between them when people started to breeze past her as she spoke.

"Wow, you're smart. So why didn't we revoke it?" Jace dead-panned with a little smile, reaching out to hold onto her arm when she almost lost her balance.

"Uhm it's a complicated process? Plus, we like each other?" Millicent watched as his long index finger tapped his cheek as if he was in a serious thought analysis process.

"Sounds good." Jace locked his eyes with the bright doe eyes of Millicent after he finally agreed to her plans. He could not see any other way out of it. They had to be the most realistic they could be. He grabbed the bags again and urged her with a head gesture to continue moving.

"Okay, let's hope this works. I can't believe I'm doing this to my mom." Millicent said in an excited manner when she thought about the prospect of being such a 'rascal' but in truth she was also terrified of what could happen if the lie was divulged.

"I'm sure it will. You have the ring right?" She nodded, thinking of the gold ring he had purchased when they were in Las Vegas. He told her not to worry about the money.

She focused on the direction in which they walked, only to once again come to an abrupt stop.

"What happened this time?" Jace drawled. He was yet again forced to come to a stop and turned an incredulous eye to Millicent who was staring wide-eyed at something or someone in the midst of the numerous faces.

"We're doomed." Jace turned around to see what she was talking about but found nothing. He swiveled back to face the lady who now had a weird countenance, leaving him confused.

"Uh, little M?" He waved his light skinned hand in front of her face to snap her out of her reverie.

"Manuela is here." Jace just lifted a brow, so she turned to face him with the look that he could now describe - she was nervous.

"Okay?"

Millicent focused on the two who stood a little too far to see them right now. Her best friend's brown braids were up in a bun with the curls flying around like boho braids were known for. She was wearing a blue cropped top on her high rise jeans. But what worried her was the person who stood next to her chatting and laughing with her. Max was with her.

"She's here with my brother." Jace shot his eyes around in panic. He was not yet ready to face the lies they were spinning. He felt himself being sharply pulled to the side.

"That was close. Here's what we'll do - I'll go to the restroom and wait for ten minutes before I come out. Make sure you guys leave by then." Millicent rushed out before turning to perform her part but before she could make it, Jace whispered her name. She turned to see a cheeky grin on his face while he lifted her bag up to her. She whispered some profanities before collecting it and rushing off to hide.

Jace chuckled and watched as her curvy body got lost in the crowd that surrounded them. Shaking his head, he sauntered to the exit to see what Millicent spoke about. His cousin was chatting animatedly with a stranger who he presumed to be Millicent's brother. They did share some resemblance, he noted as he assessed him, gradually drawing closer. Cropped hair, shaved at the side and almost the same kind of bright eyes except Millicent's was just so clear that they could reflect the person she looked at.

Manuela caught sight of her cousin and smiled with distaste before saying, "Finally, you decided to bring your annoying body out." Her eyes were darting around in search of her friend who she knew was on the same flight as him. "Where's Mimi? I told you she was on the same flight so check on her." Her hands settled on her hips in a demanding stance. She thought it might have been purely coincidental that her cousin and friend went to the states on the same day and returned similarly too but something ticked her off about it.

Jace scratched his neck, caught off-guard by the detail he had forgotten. "Uh, I thought she came out before me." When Manuela's hands dropped from her waist, he breathed out slowly before turning his body toward the new person.

Manuela spoke when she noticed his line of sight. "This is Maxwell." She smirked when Max's lips turned down at his full name. "Max is Mimi's brother."

"I know." Jace slipped out the information. Max's face depicted the surprise he felt.

"How?" Jace only nodded at Max in careful acknowledgement, not wanting to begin the drama now. He had to get Manuela out.

"Let's go, Manu. I'm so tired."

"But..." But Jace who had turned to catch the mop of thick black hair began to drag her out.

"Bye Max. It was great to meet you. I'll see you soon." Max thought the man he had just met was the oddest speaker he had met. He couldn't question him as he dragged his cousin out. Manuela cried behind to bid him farewell.

Millicent after seeing the two depart, waited for two more minutes before going out to meet her brother who was less than enthused to be running this errand for her when her home was so close to the airport.

Getting to her place, she was the first to speak. "There's something I have to tell everyone."

Max did not know what it was, but he could see that it made his sister anxious.

"Everything okay Aba?" She quickly nodded to assuage whatever worries both she and her brother were having. Max rubbed her hair affectionately. "If you say so. But promise to let me know if anything bothers you." When he got the assurance, he pulled on her hair.

"Ouch Max!" He only smiled triumphantly and quickly dashed his vehicle out of the neighborhood because she had already alighted.

Later that night, Millicent stood outside of Manuela's apartment with Jace. Their gazes locked as they discussed how they were going to break the lies to Manuela.

"It'll be fine." Jace reassured her for the tenth time. He stretched out his hand for her to grab onto as it was time to put their plans into motion. I hope so. Millicent's thoughts echoed even to her facial expression.

Manuela sat on the couch arranged to face the television in her home when she heard the front door creak open after Jace went out twenty minutes ago. However, at the sight of her best friend's hand in her cousin's hold, she stood up alert, forgetting about her phone which dropped in her shocked state. Her face pressed in angry lines of perplexity and disdain.

"What is going on here?" Her lips finally moved after they had slowly made their way into the room. She looked baffled as they turned to each other with smiles. She knew of her cousin's debauched ways and was wary whether her friend had fallen into his wiles.

"Uhm, Ella, take a deep breath." Millicent started, looking at the curly hair that dangled on Jace's face for support. She felt him squeeze her hand. Facing her friend she continued, "We're married."

They watched as Manuela looked at them, every emotion fleeing from her face. After a minute, with an expressionless look she pounced on her cousin who leaped away from Millicent.

"What joke are you playing?" They stared deep in their eyes, communicating unknown information which Millicent knew nothing about. Millicent's anxiety peaked at the way Manuela's eyes blazed, and she had not even spoken to her yet.

"Sorry little M. She's scary. You have to do the rest on your own." With that Millicent stood in awe looking after the retreating body of Jace, leaving Manuela who was still silently standing in her anger. She faced away from Millicent but turned without any indication.

"Look me in the eye and tell me the truth." From the look Manuela gave her she knew the game was over. How was she ever going to convince her family?

"How'd you know?"

"I know you, Mimi. And that buffoon is my cousin." Millicent sighed and decided to confess. She was her friend, and she was the inspiration in the first place.

"It's a ploy like you advised."

Manuela reeled back. "You listened to the stupidity I uttered?" Millicent nodded meekly.

"Aw, Mimi, if it was anyone, I'd probably help. But my cousin, he's complicated."

"It's just an act to make my mom lay back." She heard her friend sigh and heavily dropped herself on the couch. Bringing both hands to her face, Manuela rubbed it tiredly, reprimanding herself for letting her foolish idea slip out to her friend.

"How long is it going to be an act?" Millicent knew that Manuela was extremely worried for her heart, but it looked more than a simple worry. She didn't know how long the act would be. She only wished not to be swallowed up by her own plan.

Chapter 10

"So that's why you went to the US?" Millicent gulped when Manuela set her eyes on Jace who had reentered the room and was now sitting by his accomplice. "You better not use my friend."

Jace's eye twitched, speechlessly eyeing his cousin. He shifted on his seat to settle on the edge and crossed his hand before asking, "But she can use me?" His right brow perfectly lifted, but even he knew that the gesture was ineffective on her.

"Yes." Manuela replied without a thought, and that had Millicent springing from her seat to attach herself to her friend. She curled her arm around Manuela's left arm, and leaned her head on her shoulder. She caught Jace watching her with his smooth long lashes trying to conceal the fact. With her youthful tendencies, she stuck out her tongue to him to see his pink lips stretch out in a sweet smile and she reflected the action. Unbeknown to them, Manuela had caught the interaction.

"And you!" Millicent startled from beside her friend, sat up in hypervigilance, slightly orienting herself away from her. "Don't think about falling for this boy. We'll look for a man for you."

Jace frowned when Manuela turned to give her one of her usual triumphant looks whenever she was able to win an argument. He couldn't speak because she continued to add to what she was saying to Millicent.

Manuela twisted her body so that she was facing Millicent, and she drew their hands together on her lap. "You two are adults and I hope you know what you are doing. Are you ready to face your parents? There are other ways to handle the situation."

"I'm sorry Ella, you're not being coerced into a marriage that you didn't ask for. If this is the only way to live a good life then so be it." From her peripheral, Manuela caught Jace nod with a very serious look on his face. She hoped her cousin did not use Millicent, the kindhearted, spunky friend of hers, for his own gains. He told her that it was nothing like that but she knew him. Helping a stranger, even her friend, would come at a price. She found that her eyes were on him as she was lost in her thoughts, and he in turn gave her a questioning gaze.

"I know love. That is a difficult situation. I'm here if you need me." Millicent moved closer as her friend brought her arms around her for a hug.

The next day, Millicent sat in her car with Jace in the passenger seat. She slanted her head to catch the profile of the young African-American who looked better than good. He was wearing a blue polo shirt that stretched against the muscled chest wall over white pants. His slightly blue-gray irises shone in the sunlight and his hair was styled backward with a few untamed ones falling out.

He sat casually in his seat like he owned the entire world and it took Millicent a while to acknowledge that his eyes had focused on her for a while. Her breath caught when she readjusted her sight to see his eyes intently on her face.

"I'm so nervous." She whispered out softly. He unblinkingly cast his gaze to her plump brown lips, thickly swallowing the air that blocked his throat before whispering also, "I'm here."

Millicent grinned and teasingly supplied, "I'm more worried about you."

"Okay, I think we're good to go inside now." Jace declared loudly, drawing a snicker from her. But she did what he said and got out of her Toyota corolla that was parked outside the gate of her home. Jace followed suit and got out. When she rounded the car to his side, he naturally grabbed hold of her hand, its smoothness pressing to his own, and he was pulled into the yellow coated house after they passed through its gate.

Millicent didn't hear anything come from her childhood home for a while till the rushing footsteps pattering became loud enough. She didn't have time to position herself before a small body collided with her.

"Aba!" A little voice called out and she didn't know whether to be excited or scared at the encounter with her little cousin.

"Bridget!" She delightedly bounced up her five-year old cousin onto her hip, releasing her hold on Jace who stood in the room admiring the interaction between the two. Millicent tickled Bridget on her side and asked, "How are you little one?"

"I'm fine!" She responded, enthused to see one of her favorites who always provided her with sweets. Bridget's eyes moved to rest on Jace whose hands now rested in his pocket watching the little child with open curiosity. Bridget leaned into Millicent's ear and asked the question which although whispered could be heard by bystanders as far as ten feet away. "Who is he?"

"My husband." Millicent simply stated, moving closer to Jace who grinned at the delivered information. Bridget let out a scandalous gasp at the same time that the sound of a shattering glassware reached their ears.

Jace turned to see an older woman and Millicent's brother whom he had met at the airport, standing still with similar astonished looks.

"You..." The woman stopped speaking yet again lost in shock.

"Aba, what did you say?" Millicent's wide eyes looked from the new intrusion to Jace, who stood next to her with an indifferent look, only smiling at her aunt and brother who entered. This was not how she wanted the news to be delivered.

Jace moved to the two leaving Millicent behind. "Hello, we meet again. I'm Jace Elrod, Millicent's husband." Jace came to a stop, spoke and reached out his hand. The tall woman next to Max, with her hair braided in a cornrow, came out of her reverie, to look at Jace in awe. She took a while to decipher the words he spoke because his accent was different than she was used to.

But without warning she screamed, "Regina!" Millicent registered the name of her mother flying from her aunt's mouth but also caught the confused aura around Max. The said brother breezed past Jace, grabbed onto his sister who had set Bridget down with a candy she found in her purse and dragged her to one of the guest rooms on the ground floor.

"Stop pulling me so roughly."

"What's going on Mimi?" She watched her brother take an intimidating step in front of her, a dangerous frown on his face, while
his arms settled across his broad chest. She had to force her head
up as he loomed over her with his height.

"I married a guy I liked." She simply stated to see his face harden
more.

"That makes no sense. Just days ago, you were crying not to get
married. And this is not culture, the family will never recognize it
until we have proof." She tried to rack her brain for a solid response.

"We got married in the US with a certificate." Millicent rambled
on proud at how the lies were flying through her mouth without
giving herself away.

"You're not joking? You didn't even ask for consent!" If this was
Max, then Josh would be the one to kill her. She gulped at the tense
way his dark eyes regarded her and shook her head. She couldn't
back out now.

"You married your friend's cousin who lives in the states, and
who we've never heard about, and you want me to believe the
nonsense that you like each other?" Harsh breaths came out as
Max shouted moving to roughly grab her arm as if he was shaking
her into a new reality. Millicent less confidently nodded this time.
Even if they knew it was a lie, she would persuade the lie into the
deepest parts of their brains to be the truth.

Max with a long hard look, tried to see past her but looking to
see that his anger could harm his sister, angrily stormed out of the
room slamming the door shut. "I'm never agreeing to this!"

After the door slammed shut, Millicent closed her eyes and
slowly slid down the wall to which her back stood as they spoke.

With three shaky breaths, she stood up to go and deal with her mother too.

When Millicent exited the room, she was baffled at the scene in front of her. Her mother and her aunt coddled Jace who was sitting on one of the couches happily laughing with the two. Her mother was the first to notice her.

"Ei, Aba, Kwaku 'broni' explained to me that you are his wife." She found Jace's eyes, and raised her brows at him, but he looked at her concerned at how her brother stormed through the room earlier. Millicent catching onto his concern shook her head in dismissal. Being reassured that she was alright, he sent a discreet wink conveying his success.

"Oh, yes. I'm sorry that we didn't do it the right way."

"That's okay. Kwaku here was telling me how you two like each other and that's why you are here. You don't want to do the custom marriage now right?" Millicent subtly looked at Jace, maybe she should have let him deal with Max. Seeing that he was able to convince her mother who was more difficult than the brothers.

"Uh, yes?" Jace lightly laughed under his breath, taking the juice that her aunt, Anita, brought for him. She smiled in adoration making him a little wary. It seemed like Millicent's family more than liked him.

"Come and sit Aba. I brought juice for you too." Millicent warily walked to sit next to Jace for whom they were treating her like a princess.

"Thank you, auntie Anita." But her aunt was staring at Jace, particularly his hair.

"How did his hair get this curly, isn't he Ghanaian?" She asked in their local Fanti language to avoid Jace discerning what they spoke. Her mother also listened with keen interest even while she spoke with Jace.

"His father is white." Millicent awkwardly answered, feeling apologetic that they were discussing someone who was present without his knowledge. The two sisters appreciatively watched Jace who was beginning to feel the interrogation from the stares and reached out to Millicent for her hand. Her mother discreetly turned to her sister and they both shared a victorious smile. To them, her presenting Jace as her husband didn't matter as much as her finding a man to add to the family. Their claim of marriage was also not complete until the man came to pay the dowry.

"So, when did you two meet?" Max, who finally seemed normal, had joined them for supper. He was quick to interrogate the two since their oldest was not around and their mother was not seriously considering the situation.

"In 2023."

"2028." Millicent said to everyone's astonishment. Jace forced himself to hold back the snicker and schooled his look of incredulity. He shifted on the dining seat he sat on to face Millicent. His lips were tucked in his mouth while he cutely tilted his head. His hand reached out to push her hair back.

"What are you saying little M? 2028 is in four years from now." The older women watched their daughter who was being spoiled by her supposed husband with gratified looks. Even Max coughed out a hidden laugh. Millicent's leg bounced continuously under the table where they were eating their dessert. Her little cousin laughed raucously at her expense, and she turned to glare at her.

"No more sweets for you Bridget." She leaned closer to Jace to whisper in his ears.

"I'm so nervous." He grabbed onto her hand and rubbed it with his thumb in soothing circles. Luckily after that embarrassing answer, Max left them alone, refusing to admit that he had begun to like the young man next to her seeing how he carefully tended to his sister.

"I can't believe I said that!" Millicent's aggrieved voice spoke as they got out of the car in the darkness of the night after Jace teased her endlessly.

"Aw it's okay little M. You just let them know there's room for a future husband."

"I'll slap that smirk off your face." Jace felt so content in her presence that he failed to realize that this was one of the few times he could be himself around someone he barely knew.

A dark figure standing on the porch with Manuela caused Jace to stop his gait. Millicent also stopped and lightly touched his hand.

"We're doomed!" He spoke silently, still looking at the two figures who had yet to discover their appearance. Millicent scrunched her face in the direction of the lit porch before seeing who Jace saw.

"We can't catch a break! That's my mom." Millicent's heart stilled the same moment that the beautiful lady's eyes turned from Manuela and rested on hers.

CHAPTER 11

"Mom!" Jace called out excitedly, gently tugging Millicent who stood frozen at the sight of his mother. His mother watched him with a distasteful smile.

"So, you know your mother? I thought Manuela had become your mother. You know the things you want to do is the reason you left me in that big house alone." Reaching her, Jace walked over to hug his mother. Unlike other people in the country, he was presently in, he grew up with a lot of physical touch and basked in that form of affection.

"I missed you too, mom." His mother pulled back to take in his entire body to calculate the state of his health. Manuela moved to stand beside her friend while her aunt greeted Jace.

"How'd it go?" She murmured to Millicent, making sure she stood as close as the hairs of their arms could touch to keep the conversation between them.

"You'll be surprised." Millicent responded and smiled while keeping her eyes on Jace and his mother. She had yet to acknowledge her.

"Just so you know. She knows you guys are married. She doesn't know it's fake. S-" Manuela's words were swallowed back when her aunt finally called out to Millicent.

"And who is this with you?" Millicent then realized the sophistication that hovered around his mom even in the African print maxi dress she wore. She looked regal. Her natural hair was put in a sleep gelled form with a braided extension attached as a pony tail. She was almost as tall as her son but that could be an advantage her two-inch wedge heel that peeked out of her dress offered.

"This is Millicent. She is, uh, Manu's best friend." Millicent saw the ends of the woman's lips curl up in a sly way. Manuela just shook her head but was also surprised at her aunt's calmness.

"Is that so?" Jace doubled trying to call Manuela with his eyes, but the latter was reassuring her friend who didn't know what to do. "Let's go inside. We can't stand out here forever."

"Uh, yes, Mimi is my friend, aunt Josephine." Manuela spoke while she ushered Millicent into the house after her aunt and cousin entered. Josephine just hummed to acknowledge what she heard. They all settled in the blue leather couches in the living room.

"So what is this I hear about getting married in Las Vegas." Jace's complexion paled, stiffly sat up and let out a quick laugh. He turned to his cousin who watched in mirth but nodded all the same to his questioning look. He turned his head to Millicent who for the first time looked more composed than he did. He relaxed his form and found his mother's waiting gaze. She had fully crossed her leg and leaned back elegantly in her seat.

"Yes mom, I got married to a girl I like." His mother silently watched Millicent who kept her watchful gaze on the woman but had yet to talk. Both of them seemed to be assessing the other.

"Introduce us then."

"That's it? You aren't going to roar?" She watched her son amusingly. Because he grew abroad he seemed to be lacking knowledge of their culture. No family would accept the marriage until the dowry or the bride price was fully accounted for. She thought the girl should know better. Looking now, she saw her son's gaze resting on Millicent. He wasn't aware of how his eyes searched for her so she knew it was an attraction and nothing more. But she was happy he had found someone she would probably like.

"When did you two meet?" Millicent and Jace's matching grins went unnoticed by their company as they simultaneously responded, "In 2023." Manuela stilled and shook her head in wonder with her mouth agape as she looked from one to the other. They were crazy.

"And where did you meet?" Josephine interrogated further.

"On Instagram."

"Facebook." A breathy laugh escaped Manuela. The two just went head straight into the plan without any plan. Which was surprising for someone like Jace who was usually calculating.

Josephine's lips twitched and she relaxed herself into her seat, untangling her legs. She stared intently at Millicent. "You know nothing about each other, do you?" Millicent shook her head, admitting to the statement, before she could stop herself.

"Why did you get married?" Looking at where her eyes were, they knew the question was directed at Millicent. The latter didn't have to think hard about the question.

"Since knowing Jace, I've found him to be extremely caring even though he hides behind the curtains of a harsh face or playful shenanigans, he also loves with all he has- he withholds nothing."

Her eyes quickly found Jace, who was already looking at her, and she softly smiled to which he felt his heart skip a beat. "That's why he is scared to open up to anyone he hasn't known for long; he's afraid of being heartbroken because he wants someone to love him in the same capacity. And because I've seen it all, I want to be the person that does that. Loving him the way he deserves."

Jace almost believed her words. It felt impossible the way he had seen through him like no one else had. Manuela was awed by the potential her friend had to become an actress. She had said all that so earnestly that it almost moved her to tears. And the way she looked at Jace, almost as if they were in love!

Millicent spoke the truth. Well, she didn't want to marry him, but she spoke everything she had seen when they traveled.

Josephine regarded the young woman with a neutral face but inwardly she was overjoyed that someone who understood her son almost as well as she did, had come their way. She was going to leave fate to play its game with them. Unwinding herself from the couch, she stood, her presence instantly filling the small space.

"Well, we do need to bring your bride price to make it official." Millicent and the cousins were instantly on their feet, all shaking their heads in denial.

"No! I mean we want to be around each other physically for a while before having the traditional marriage." She was astonished at how she was making such realistic remarks.

"That's fair. Young kids in love." Josephine spoke wistfully while Jace moved around to stand beside Millicent, draping an arm around her before leaning down as if giving her a peck on the cheek when he was actually making a silent conversation.

"Have I told you how smart you are?"

"And you never follow rules."

"We need to touch to make them believe, little M." They jumped apart when Manuela cleared her throat. Josephine finally smiled broadly at their interaction. Millicent could be the hope of her son which is why she did not want the said son to destroy this opportunity.

"And you, Kwaku, your dad is coming in two weeks." Jace was again startled. "And remember that you are not married until you pay the dowry even if you have the certificate." She pointedly said to the 'couple' hinting again that their marriage was not official to the families even if the entire world accepted the proof they had. That was how Ghanaians, honored their families before they left for marriage.

"That's early." His mother ignored him and continued.

"Solve it and don't hurt Millicent otherwise I'll personally skin you." His eyes widened at his mother's words. The turn of events for the day was making him lightheaded.

"Aw my sweet, sensible auntie." Manuela eulogized her aunt with a hug, teasing her cousin behind the woman's head. Jace only stood there in deep thought, coming down to his usual solemn look. Millicent stood in fear. Hell was going to fall on earth if everything was disclosed. Also, it was so bizarre how the adults received the news, as if the broken traditions were the least of their concern.

Josephine moved to hug Millicent after she separated from her niece, leaving the woman stunned. Even Jace had a shocked look. "I'm sorry about my foolish son. If your family is angry at the lack of consent, my husband and I would pass by." Josephine spoke, pulling her to arm's length.

"I think my mother is fine with it." Josephine shook her head.

"We need a family introduction. We know nothing about each other, and I don't want to be the disrespectful elder." Millicent helplessly looked toward Manuela.

"Auntie, let's take it casual for the time being. No one but the immediate family knows, so we can relax." The woman nodded after thinking a while. Turning to her son, she smacked him on the back of his head.

"Ouch." Jace stared open-mouthed at his mother. He was receiving the punishment of a ploy he was helping out with. He never knew all these were requirements and Millicent never said it.

"How do you secretly marry the girl-child of a family without approval first? Did you add your money for her upbringing?" He sent a discreet glare to Millicent who grinned and shrugged. Checking her phone that she carried in her hand beside her yellow purse, she muttered some incomprehensible words, before continuing to address her son.

"I have to go now. Make sure no one else hears of your stupidity before we correct it." He gulped at the threat. His mother never uttered empty threats.

Jace discarded the words like floating letters carried by the wind before stepping in to embrace his mother. "I like her." Josephine whispered while her keen eyes faced Millicent with a hint of a smile in them. Jace only snuggled closer wishing he could let her know that though he liked Millicent for who she was, eternity with her was far from the picture he had, even if he thought he was attracted to the said girl. Ultimately, an attraction is but for a moment. Jace's thoughts calmed his distressed mind and heart after he broke apart from his mother.

"Come visit me, Millicent. Just let this one know and he'll bring you. If he doesn't let Manuela know, I'll send you a car." Josephine affectionately offered, holding Millicent's hand in her own before giving her a quick side hug.

"I'll see you out auntie." Manuela saved the two, silently telling them with her eyes to discuss what they needed to.

"We'll come too." Josephine grinned at Millicent for the first time in the entire night, warmly shaking her head with disapproval.

"No, no dear. You two enjoy your time together. Manuela will see me out." Manuela threw her cousin a displeasing look- she did not like that they had just deceived her. However, seeing Millicent's pleading eyes, she only sighed and continued to escort Josephine. She walked out with Josephine leaving the fake couple behind.

Immediately the door shut behind them, Jace sharply turned to Millicent who was busy taming her long wild curls with her hand. Her eyes shot up in surprise when he exclaimed, dispersing the moment of calmness she was basking in.

"You!" Jace's smoldering eyes set on the woman who he had come to find as extremely intelligent. He stalked toward her but Millicent stepped back, a step at a time matching his predatory movement, till her back hit the wall. She watched as the attractive young man hovered over her both in fear and growing excitement. Jace clapped his hand on the wall above her head, causing her to sink lower and he bent lower intensely staring into her doe eyes with their dark brown irises. Her smooth skin shone up at him.

Millicent, gulped and shyly looked back into his eyes, cowering from their attractive intensity. "Me?" She asked.

"Yes you." Jace whispered, his smoldering eyes turning soft. His hand snaked around her waist pulling her up as his chest raced with the same speed hers was. The air thickened around them. His hand was soft on her, making Millicent squirm in an unknown delight.

"We need to get to know each other." His breathy voice continued. "We sound stupid with the answers we give." As he stood watching her, he realized he was indeed enticed by the beauty he held. His eyes always searched for her radiance so that it could brighten his gloomy days, and this was just someone he had just met. For some reason he was almost always instantly calm and content in her presence and he craved that feeling whenever she was away. His voice in the moment they shared was proof.

"Okay." Millicent whispered.

"We have two weeks." His eyes drifted to her plump lips that were currently parted. Millicent's chest rapidly rose and fell when she caught his eyes falling on her lips. She couldn't believe how quickly the air changed between them. Jace's hair lowered a little while waiting for her and she did speak.

"Manuela?"

"My mom likes talking." And seeing no more resistance, he dipped his head and captured what troubled his dreams since he met her. She didn't know she troubled his dreams and this kiss made it reality.

Chapter 12

The rooster crowed being highly exuberant to see the first rays of the sun, waking up most in the city of East Legon. Meanwhile, the hens like most mothers started clucking in preparation for the day at dawn right before the daybreak. Millicent laid in her bed oblivious to how nature sought to wake up the light sleepers in its own way. Her legs wagged in the air, with the rest of her body laying face down on her blue floral print silk bed sheet. A pillow propped up her chest and her head was held up by one of her arms to accommodate her posture and enable her to read her bible that was open up before her for her devotion. She knew she was not as devout as she wanted to be but she never left her home in the morning without seeking out the book.

She hummed out a tune she learnt from her Sunday school days, smiling at the memories the tune evoked.

Out of the blue, the image of thin pink lips engulfing her dark full lips took over the words she was meditating on. Millicent quickly shut her eyes to try to dispel the image; however, the tighter the lids of her eyes pressed together, the more vivid the image played behind her closed eyes. Her eyes again snapped open, and she hit her hand on her bed in frustration when she felt the loud and hard beating of her heart within its cage.

"This is why I didn't want him to touch me. Now I'm seeing these unholy images during my devotion!" She muttered out, feeling especially confused at the way her body was behaving at the mere flashback of Jace. She sat up fully on her bed unable to enjoy the peace she craved. She was going to put her heart in a perilous situation like Manuela had said, if she indulged in her new feelings for a man who probably did not care; not that she was looking for a love life. The said man was just helping her because of his pity on her unfamiliar predicament.

Her doorbell associated with a loud knock from her front door drew her out of these thoughts. She turned to the bedside table where her clock gloriously sat to see that it was just ten minutes after six. Frowning in displeasure at being woken up earlier by unceremonious dreams or rather memories and the notorious pounding on her door, she stepped down from her bed and trudged out of her room grumbling. In her state of chagrin, she forgot about her slippers and was attacked by the biting chill of the marble floor of her hallway outside of the living room's silver gray rug. Unlocking the heavy, lustrous, wooden door, and pulling it open, her slightly squinted eyes were met with dark curly hair, and traveling her eyes down she came to face the blue-gray eyes of the man who plagued her dreams the entire night.

"You!" Millicent exclaimed and her eyes gradually widened to express her astonishment.

"Hi." One of Jace's fair hands simply lifted up in a wave while he possessed one of the most beaming smiles on his face. While he was excited to see her, the smile looked almost unnatural on his face. His own eyes lingered on her exotic look in her short peach colored silk pajamas.

Millicent to a defensive stance, widening her legs and placing her hands on her waist, positioning her body so that it held her door open. "What are you doing here?" She asked in a low tone to prevent her voice from being carried away by the stillness of the morning.

She saw his hands move from the corner of her eyes, so her gaze naturally traveled there only to be met with confusion as he held a rather huge suitcase in hand.

"Why are you holding your suitcase in front of my home? How did you even know where I live?" Her sharp eyes moved to find his, which still lingered on her body. Traveling her gaze down she found that she was still in her nightwear much to her embarrassment. She rushed back in to get her robe.

"I didn't say you could come in." Millicent drawled out tiredly when Jace seated himself as if he paid her rent with her. She was now covered in her robe. A shame. Jace muttered under his breath.

When Millicent's full body appeared in front of him with that cute intimidating stance where she placed her hands on her hips and regarded him with eyes resembling glowing coals, he sat up from his hunched position and spoke, "You never told me to stay outside either, little M." His lips twitched when her eyes narrowed even more at his audacity.

"Don't get smart with me young man." Millicent sighed when she saw him raise his hands up mischievously in surrender. His meteor gray -blue eyes this morning though easy was holding unbridled interest in them as they caressed her, making her squirm. "Tell me, why are you here so early in the morning with your luggage?"

Jace ran his hands through his hair quickly letting the curls bounce off to his forehead before speaking. "Manu threw me out." Millicent's brows arched higher in surprise. Dropping to a squat in front of him, she held onto his thighs for leverage. She was worried something had gone amiss between the cousins, hence the imploring crease on her forehead.

The heat of Millicent's warm hands pierced his skin and crawled up, inciting him to draw in a quick breath through his parted lips, his commanding eyes guiding hers to seek them. "She was affronted by our session by the wall." His lips stretched wider when he felt Millicent reel from his mention of their kiss and Manuela running in on them. His hands unconsciously trailed up to the corner of her full lips, rubbing it and catching her in a daze.

"I told you not to touch me." Millicent whispered, recalling how her friend had screamed when she interrupted the moment when their lips were locked. Needless to say, Manuela was disappointed in her cousin.

Their eyes were drowning in each other, reflecting their desire to engage in the memory that plagued both unknown to them. "I can't stop myself." Millicent relished the feel of his almost calloused hand on the delicate skin of her face. Her eyelids almost shut at the attention. Jace was fascinated at how one woman stole his thought process with just some few shared kisses and how she was holding him captive with just her eyes. She was like a magnet to him, always drawing him. Her beauty, radiance, smile, voice, everything about her disconcerted him.

The spell was broken when Millicent's alarm went off from her room. Jace withdrew his hand as quickly as he could while Millicent scrambled to her feet quite ungracefully. She cleared her throat and looked anywhere but him. He couldn't stay with her, otherwise she wouldn't know what immoral thing she would do next. Her heart was racing and she felt the thin layer of sweat that coated her neck when she rubbed it in her awkward state.

"You could go to your mother's place." She spoke, finally turning her head to Jace who was now leaning back comfortably on the couch, a stern look marring his features. Yet, promptly the grave look was smoothed away with a jolly look.

"She thinks we are married, remember." Jace's eyes remained constant on her movements even as she casually dropped into the couch opposite him. Her home had the same layout of her cousin. They did stay in the same estate, although it was odd that they did not decide to rent out the same. She made the house feel full and homey with her intricate taste in eclectic decor with a more modern organic decor and contemporary outlook. She pulled on her hair that had been twisted and pulled up to a bun- one of her many features that intrigued him.

"Aw don't look too down babe. We can get to know ourselves better." If only he knew that getting to know themselves was what made her worried. She was scared of her own self in his presence.

"How did she even throw you out this early? She normally sleeps in." Millicent shot up in fright, bumping her leg against the couch throwing Jace a panicked look. "Wait, what day is it?" She rushed out, already moving away to get her phone.

"Uh, Monday." Jace replied, unfurling himself from the couch as well and following her through the sun lit space of her living room.

"What the hell! I thought it was Saturday! Gosh I'm going to be late." Jace stood in the hallway disgruntled from her sudden burst of panicked energy. He was amused at her misplaced dates.

"Little M, we arrived from the states on Saturday."

"Oh we did! I should have gone to church yesterday. Look how muddled I am." She paused when she reached her door and found his shadow around her. Swiveling to face him, she remembered he was homeless now. She shuffled closer, grabbed his hands and turned him in the opposite direction to the second room she had.

"What time is it? I doubt you're late." Jace called out exasperated at being dragged around like a dog.

"Starts at nine. It's already 7. A forty-minute drive. From a lady's perspective I'm, ohhh, very late." Her ranting was a new side that he had seen and he found it endearing. Shaking his head to dispel the thoughts, he was pulled into a room that seemed unused. She had not decorated it like the others. He caught a glimpse of her own room and it was decorated to full capacity in a modern organic way.

"Here's where you stay. When I come back, I'll lay down the rules."

Jace grunted in disapproval. "Again?" He asked to see her fierce eyes set on his.

"If not, you know where the door is." Her retreating form was the only indication that she once stood with him. He walked back to the living room for his luggage, smiling softly as the idiosyncratic redolence of Millicent.

An hour later he heard her call for him, her footsteps frantic. He poked his head and naked torso from his room, "Yeah?" Millicent pirouetted on her feet to face him and was met with his bare and very toned shirt. She quickly adjusted her head so her eyes rested on his face. A bashful look occupied her face when she found his smirking, gleaming countenance.

"I'm leaving. There's supplies in the fridge and food too." She was rooted when Jace walked straight out of his room and stopped when he was foot to foot with her. Something on his neck gleamed in the ray of the sunlight from the window and her head dipped to see a thin gold necklace around it. It made him look more masculine like an alpha male. It did not droop down to his broad, muscled chest. Catching herself for the second time in the morning, she looked up to see a disturbed scowl, crossing his thick, sharp arched brows. He brought his bare arm around her shoulders and crushed her into him. Millicent stood with her arms dangling at her sides while he embraced her.

"Take care." She breathed again when she was released and worriedly glanced at him to see him. "Don't worry, little M, I've not fallen for you. It's not going to happen either." For some reason, the end of that statement disturbed her but she brushed it off.

"Right!" Her eyes shuffled around, drawing the strap of her bag closer and turned to move away from Jace. "Bye."

After a long day of being out from the comfort of her home and surrounded with colleagues and a boss who was difficult to please, Millicent's eyes shone when she locked her car and saw her residence. With hurried steps, she bounded to her house. As she opened the door, the air that rushed out of the room was filled with ashy smoke. She hastened inside and meandered directly to the kitchen to be met with more smoke and an empty room.

"Jace!" Millicent's eyes roamed through the expanse of the room for the source of the dispersing smoke that burned her eyes to tears. She opened up the windows and stepped back to the silence her call received. She was just about to call out again when she saw a body curled in a corner next to a cabinet with a saucepan in hand. It was Jace and he was not moving!

"Jace!"

CHAPTER 13

"Jace?" Millicent questioned in a hoarse, dreadful voice coming to squat beside his body. His eyes were shut with little squeeze lines at the edges. There were angry and pained lines along the crease of his forehead. Millicent raised her hand to lightly rouse him out of the state he was in. He had yet to open his eyes but the expressions on his face let her know that he was alive. Beads of sweat lined his forehead and when she grabbed onto his hand, his eyes blinked open, sending her scampering backward on her butt in fright. He hissed in pain when he tried to move which sent Millicent rushing toward him in worry.

"Jace, what happened to you?" She called out again, moving to sit in front of him still in her black solid cotton trousers which she wore below her top covered by its blazer. His eyes portrayed instant relief when they settled on her.

"Little M, I think your kitchen hates me." Millicent's hunched shoulders dropped in consolation at his words.

Jace tilted his head back and sighed thankful for the appearance of the owner of the house. "Is that Mimi?" The device beside him which he had forgotten about transmitted the voice of the person on the other side.

Millicent strained her neck around him, looking to where Jace's neck had bent to. "Sean?" She questioned. Looking at the dark screen of Jace's phone. It was on speaker.

"Oh, good." Millicent's bright eyes had questions in them at the way Sean moaned distressingly. Jace jerked his shoulders upward and dropped them, lifting his eyelids conveying that he had no clue what his friend was talking about.

"I thought he was going to burn down your home and himself too." Sean teased with a chuckle and that was the moment Millicent raised her head to see the mess in the kitchen. She choked on her breath with her mouth open, her pair of doe shaped eyes turning accusingly to Jace.

"What did you do?" She asked in a flat, demanding tone. Her usually calm and smiling face now looked unimpressed.

"Uh, guys, I'll leave you to it now. Take care of him, Mimi. His hand is worth millions." Jace sharply turned to his phone next to his leg, on the tiled kitchen floor and grabbed it bringing it to his mouth.

"You have not been helpful since this began. If anything the house would have turned to ashes if I listened to you." But the line went dead just after he spoke. He stared at his phone as if it was an alien. Noting the silence in the room, he twisted himself very slowly to meet the glaring eyes of Millicent. Her right brow twitched.

"Spill."

"I was craving plantain and tried to fry it. I could promise that I saw my mother even drop her hand into the hot oil without flinching." Millicent couldn't help but be entertained at how the thought seemed to vex him, watching his scrunched up eyebrows and how he furiously regarded the frying pan in his left hand. Slowly leaning forward, she grabbed it from him, recognizing that it was warm and stretched up to put it in the sink above her. She tilted her head for him to continue.

"Well, I drop these plantains in the hot oil, and it starts spritzing everywhere. One of the shooting oils hit my face very close to my eye. I lost my balance, hit the pan of the stove and everything went flying." Jace surveyed the kitchen himself after he heard Millicent's deep sigh. It was a workout of a horror movie. The half-fried plantain littered the counter and the floor, the floor itself was greasy with oil and even the area where they sat had water dripping down. He was not born for the kitchen, and with that thought he clucked his tongue drawing Millicent's tired gaze to him.

Millicent stood up listlessly, rubbing her face tiredly with one good hand, questioning why she had someone so disastrous in her living space but turning her gaze to the man who looked more than tired himself with his swollen eyelids, she felt her compassion spike. She stretched out her hand to him to help him out. As Jace lifted his hand, she noticed the red angry marks on his palm, and reacting before she could think, she agitatedly grabbed onto his left hand with worry clouding her gaze.

Jace was taken aback by the change in her demeanor after she brought his hand closer, turning and observing so worriedly. "What happened?" Her wide eyes shot up to look into the blue-gray tired ones hooded by his currently heavy lids. He tried to pull his hand back but she had a firm grip on it. Her hair fanned around her face as she dipped lower, softly tracing her finger across the burn causing him to hiss.

"I think it's from grabbing the pan."

"Why do you think the wise people added a handle?" Her exasperation could not be put at bay. But taking a closer look at him, he seemed tired not because of the day's activity but something that seemed beyond his control. She suspired once again with their eyes and hands locked together. Shaking her head a little with a pained look she asked, "What am I going to do with you? Come with me."

Jace could not utter a word after he saw how anxious she looked for him. No one except his closest family had given him such a genuine look of care. It was probably because he never lifted a lip to them, never regarded anyone outside with close to a smirk. That's because he learnt the hard way that some people enter into your life with smiles just to exploit you and after they succeed in destroying you, the smile disappears. But Millicent made his lips stretch without trying and it worried him. He stared at the said woman whose back was to him naturally walking like a model with that subtle movement of her curves in the right places. Her hair swooped back and forth calmly and when they entered the bathroom, her bronze face turned to him. She beckoned him closer with her hand and opened the tap.

"I bet you didn't even put it in cold water." He heard her, yet all he could do was stare with a sweet pain clenching his heart. Her eyes focused on his hand with attention. She did not even know who he was. Could it be real that she really cared? He allowed her to pull him to sit on the toilet before scavenging the drawers for the supplies she needed. She squatted before him and started to disinfect oblivious to his prolonged eyes on her. Her hair obscured her view and without thinking, Jace sent his right hand to push them back yearning to see her face. He smiled again when she was in his view.

Millicent was caught up in the role of a nurse that she was not attuned to the environment and what was happening. Placing the disinfectant away, she jerked when the sudden vibration and ringing from her butt attacked her. Jace's hand was on her as quickly as it happened, helping her stay still. She sent a quick smile in appreciation while reaching her phone. She brightened when she saw the caller and turned to Jace. "Manuela!"

"Hey Ella!"

"Mimi! How are you?" She sent Jace a cheeky look to which he gestured with his eyes in question. Millicent placed her phone down and continued to tend to him. "I could be better and you're on speaker."

"Why? What's up?" Manuela's worried tone drifted and her cousin understood her concern. She really cared about Millicent. Jace's quiet and intrigued eyes strayed to her again as she shared the story with her friend.

"I knew he was a little clumsy in that department. If I knew he came to your place, I would have come to drag him out." Millicent chuckled. "I'm serious Mimi, don't be charmed by him. Has he told you anything?" After hearing this, Jace frowned and interrupted them. Millicent only looked confusedly.

"I'm right here Manu." He grumbled.

"Good!"

After the call, Millicent found him in the living room according to her request. She leaned by the doorway and crossed her arms, a frown settling on her smooth features as she remembered Manuela spoke about him saying something. She had changed into a simple dress. She cleared her throat which had Jace's eyes settling in her direction leaving the movie he was focused on.

"Is there something I need to know?" She was only met with the blank stare on his tanned skin. She watched him look at her with the same expression for a while before a wide smirk overtook it.

"Not that I know of." She nodded resolutely, accepting his excuse. Everyone hinted she had something to know but the person to say it was not and she wasn't close enough to probe him.

"Come let's eat." Jace bounced out of his seat at the mention of food. Chuckling Millicent entered the kitchen.

"Okay, here's the rule for the meat." Jace stopped munching on his plantain and watched the woman opposite him in wonder.

"Did you ever think that being a lawyer or teacher would work for you?" He asked so seriously that Millicent had to think through the question.

"You don't even know what I do for a living. Which brings me to the rule. If you guess an answer correctly to the question, you pick one meat." Jace grinned in response, propping his head with his hand as he dropped the rice he brought to his mouth.

"What? It's a good way to know more about ourselves." The kitchen was sparkling clean now. The gray counter was shining and the midnight blue tiles as well. The coffee cabinets were all closed and the window was shut after the smoke receded. Jace nodded urging her to begin, the smile resting on his face mirroring hers.

"What do I do for a living?" Jace looked skyward, pretending to be in deep thought as he tapped his index finger to his chin.

"A teacher!" The index finger popped up like a light bulb as he answered.

"Dang! Nope!" The almost smile on his face faded when Millicent took the chicken from the platter.

"Hey! You said if we get the answer correctly." His eyes accusingly watching the chicken as his throat bobbed.

"Well, who did you think was going to eat it if you lost?" Millicent's sassy answer shut him up with an envious stare on the meat she tore apart to eat.

"I work as an accounting manager at DLG Energies. An oil company." Jace's eyes flitted in surprise, impressed that she worked that high up at such a young age.

"That's super impressive." He decided to speak his thoughts. He believed in praising people the way they deserved for their hard work and was happy to see her eyes light up.

"Okay my turn." His eyes glittered watching the meat in anticipation, forgetting all about his food. "What is my favorite TV show?" Millicent gamboled on her seat in excitement. "There's no way you know." Jace cried out in spirited annoyance. He slipped lower into the high dining chair.

"You're so funny. You've been watching one show since I came home. It's got to be 'house of the dragon'." She laughed when Jace groaned out. In some ways he was a really simple home boy but his business side was the more complex part of him.

"This is not fair."

"Oh but it is! Take it as pay back for what you did to my kitchen." Millicent was just very perceptive and that too more than the cunning Jace. You need truth to find truth.

Thirty minutes later the two were howling in laughter.

"Wait! The man teased Sean, so you decided to put half a cup of apple cider in their tea? The one they served at the shareholders meeting?" Jace could not respond as tears dropped from his eyes. He was falling off his seat, slapping the table at the memories he was sharing from his teenage years. Even Millicent had cackled so much that she was now in a fetal position to accommodate the laughter she heaved.

"You should have seen their faces. Like a baby who was pushing out hard shit." Millicent imagined the image and was sent into further rows of laughter.

Jace looked at the woman who was unashamed to be herself, frowning at what was annoying and laughing at what was funny. They had been sharing funny moments from their lives after she had managed to eat more than half of the 20 pieces of chicken, leaving him to miserably enjoy only four of them. He loved getting to know her- the layers of her underneath her calm and composed demeanor. She was so much more and he found himself lost in her tales wanting to know it all. So simple yet so complex. His eyes sparked at her enlightening smile with a new motivation and afflatus discovered.

Chapter 14

R ays of sunlight rushed when the curtain parted to allow for its greeting. It bounced against the warm gray wall as well as the green color of the plants in the room. The sun did not withhold its glory from dazzling the bronze skin of Millicent as she stepped out of her room clad in her black and white polka dotted blouse tucked in midi in her knee length pencil skirt which enhanced her figure. Her heels clicked on the ground with each step hoping that the man in the other room would come out to fulfill his ritual. A smile brightened her countenance as her loosely curled hair bounced around the low ponytail she had placed it in. Her bright doe eyes turned to check his door which had no evidence of him making her glossy lips tilt lower.

Over the past week, it had become an unspoken ritual for Jace to meet her in the doorway for his early hug. Some days when she was able to prepare breakfast, he would hug her after they had eaten. Her smile dimmed more when a minute had passed. She hadn't realized that she began to wait for him like a habitual affair just to feel his arms around her. Just a week of being around each other and she was already used to it all. Her smile dimmed further when he didn't show up after a minute. Checking her phone she decided she had roughly ten minutes to spare, so she leaned back on the wall and dropped her head to watch her shoes as she waited. Her arms crossed with her blue Prada bag.

Jace sat on his bed in his room with his phone next to his ear. His bare chest with stretches of hair evenly grating it was visible as the duvet covered his legs. His manager's grave voice assaulted his ears.

"You need to get the inspiration to start the work, Jace. Many people are awaiting your new collection with bids already in place." Jace grunted in a low voice.

"I think I found one Cole. I told you traveling would be great. It'll be done by the end of summer." Jace's bored tone commandingly asserted to the man on the other side. He could picture him pulling the roots of his brown hair in frustration in dealing with a notorious artist like him, but that was Jace, he liked to do his things his own way and that's what brought in the great value and big bucks.

"As always, I trust your capability, but I have never seen you more blank than the previous months. Even Sean was worried." Of course, he called Sean. Jace thought with distaste, a scowl as cold as an executioner's ax imprinted on his face. He had been woken up at 5am by Sean who was everywhere in the states, probably just after 9pm in California, so of course he was grumpy. He brought the phone away from his ear to see that it was five minutes to eight, making him shoot out of the bed with hurried steps.

"Cole." He cut off his manager from whatever he was saying. "I have to go." With that he did not even listen to what he said and threw his phone in the heap of his bed. Millicent left for work at eight to accommodate traffic in the forty minute drive. He always made it out to see her dressed and embraced her, drawing in her smell before he sent her off and began his day. Today was Friday and close to the weekend so hopefully she didn't rush out. Throwing on one of his white shirts because Millicent couldn't stand to see his bare torso without getting shy, he pulled the door to his room apart to find a feminine figure leaning on the wall with her gaze dropped down. He breathed out in relief feeling his chest uncoil at seeing the radiance of her beauty though her eyes were not on his yet. And she waited for him! His feet padded across the floor lightly ignoring the coolness of the tiles as he forgot to put on slippers in his haste.

Millicent did not hear his door shut nor his footsteps, so her face held some bewilderment when his bare feet appeared in front of her heels. She raised her head, her eyes glinting when she was met with his smile.

"Little M, hi." Jace's hoarse, thick voice called with delight.

"I thought you were sleeping." She spoke in her soft, musical voice, watching him with a sweet expectant look.

"When you're going out, especially dressed like that? Never." Jace's eyes swept down to take in her form and what he saw made him gulp. She was such a majestic and regal person but she had no idea about it. Opening his arms, he waited for her to walk in, and she did, almost crashing into him. He gripped her perfectly curvy frame with his hands roaming up into her hair and he felt her grip on him making him smirk. He had to bend down a bit to drop his head fully on her shoulder.

"My mother wants me to come home for food." Millicent's voice captured his attention even as they were warm in each other's embrace.

"Come and pick me up. I'll go with you." He felt her pull back to see her smile.

"I don't have a choice. It's more like she wants to see you." She grabbed her phone from her bag to check the time and it was just right. Jace was holding onto her hand or rather she was holding his. Looking up from their hands, she found Jace's calm eyes on her, a smile in them though his lips rested in place.

"You have to take me to the route where I can jog."

"Are you sure you haven't even been going out to jog?" She chuckled at the childlike shake of his head. The hair that many like herself admired in a cute disarray. "Okay, we'll go for a walk this evening and we'll see my mother tomorrow." She conceded and a grin displayed on his face.

"Good." He brought her into his arms again.

"I have to go."

When Millicent stepped out to work, Jace also sat on the porch with his drawing pad in his hands, only able to trace out the face of the one woman who had occupied it, the past weeks. He remembered vividly the slant of her forehead, the shape of her eyes and how it curved bewitchingly at the ends with the one lash on her left eye sticking out of her full lashes, the dip of her diamond-shaped elegant nose, and the gestures of her full lips. This one he captured in memory had her eyes squinting in humor making her lids look heavier; her top brown lip spread with her faint pink bottom lip stretching.

Jace held the pad afar and let the natural light spread on it. He just needed his canvas and an easel to make it come alive. His hands were itching to have her up and his meteor-gray-blue eyes glowed in the sun looking at her on paper.

"Such a beauty." He whispered to himself. He shook his head in disbelief when he realized what he had drawn. "What am I even thinking? We're not dating."

Millicent returned to a very quiet house, meaning Jace was probably out. He liked exploring the city or probably having fun somewhere as he had done for the past three days. He frequented the bistro and left the kitchen to rest. She shook her head thinking about how wild he could be. However, she was surprised to see him come out of his room in sweats and a tank top. His hair was wet almost as if he just exited the shower. When his eyes fell on her, he blinked once and instantly his entire face beamed, and unable to contain her happiness at seeing him she grinned in return.

"Little M, I'm starving." Millicent's expression turned sour and she steupsed listening to his words. Now she understood why her mother was annoyed when she had to prepare their food after a long day.

"Can you boil water?" She lowered herself on the couch and he came behind her as she took off her heels.

"Of course!"

"Great, you can survive in the desert!" She responded flatly. Her head rolled back when Jace placed his hands on her shoulders closer to her neck and began massaging. She tilted her head back and her eyes met his blue-gray ones. They shone with an unreadable emotion. Jace swallowed thick, already mesmerized by her beauty and without thinking had dipped his head a little and his hands slowed down in doing their work. Millicent's heart thumped loudly with emotion; this startled her and caused her to widen her eyes while sliding lower into her seat.

"You. Don't try anything funny." Her voice couldn't go an octave higher than the soft, breathy whisper. Jace's eyes tried to find what drew him into her dark brown irises. His skin had gotten hotter and the tension around them now was palpable as she also could still not take her eyes off his. The moment she opened her mouth to speak, it was as if he had been hypnotized to look at her plump lips which were slightly parted at the moment like she was calling for him.

Snapping his eyes shut for a moment to regain his composure, he felt his hands tighten their hold on her shoulder. Every part of him was taut. He was sure that if he released himself, he would indulge in the images that floated through his head, ones that he was sure Millicent was not ready for. Opening his eyes he said, "You don't get to blame me without blaming your eyes first." His hands loosened a bit and traced her hairline.

Immediately Jace's hand touched her skin, she bounced up from her seat in fear of the temptation in the room with her. "Uh, let's eat out for dinner and we can continue with the walk." With that being said, she scurried to her room.

"Do you plan on getting married soon?" Millicent question, walking beside Jace on one of the streets away from the street food restaurant was. They walked so close to each other that there was no room between their adjacent arms for air to escape. The hairs on their arms interacted in their own attractive way but neither seemed to care as they were engrossed in their own bubble.

Jace shifted his gaze from the front of the street to see her side profile with her still staring right ahead as they walked. "Why do you ask?"

Millicent grinned at him, catching his gaze on her and letting her voice drift through the cool evening breeze. "Well, Mr. Elrod, it is a truth universally acknowledged, that a single man in possession of a good fortune, must be in want of a wife." Her eyes twinkled in mirth when she saw the streak of recognition pass through his eyes. She just jumped the gun without knowing what the outcome would be.

"Little M, if Austen was alive as a gen Z, I'm sure she would have changed that opening statement." When Millicent chuckled at his statement, she saw his straight, pearly white teeth shimmer in the presence of the twitching streetlight. She felt safe walking with him in the dark and it felt weirdly intimate with the way they were attached to each other's skins.

"I didn't know you read books, classics for that matter." His soft smile warmed her heart.

"There are a lot of things you still don't know about me. Besides, I could say the same for you. I didn't think you'd understand it." She said quietly when a group of girls dressed in expressive clothes walked past them with hearty laughter.

Jace stopped walking, grabbing her hands which drew a sharp flow of air out of her chest at the heat of his touch on her skin. She felt like she was going crazy anytime he touched her. "That's what we are doing. Getting to know each other. You never know, we may become amazing friends." Millicent felt her heart clench at the same time Jace felt the piercing pain at the term he used.

They became lost in the embrace of their eyes once again, unaware of the things that happened around them; not the cars that passed nor the people that walked, that was until Jace's ears caught a noise.

"Do you hear that?" He whispered with an air of urgence.

Millicent lifted a brow and tilted her head trying to listen. "Hear?" She searched around with her eyes till she saw a local brown dog with white spots behind them under the buzzing streetlight in front of a house they had just passed by. The dog was not bulky but with how it had hunched and its growls, it was not up to good.

"Is that dog growling at us?" Millicent was still trying to assess the friendliness of the dog when she heard the slight panic in Jace's voice. He's not going to...

"Jace-" She began to reprimand but what she feared had already happened. She swiveled with her mouth open in fright when the dog dashed past her and after the running form of Jace.

Chapter 15

"He did not just do something that idiotic. Jace! Stop running!" She groaned with disbelief. But as she turned to see him two blocks ahead still running with the dog chasing her, she couldn't help but buckle at her knees and double over in laughter.

"Millicent!" Jace's frightened voice called her when he ran around her for the second time. She could hear his heavy breath, but she could not stop her laughter. Jace's agitated voice called out when he reached her, and she could hear the dog bark quite ferociously. "This is not funny little M."

She coughed and tried to stand. "Oh– I'm- I'm sorry." Her last giggle bubbled, and she jogged to his side motioning him to stay calm as the dog leaped around him. "I think it's tired now too. Look, it just wants to play."

"You call this playing? He obviously wants a piece of my meaty flesh." The dog barked wildly in the night.

"Young lady, won't you help the man?" A passerby called in their local language as she took careful steps to the pole that Jace was currently climbing with the dog barking up. Luckily, he was the only one who saw what was happening.

"I'm helping." The scene reminded her of Tom and Jerry and that erupted a random set of giggles from her. She grabbed a stick from the side of the wall of the house they stood by and stood in front of the pole. She shoved it in front of the dog. After three attempts of frightening it, it turned and trotted on another path. Tossing the stick away, she turned to see he had slid down.

"Have you never been warned not to run from a strange dog?" Her humorous statement had him frowning.

"I think it bit me." Millicent startled. She grabbed his leg that he had turned to check and saw a faint red mark on his left leg. Patting his blue shots, she stood again.

"Looks like a scratch. Come, Ella's house is two blocks up. Let's go and disinfect it." Jace immediately grabbed onto her hand, starting another set of laughter.

"Shut it, little M." But that made her howl louder. Even he could not deny the humor in the perilous situation. "How would I know that the dogs in this part of the world are this, I don't know, fierce."

"Their primary purpose in most homes is to safeguard it, and for some reason they seem to know. So, they're pretty much aggressive to people they don't know. We don't adopt them as children because we kind of respect their species for who they are and what they do. No offense." Millicent quickly added when she saw his mouth open to argue. "I mean they are cute, but we leave them to their own doings. Also, they're free to walk around and form friends with other dogs around. It gets scary, sometimes, how they act more human than humans."

Jace grumbled understanding what she was saying. "Someone needs to let them know that they could be nicer." Millicent giggled and they stopped in front of Manuela's house which was two streets from hers. In an attempt to visit her friend, she suggested that they stop by.

Millicent lifted her hand to hit the doorbell, but it was grabbed by the man who was with her. She faced him at her side with an interrogative look and her eyes narrowed.

"Just saying, little M, doorbells are overrated for Manu." With that he ignored the doorbell and banged the door.

Jace was always succumbing to being a teenager around his family and close friends, so his cousin was not surprised to find him as the culprit. Manuela stepped down to hug her friend, bumping Jace away. "I was just about to call you for something exciting! But why is this raccoon with you?" She noticed the mirth in Millicent's eyes as she watched Jace who seemed to be pleading with his eyes.

"I'll tell you one day. He needs to clean up a wound." Manuela opened the door so they could enter.

"What happened to you now?" Jace sauntered past her into the house with his head high, ignoring her to avoid recounting the embarrassing moment. Manuela raised a brow at Millicent to which she just shook her head with a suggestive stretch of her lips.

Millicent stopped in her tracks just as Jace who stood watching the person sitting in the couch who stood to his feet one his eyes met Millicent's. Her eyes scanned him from his buzz cut faded hair to his stylish bushy eyebrows and into his deep-set of brown orbs. His dark lips stretched wide and Millicent's doe eyes widened at seeing the man she had the most unfaltering crush for during her university days. Her face brightened just as Manuela spoke, "Surprise!"

"Aseda!" Millicent exclaimed and rushed forward, delighted to see him again. She could already feel his characteristic calm aura. She was brought into Aseda's warm hug, and they drew back excited to see each other. She looked at Manuela with disbelief.

"Yep, in the flesh."

Jace, who had still not moved away, stood watching the interaction. His forehead scrunched and his knitted smooth brows wiggled like ugly caterpillars at the new man who looked like an unwelcome suitor.

"Weren't you in Germany for your PhD program?" Millicent implored with sparkling eyes. Aseda towered over her slightly but not as much as Jace.

"Yes, I finished it about three months ago." Aseda replied in a bold and deep voice. He saw Millicent's cheeks broaden. But his gaze was drawn to the commanding man who stood in the entry to the open hallway, almost as if he knew Aseda was wondering about him, Jace loudly cleared his throat to gain their attention. Millicent turned to him with imploring eyes.

"I need help little M." His eyes drifted to the cut.

"You haven't cleaned it yet?" She walked to him with worried eyes without another thought after giving Aseda an apologetic look. But Manuela caught onto her friend's hand before she could reach him.

"I'll help him. Go ahead and chat."

"No! You scare me, Manu. I want little M to help me." Manuela directed an icy look at him battling with his own daring look. Her cousin had taken a fancy to Millicent even if he could not tell it and right then she could tell he was jealous. They may fight like crazy siblings- as weird as it was that they lived on different continents- but she loved him and could tell that Millicent might be his saving grace, but she still wanted him to do it right with her friend. Millicent patted her hand, and she dropped it before addressing their mutual friend when the two disappeared.

"You could do this yourself; you know?" Millicent spoke sweetly as she tended to the wound which did not look to be that trivial after all.

Jace sighed, meeting her eyes from where she squatted in front of him after placing the band aid on his leg. "I just realized that I'm envious of the places your bright eyes look. Your eyes make me selfish. There's a look in them that I want for myself." Millicent held onto his leg for support. What was it with him and caring for his wounds that made him so bold? The way his unblinking eyes lingered on her eyes unnerved her.

"You can't say that, Jace. None of this is real." His hand roughly, yet gently grabbed her hair and dug into her scalp causing her to tremble to his delight. Her lip parted lightly and her eyes widened in curiosity. Bringing her head up while his other hand grabbed onto her waist to lift her up to a standing position, he held her close, getting up himself.

Millicent felt his warm breath fall on her lips, but he refrained from moving any closer. His back was to the counter, so she faced the mirror and could see her face. The image in front of her mirrored a look of helplessness. She was already drowning in this attraction and all that kept her sane was her neck above the waters of temptation.

Manuela who was laughing with Aseda caught Jace before he could leave and whispered as they stood on the porch. "When are you going to tell her, Kwaku? I don't want you to betray her trust."

Jace looked conflicted. "It's all fake, Manu. She said it herself."

Manuela scrunched her brows. "Don't make me regret not telling her myself. I feel bad as it is, but I think it's yours to deal with." With those words, she allowed him to leave.

The situation forced her to escape from her friend's house with just a simple chat to her ex-crush. She made sure to withdraw herself from Jace as they walked to keep her head in a safe space.

At the brightness of the sun the next day, the two set out for Millicent's mothers. She had instrumental spirit music flowing through her speaker. She sat in the passenger's seat riding shotgun and Jace drove.

"Why don't you have a car if you have a license?" The easy atmosphere had returned between them after putting the igniting emotions behind them.

"Babe, that's called sustainability. I don't live here remember?" She saw Jace quickly turn to her with a casual teasing smile. He said it would be good to casually call out the pet names for practice. He wore his shades up and his brown Burberry T-shirt stretched along the expanse of his chest. She looked out and saw a brand of bread that her mother preferred.

"Here! Pull over please." Jace's ears tingled as he pulled over to the side of the road. "I'm going to get the bread that my mom likes. It's on the other side of the road." She spoke as she searched for her purse in her bag.

"Be careful!" Jace's brows arched up in surprise when she cheekily threw him a wink after she shut the door.

His eyes followed her, rolling down the window so that he could see her properly with the cars rushing past and the numerous hawkers all around. It was loud because the Madina market was a few miles behind them. He saw Millicent cross over to the middle of the road waiting for the other cars to move along. It was a bustling road, larger than their normal streets. A hawker carrying water passed in front of him, calling out for buyers, sweat trickling down his forehead in response to the heat. Jace looked curiously as the boy did not look older than sixteen.

He wondered about his schooling and normal day life. His attention was still on the passers-by when a loud screeching on the other side of the road caused everyone to stop their business and turn to the continuous screeching of tires. Jace's hand shot out to open his door when he saw a motorcycle strewn at the edge of the road and a seriously bumped car. There was blood and the place Millicent had pointed to was right behind the car. He anxiously searched for the thick mane of curly hair and pink dress. But she was nowhere. That was until he strained his eyes to look down and saw the familiar pink dress on the floor with something red next to it.

CHAPTER 16

"Millicent." Jace's lost voice distractingly whispered as he stumbled through the road to the opposite side where a massive crowd was forming. People had their phones out, filming instead of calling for help. His disgruntled steps caused him to bump into people while his eyes furiously through the ground to find where she was. His breaths came out in harsh pants. His entire environment was lost to him; everything was muffled and discolored until his eyes fell on her, sitting on the paved pathway, a few steps from the car that had crashed into the motorcycle. There were spots of red on her pink dress. Her legs were propped up, hands splayed on her ears and her face was tucked into the cocoon that she had created. Millicent was shaking like a feather. Jace saw a man try to shake her out of whatever stupor she was in but she did not even raise her head. With his heart beating wildly and anxiously, he rushed to squat in front of her. The people who surrounded them began to whisper.

"Little M." Jace called her in a soft voice. She stopped shaking immediately she heard him, but her head was still hidden from him. Jace cautiously put his hand on her shoulder.

"Bro, you should send her to the clinic." He heard one of the spectators comment but everything they said was like smoke drifting liberally in the air to him. His stormy eyes were searching and waiting impatiently to see the doe ones he was used to seeing.

"Little M." He repeated and felt her shiver. Very slowly, her head lifted from the crook of her arm. Jace slowly exhaled in relief. His eyes dragged along the length of her body to reassure himself that she was not hurt anywhere. Those bright doe eyes were now dull and absent like she did not recognize him. He lifted his hand up to her cheek and seeing no change in her expression, he slowly guided her into his embrace. He felt her breathing stutter as his hands gripped onto her tightly coaxing her to come out of the darkness she was in. After about two minutes he sensed her hands grip onto his shirt, and he finally visibly relaxed.

Jace untangled himself after close to five minutes, when he felt her body shake uncontrollably. She was weeping and he could feel his heart break. Whatever was happening to her was more than the accident that had taken place in front of her.

"Let's go home." He wrapped his arm around her and gradually eased her into an upright position. That was when he saw the pool of blood that she sat next to and how people were dispersing after the victims were sent off in taxis. There was no sign of any police yet so he led her peacefully back to the car, strapping her in and driving her back. Millicent did not utter a word, still holding a lost look with streaks of tears dried on her face.

When he led her to the bathroom to clean her up, she still did not say anything. He wiped off the spots of blood from her and urged her to go change. He had not seen her in such a state and it frightened him that she was in such pain and it frightened him at how much he cared. He wanted to do anything he could to wipe off that look from her. So, though he was currently in bed trying to sleep, he could not because he worried about what was going on in the room adjacent to his. Jace shot up in bed when he heard the light knock on his door in the stillness of the house. He immediately descended and crossed the room to open the door where Millicent stood timidly with an aching and exhausted expression on her face. There were pools of tears gathered under her eyes.

"Little M?" Jace implored with a soft murmur. He saw her shuffle on her feet dressed in nightwear. When she failed to respond, he became increasingly worried and the crease appeared on his forehead. He called her again. "Millicent?" Millicent's eyes, which were looking at her bare feet, drifted up to look into his dark eyes.

"I'm sorry. I can't sleep." Jace simply held open his door and opened his hand to her. She looked at the open invitation for a second before steadily slipping her smaller hand into his. Jace led her to his bed, pulling open the duvet and she quietly slipped in. Slipping in himself, he slid down and turned to face her. She was staring even after ten minutes; her eyes were open and staring.

"Want me to read you something?" Millicent blinked and nodded, shuffling closer to him. She saw him turn to rummage through his stuff and bring out a tablet. "I normally like the hard copy but I'm going to turn off the lamp now. Don't get too excited and forget to sleep." He smiled when a hint of a smile appeared on her face.

After he turned off the lamp, his deep and calm voice rolled out the words.

"Happy families are all alike; every unhappy family is unhappy in its own way. Everything was in confusion in the Oblonsky's house..." Millicent's heart calmed at the familiar words and the soothing voice of Jace led her into a peaceful dark place. It was two minutes later that Jace realized that her breathing had calmed and her face looked untroubled. Brushing away her tightly coiled hair that had escaped the braid she placed it in, he also slowly drifted off.

Millicent, who woke up with a start after realizing she was not in her own room, quickly crawled away and was met with the sound of her doorbell. She opened it and was surprised to see her brother, Josh, dressed in dress pants and a shirt with a concerned look etched on his smooth features except for the neatly shaped beard he had.

"JJ?" Josh stepped forward and engulfed his sister in his arms.

"I heard what happened, Mimi." Millicent's sunken and dull eyes widened, stiffly regarding her brother who walked around to stand right in front of her. "Your 'husband', a topic for another day, called to let mom know why you couldn't come." He put the word husband in air quotes but had that soft look of pain as he took in his sister's features.

"Dress up and let's go to church." He spoke after he realized she wasn't going to say anything like this.

A few minutes after Millicent left Josh in the living room, he heard another door open and a tall man in sweats and a loose shirt stumbled around the hallway anxiously looking around before his surprised eyes landed on Josh. Looking at his curly hair and naturally tan fair skin, Josh assumed it was the husband rumored to be his sister's. His football brown eyes quickly changed from its normal perceptive look to cold and steely when Jace marched to him. He noticed his gray-blue eyes also looked stern.

"Who are you?" Jace's voice was still raspy from his heavy sleep.

"Joshua Arthur, Millicent's brother. And you must be Jace." He responded drily, still skeptical about the entire marriage.

"Jace Elrod, Millicent's husband. A pleasure to meet you." Jace retired to his usual impassive and unreadable gaze when he spoke to people from outside his close circle. His voice sounded almost bored but his eyes were sharp enough to regard the man in front of him with respect. As someone who commanded an air of respect easily, he could tell that this brother of Millicent was fiercely elegant even with his placid look. Jace stretched his hand out.

Grabbing onto his hand in politeness, Josh spoke, "I don't know how you did it, but this marriage is not acceptable until you do it right." He released Jace's hand after the latter nodded in agreement, albeit false. "Thank you for looking after her yesterday."

Jace could not respond as heels clinked around. He turned to see Millicent in a purple satin dress with pearls lining the waist band. She looked radiant but her eyes were turned away from him, but she still offered a smile making him frown.

Millicent's eyes focused on her brother, trying to ignore the man she spent the night with.

"Ready to go?" She heard Josh call out to him. Before she could move, Jace gently grabbed her hand, but she still refused to meet his eyes.

"Where are you going, little M?"

"Church." She spoke nothing more but walked out with the man he had come to know as his brother, who gave him a final stiff nod.

Jace thought that she would no longer be returning to him to seek refuge as she did the previous night, but she returned in the same manner, that night, listening to him read and falling asleep. The night after and the next was the same. The hug he received from her before she left to work even seemed lifeless. He called Manuela to find out something, because Millicent behaving anything other than assertive, strong, funny was tormenting him so much that he could not comprehend. Manuela gasped loudly after he shared the details and only sadly responded that it was her friend's choice to share. She said it was a difficult time for her and all Jace could do was to be there for her. The sketches of her he had now lacked the shine he wanted; the one he craved. So, he sat up at night, just like he was doing this Friday as she slept facing him and attached to his side, burrowed in him to capture her beautiful and peaceful face on his drawing pad.

He heard her choke on a breath before shooting up into a sitting position, immediately heaving and looking for more breath to occupy her chest while in thick torrents of tears fell. Jace dropped his pad on the ground and quickly turned to grab her.

"Millicent! Little M." Her eyes were wild as she searched around the dimly lit room for his face. Jace's hands were firmly gripping her shoulders with fear clouding his gray eyes. "I'm right here, little M. It's just me."

"Jace." For the first time in the entire week, she spoke his name, broken, choked, miserably, eyes red-rimmed before chucking herself into his arms. She tightly gripped onto him and for a moment she was just silent before she shook and started to weep.

Jace continued to sooth her, running his hands through her hair and patting her back with his face scrunched up in pain at her heartache.

When her cries quieted and receded to sniffles, Jace spoke, "Little M, I don't know what is going on, but I want you to know that I'm here to listen. I won't judge and my ears can be yours whenever you feel like it." He felt her grip strengthen while she let out a shuddering breath in the crook of his neck.

"He's gone." Millicent whispered. Jace slowly untangled them so that he could see her. She had a far off look, but he waited for her to continue. "It was just like that- blood was everywhere and the motorcycle was on the side of the road." Millicent anxiously pulled on her hands. This was her nightmare and she did not know how Jace was going to take this. She felt him grab onto her hands and he rubbed them, his eyes focusing with a reassuring look.

"I was returning from school with my dad. He was driving us, and I saw a cookie that I liked. It was on the other side of the road from us. I remember he promised we could get some ahead of us but I was not relenting or taking no for an answer. So, eventually he pulled over to get me the cookie." Millicent blinked away the tears and saw the impassive look on Jace's face as he leaned closer to wipe the trail on her face. If he could tell what she was going to say, he didn't show it. He cued her with a bob of his head that he was listening.

"I was waiting when a loud screech, similar to Saturday's, was heard. It was a mess. The people who stood around said the cyclist crossed the car and it deflected its course, knocking into my dad who was by the stall away from the road. I saw his head." She whispered brokenly. There was a hint of fear in her eyes and her voice. Jace could tell where it was going and pulled her back into his embrace as she began to cry. "It was split and blood." Millicent could barely speak now, and was only held by the strength of Jace's arms.

"Jesus! I'm so sorry, little M." Jace's voice cracked in agony. His eyes shut firmly, holding her closer. But he knew her thoughts wouldn't be the rainbows so moving her back, he coaxed her with his hand to open her eyes.

"Listen, little M. That was not your fault. Your father could have easily gotten it and walked back to you if a reckless cyclist was not on the road." Millicent's heart was calmed by the fierce look in Jace's raging orbs. She nodded feebly and sought his arms again.

"Thank you." She whispered thickly to feel the little pat on her head. In his arms, she was lulled to sleep, entwined with him without nightmares.

The loud ringing of Jace's phone drew him out of his slumber and searching for it, he slid his hand to answer without checking the caller.

"Kwaku." He heard his mother's melodious voice. "Your father is here and wants you home for dinner. I think you should bring Millicent." She whispered the last part. His face paled and he turned to see Millicent, whose arms were around his waist with her face attached to his side. He pinched the bridge of his nose, thinking of how to deceive his smart father.

"Okay."

Chapter 17

"Are you sure that he is going to like me?" Millicent's large questioning eyes looked up to Jace's blue-gray ones for a second before he refocused on driving to their intended location. Millicent sighed and then unable to help herself she asked, "What's he like?"

She saw Jace stretch his hand to pat her knee and he turned to offer her a reassuring smile.

"My dad is a great person, you'll see. He's just a little perceptive, so we'll need to be careful." He said in a light tone. And then muttered a bit condescendingly. "A great person until the past few months at least." His eyes narrowed with a dark fierce look.

"I'm sure we can keep up without messing with the dates." She spoke when he did not clarify the last words he spoke.

"Ha! You're the messy timekeeper. At least, we have a good idea about ourselves now." His deep voice chuckled to hear her groan. "You're going to like him and he you." With a rueful smile, he continued down the road.

The sun was high up by the time the two got to the Elrod residence - more of a grand mansion. Millicent looked around in awe. It was at the Airport Residential Area and all the homes that area a very lush landscape. It also bordered between chic apartments and townhouses, depicting the elite district. It was extravagant than her estate in East Legon mainly because she preferred to have a personalized home.

"Do you all enjoy..." Millicent waved her hand around the mansion they had parked in. Jace walked next to her and slipped his hand into hers. It felt natural to her especially after sleeping and waking up consciously in his arms. This morning, she did not escape before he woke up, so she shared the bliss of waking up with his awestruck gaze on her face.

"Growing up as part of the family of the biggest business magnates in the world who owns an international architectural company and is an architect himself, introduces you to a world of crazy wealth." Jace capriciously started walking towards the front of the house.

"What?" Millicent pulled on his hand, her hair floating back with the strange breeze that blew past them. Her yellow-patterned dashiki glinted in the sunlight that reflected the tall glass window above. Her glossy lips parted in anxiety.

"Who are you people?" Her voice rushed out in unease, looking back and forth between the house and Jace whose hand tightened on her own.

"Relax, little M. Trust me, everyone is going to like you." Millicent's eyes fluttered shut when his hand came up to trace her face and set her hair in order. He also rearranged the shirt-dress she wore, dusting it after he set it to his liking. He had been doing that since this morning - dressing her up and pampering her style- and his eyes shone with a deeper intensity whenever he did so.

"I'm right here." Millicent was lost in the colors of his prying eyes; his soft smile that he always had for her was in place while he continued to play with her hair. She nodded after seeing his unwavering, promising look. "Good, let's go."

Her steps matched Jace's as he opened the door for her and led her inside. There was no one in sight when the ultra-modern white interior of their home came into view. The colors of their home ranged from gold, white and silver. The silver couches were placed further from the 170-inch television which was displaying serene nature videos.

"Come. She must be in the kitchen." Jace directed her to their right where a dining space was visible an entryway that was connected to the kitchen. "Explosive food." He grumbled and Millicent just snickered in response.

Millicent was awestruck by the complete elegance of Josephine who stood with her back to them, stirring the content of a pot. She felt Jace slightly rub her hand before he dropped it and bounced toward his mom, wrapping his hand around her shoulders. The poor woman jumped in fright and almost sputtered the ladle of stew on his handsome face. He was so different from when they first met - his usual playfulness was not a charade anymore, but she could feel the warmth and love he had for those he regarded as close.

"Kwaku, do you want to give me a heart attack?" Josephine slapped his back with her good hand, drawing a yelp from him who had a lost puppy look in his eyes and his tall form hunched in apology. After a moment Josephine fully recognized his presence and exclaimed, "You're here!" Jace was going to open his hands for a hug when she pushed him away and asked,

"Where's Millicent?" She asked in an excited tone, looking back and her dark pupils found Millicent. She pushed the ladle in Jace's hand and gestured with her head that he should continue to stir, ignoring his groan of protest.

"Millicent, my dear." She took off her apron and hung it on the highchairs next to the center counter. She embraced Millicent in a motherly embrace with a warm smile which made Millicent's tense form relax and copy her bright smile as well.

"Hi aunt Josephine." She greeted heartily, smelling the sweet smell of ambrosia.

When they pulled away, she heard Jace ask, "Mom, where's dad?"

"Come sit dear." Millicent walked to the high seat she showed her, and Josephine turned to speak in a low tone to her son who was warring with the flying red substance from the steaming pot.

"He went to get some drinks but beware-"

"Sweetheart, we're back!" Millicent's ears perked and her heart rate picked up when the masculine voice called out after a door was shut. Without even seeing him, she could tell from his tone he was a commanding and formidable man. She could also hear the unmistakable clicks of footsteps, lighter than a man's.

"We?" Jace arched a brow at his mother who stood next to Millicent with the same expectant gaze the former searched the entrance with. Remembering why she told him to bring Millicent, she rotated her upper body and inspected the curious eyes of her son with an apologetic look.

"Sorry, Kwaku." Jace blinked surprised, moving away from the heat. Millicent's concerned eyes found the pair staring but before either could speak, a massive presence was felt.

"Jace!" A high- pitched feminine voice squeaked causing both Millicent and Josephine to visibly cringe. Millicent turned and saw a very white man, tall and well-muscled. His cheekbones were high and sharp and his eyes were naturally narrow and denim blue. His hair was brown and wavy and looked almost as soft as Jace's own. Jace looked so much like his father except his father had sharper features and now those sharp eyes were looking above where she sat, at Josephine with a fond smile. In her assessment, she had not seen Jace move to stand in front of her seat.

"Gwen?" Millicent was shocked at the icy emotionless tone with which Jace spoke. Her head lifted to see his stiffened neck. His body was tense too and though she could not see his face, she was sure that it was just as cold. Millicent slipped her hand into his and squeezed it, not liking the change in his attitude. Jace turned to look at her with a fierce look.

"What is she doing here?" Millicent peeked around him to see who it was.

Josephine leaned closer to Millicent who could not see past Jace's back. She was hidden away by his broad back. "I truly apologize, Millicent. Expect the unexpected." Millicent cocked her perfectly thin brow at Josephine's displeased expression. Doesn't expecting the unexpected make the unexpected expected? Her thoughts were disrupted by the astonishing answer Jace's father gave. He was still standing by the doorway with the new woman.

"What is she doing here? She is your fiancée!" Millicent let out an inaudible gasp and her hand loosened its grip but before it could fall, Jace grasped it even harder. She felt the feminine set of Josephine's hands on her shoulders while the woman glared at her husband who looked firm in his decision.

"Then I hate to destroy your pretty imagination, dad, because I'm already married." Jace declared with his posture still as rigid, controlling his rugged breathing in his anger. Millicent staggered to her feet when Jace suddenly pulled her to his side revealing her to the world.

Josephine also stood next to her and spoke in a hushed voice saying, "Just think of this as being in a den of lions who are already full, dear."

Millicent's face broke into angry lines of displeasure at the new woman who stood on the opposite side of the counter. The fact she heard that she was Jace's fiancée made her even more baffled, and she was impaled with both anger at being deceived and an ugly feeling of dislike for the woman. Her hair was strikingly red but the roots showed to be blond on closer look, her dull olive eyes were eyeing Millicent condescendingly, but when she turned to Jace she puckered her lips in an ugly pout. It took a while for Millicent to acknowledge the scrutinizing eyes of Jace's father on her and it dropped to their conjoined hands in bewilderment even though his expression gave nothing away. His lips thinned and twisted to the side as if in thought.

"What the hell do you mean? You're supposed to marry me." The sudden exclamation of Gwen shut all their mouths as she looked from Millicent to Jace who looked like he would explode. His entire expression when he turned to Gwen was hard and dead unlike the affection Millicent was used to. "I mean, it can't be true." She chuckled sheepishly after she turned to see Josephine's exasperated eyes.

"What did you say? How did you get married without none of us knowing? Any certificate?" His father spoke after recovering from the screech. Millicent felt Josephine shuffle around her and stand upright.

"Anthony, he got married to this beautiful and wonderful woman. I know it was wrong that they did not ask but you did worse than that." Josephine walked around them leisurely to her husband who could not keep his eyes off. Her floating maxi dress added to her power. It was obvious her husband was smitten. Millicent felt Jace squeeze her hand and she looked up to see him still watching his parents with a calculating look.

"You can't have married this woman, Jacey." Her eyes snapped back to the red-haired who strutted with a practiced poise after her squeak reached their ears. Jace moved his hand to Millicent's waist and Millicent winced at the nickname. She would have stepped away from him if she didn't despise the new woman more. Gwen came to a stop in front of him and grabbed onto his hand, but she immediately dropped it when the blazing and icy orbs of Jace dared her. Jace hated the rich snob more than he let on, but his father seemed to be blind.

"You're going to get divorced and fulfill the end of the deal." Anthony spoke again and Millicent found Gwen's proud eyes on her. Her pale skin shimmered with the glitter on her lids and her deep-set eyes glinted alongside the sly smirk on her pink lips.

"Anthony!"

"I told you; I'm married. I did not agree to this, so settle this on your own." The pure impassiveness with which Jace spoke frightened Millicent. She tugged on his hand, and it took a minute for him to stop the eye battle he was having with his father. She shook her head calmly and saw him inhale a shuddering breath. Ignoring the annoyed humph of Gwen from his side, she turned to see Josephine smile while Anthony looked surprised, his eyes a little wide, at the interaction because his son never listened to anyone except his mother.

"Enough! We eat and you sort this out. I told you the moment you did this what it could cause." Josephine's subtle spiteful gaze pried Gwen even though her smile was intact, and she frowned disappointed at her husband, thumping his chest, who rubbed his face tiredly.

Surprisingly, Anthony interacted civilly with Millicent and even found that he signed a contract with her company for their American branch. The common knowledge was a great foundation to improve their new relationship. The man admired the intelligent woman which made Jace excited. His father was very picky with humans. Gwen sulked increasingly at the interaction while trying to grab Jace as she spoke in an awful nasal voice while the latter turned to Millicent at each instance to escape her.

Millicent, who struggled to avoid Jace for the feeling of betrayal that lingered from his lies, was shoved right into his arms when it was time to leave.

"It is great to meet you, Millicent. I apologize for the ruckus in my home." Anthony said still with an air of supremacy but more warmth. Josephine hugged her as they stepped out also apologizing but she smiled politely and reassured her that it was okay. The person she was most disappointed in at least was their son.

When Jace walked away to bring their car, a sharp perfume wafted through her nostrils, and she looked next to see the red-haired woman with a scornful look. Her long pink nails roughly curled around Millicent's slender arm, and she leaned closer to Millicent because she was taller. Gwen's eyes held obvious hatred and she was even more irked when Millicent showed no reaction. Her facial muscles were calm, and her eyes gave nothing away.

"Stay away from him! You don't even meet his class. I have no idea what kind of jest you are playing, but he is mine!" Millicent's brown eyes lingered on the woman and then she smiled sweetly, catching Gwen off guard.

"Funny! Did he sign a contract of ownership under you?" She grinned when Gwen's deep-set eyes widened, befuddled.

"How dare you? I'll make sure to tear you apart." Millicent clicked her tongue and stepped back from her as her nose itched in the presence of her perfume- she just used too much of the nice smelling product.

"I'll be waiting." Her grin remained in place till Gwen hoisted herself disdainfully and walked back into the house. A furious and murderous frown creased her forehead just as their car came ahead making Jace gulp inconspicuously in apprehension.

Chapter 18

"Little M." Jace called her for the umpteenth time but the woman who looked out her side of the window refused to talk. "Babe." His deep voice called distressed. He was so worried that she would never want to talk to him.

Millicent refused to admit how over the time that passed, his little pet names had become sweet sounding in her ears and a delight for her. She was so upset that she worried that if she opened her mouth, she would say all the wrong things. This was just a game but the fact that he lied to her even when she explicitly asked him, cut her deep to her heart. She suddenly turned to him in awareness.

"Was that what everyone was hinting at?" Jace almost grinned at hearing her voice but her question made his hands tighten considerably on the wheel. He had a pained look as he turned to look at her and feebly nodded to her dull awaiting expression. They were almost to their street.

"Drop me off at Manuela's." Jace clenched his jaw and snapped his head to her. They could have talked it out if the woman next to him was not a stubborn one. He was on edge with his need to have her forgiveness.

"Little M." He said disapprovingly. Millicent heaved out a breath before turning in her seat to him.

"If I go back with you, my head will still be muddled and that won't get you anywhere." She spoke in one breath and watched him frustratingly drag his hand through his hair, and she looked mesmerized as the wavy-curly hair deliciously bounced back to their place. Even though his lips twisted in displeasure, he agreed and stopped in front of his cousin's place.

"You'll be back tonight, right?" He called out after he got out of the car to see her at the front door. She didn't smile, nor did her muscles pull to show any reaction as she nodded. When Manuela opened the door for her moments after he sat in the car, he felt as if he was going crazy. He just wanted her around him and smiling. With a final pull to the roots of his hair, he drove away.

"What's wrong, Mimi?" Millicent sat on her friend's bed with vexation written all over her face and that increasingly worried Manuela.

"You knew about it, didn't you?" Millicent suddenly shifted to scan her friend's face with an accusatory frown.

Manuela's brows squeezed together in confusion as she asked, "What?"

"That he was engaged!" She saw her friend's eyes widen in realization and when Manuela carefully analyzed why her friend was this irked, she knew that Jace had messed up.

"He didn't tell you himself, I suppose."

"Oh, he didn't! I had to meet Ursula red-hair myself with his dad." Millicent ranted, throwing her hands about, still aggravated by the contact she had with Gwen before she left. Manuela giggled at the name she gave Gwen. "And she thinks she owns him."

"This is not good. Jace is going to flip. I'm sorry I didn't tell you Mimi, but I thought it was his life to share." Manuela laid her hand affectionately on the back of her friend who was still raging.

"You like him, don't you?" Millicent's eyes grew bigger at her friend's question.

"That's silly, no-"

"I know you, Mimi. You're not just annoyed that he did not tell you." She tried to weave through her feelings to detect what Manuela suggested but she was scared at the outcome, so she stopped and shook her head vehemently in denial. But she saw the look of knowledge in her friend's brown eyes and grew even more anxious. "If you say so. Just talk to him."

"He wanted to use me. I mean I'm using him, but he could have told me if it was the same! I would be hypocritical to deny him." Manuela sighed, going to respond when she received a call. As she spoke, Millicent threw herself back and slept on her bed. Her friend came to join her after she was done speaking.

"That was Mawusi." Millicent's arched brow raised a little higher at hearing their friend's name. "Asantewaa's father remarried." If the size of her eye could double from all the news she had received, it would have done so.

"The sixty-year-old man? What about her mother? Isn't she in Belgium or something?"

Manuela propped her head up with a frown while thinking through. "I don't know if they divorced, but Asantewaa is pissed because her new stepmother is almost the age of an older sister." Millicent's nostril lifted and twisted.

"That's disgusting! How old is she?" Manuela's frown deepened again as she thought back to the conversation.

"She's thirty-five, eight years older than us." Millicent opened her mouth in aggravation and let out a scandalous gasp.

"That's horrid."

"Yep! And that is why we are going to Cape Coast next weekend!"

After spending time with Manuela for a while and planning out their trip, Millicent walked out in the dusk of the evening. When she reached home, she had a clearer mind but she still used the back entrance to avoid seeing Jace. She settled in for the evening but when it was time to sleep she realized she could not fall asleep. She was yearning to hear that deep voice read Tolstoy to her. She sat up in her bed and cried out a short quick laugh, her eyes narrowing in awareness of the situation.

"We need to talk anyway." She muttered as she picked herself up with her phone and walked out of her room to the opposite one. The door was creaked open, yet she heard nothing from inside. Knocking it lightly, she heard a hum and opened it to enter where Jace sat up on the bed with his tablet in hand. His lids shot up in surprise and anticipation at seeing her.

Jace got down from the bed and silently watched as Millicent shut the door. "Little M?" He questioned. He had been waiting in the living room for her all day, only to realize that she used the backdoor to avoid him.

"We still have to finish Anna Karenina." She inched her neck higher and swayed to his bed. "And we have to talk." She decided to add after seeing the pleading look, he had.

"Levin had meant to tell his brother of his determination to get married-" Jace's voice trailed off from the part of the bed where he sat with his legs crossed over the other in his gray sweats. The book seems to be mocking me. Perfect! He was going to peer up when the person he feared to speak spoke.

"So why didn't he?" Millicent challenged. Who knew that Tolstoy gave them the best opening statement. She saw Jace set the tablet aside and faced her who was sitting in the same manner as he did. They sat in the center of the queen-sized bed.

"Well, if he wasn't the one who proposed to have the marriage, is it still valid?" He asked in a soft voice but the fierceness behind it was not lost.

Millicent brows battled to get closer as she asked, "What do you mean?"

"It was all a business set-up between my dad and one of the rich entrepreneurs in the US. The owner of Aston motors." Millicent did not hold back her gasp and her hand flew up to her mouth. She just understood why the girl said she would tear them apart. She was no match for her. That motor company was an international sensation.

"I don't like her, little M. There's no way I'd marry her." Jace smiled as he moved to grab her hand. He loved that she communicated about things rather than getting angry beyond reason.

"But- but she wants you!" She all but exclaimed.

"And my mom doesn't like her neither do I. Trust me, if mom doesn't like her, there's no way she can get close to me. Even my dad won't get in her way." She could tell that was true. Josephine had the man around her pinky. "I'm sorry, little M. I should have told you."

"You wanted to use me, didn't you?" She saw his eyes change to a blank look.

"Initially, I thought it would be nothing. I'm so sorry. Please don't be mad." Millicent sighed and rubbed his hand, smiling lightly.

"Is that all?" Jace nodded. "No more lies, otherwise I will break your neck." Jace blinked at her threat and started laughing.

"You'll have to try to actually break it, little M. You don't even reach me." When his mouth opened to laugh, a pillow was chucked at him causing his laughter to die down abruptly. His eyes shone shrewdly, reaching slowly for the pillow behind him before he launched it.

After running around all over his room, trying to throw and evade pillows, Millicent on a quest to evade one, tripped on her own feet and hit her body into his before they tumbled down on the sheet. Millicent laid on the bed with her chest surging almost out of her nightwear. Her hair was splayed around and her blazing wild eyes drilled into Jace's cool, magnetic ones. His eyes were fiery and devouring her face. He didn't dip it down but it was a trail of fire along her face. His chest heaved so hard that she could see the outline of his muscles.

Jace reached down his hand and dragged his finger in the ghost of a touch from her hairline. His eyes followed as it dipped down her nose and his hand holding himself up grabbed her waist. He traced along her cheek and just as he reached the corner of her lip, their doorbell sounded.

Millicent's eyes shot open in astonishment. She completely surrendered herself to his touch. Her body was seriously seeking trouble. She scrambled up with wide eyes causing Jace to roll over.

"Uh, let me go check." As soon as she left, he groaned softly in torment and rubbed his hand on his face. *What is going on with me? What am I doing?*

Millicent was surprised when a frantic Max burst into her home with a fuzzy creature in his hand.

"What is that, Max?" He dropped himself on the couch and let the animal go. It was a pup.

He grinned wickedly as his sister cooed at the dog saying, "That is mimi."

Millicent's eyes shot up with a glare. "You called it by my name. I swear I'll kill you, Maxwell." She pounced but he leaped away and even the dog barked. They stood opposite each other with a couch separating them as the brown furry animal marched around sniffing her.

"Why did you bring it here?" She smiled when his expression changed. It was that sweet look he had whenever he needed something.

"Mom wants to give it to those who eat dogs. She hates the little darling. Something about how I disrespected her only daughter." He frowned at his sister before puckering his mouth. "Take care of him."

"I love mom. Why are you even leaving it at her place? Don't you have a home?" She lifted her eye in question.

"You know your mother doesn't like being alone. Plus, I'm not at home most of the time."

"And who says I'm home?"

"Josh said your fiancé is here." Millicent sputtered in anger while her brother danced about daring her to question the term. She threw her hand when he wasn't looking and hit him square on the head. "Ouch! Aba!"

"Man, that felt good. He's my husband."

"Not until I receive my 'akontasikan' and I'll only accept it if he passes the test." Millicent grabbed her slipper and he dashed to the front door before she threw it.

"Mimi?"

"What?" Millicent answered just as the dog barked. Max grinned.

"Not you, my baby pup."

"I'll kill you and sacrifice your pup after that." At that he opened the door and stepped outside. But a surprised Jace also stood to the side petting the pup after he found it and lifted her.

"Hey Jace, take care of him and you'll be officially accepted as her boyfriend." Jace lifted his brow in question. As he stalked away from the porch, Millicent stood by the open door and found something amiss.

"Max, what did the pup really do?" Her voice echoed in the dark night. It was almost ten. The impish smirk was telltale that she might actually strangle her brother after he answered.

"Oh! She took a dump on mom's back, b-u-t-t, when she was sleeping." He dashed away and into his car, cackling. He knew that was the end for him. He could only hope the pup would be alive by the time he returned but he knew his sister was too kind to do what their mother said which was why he brought it there.

"MAX!" Millicent roared into the night before slamming the door and charging at the dog.

"I'll kill you." She screamed at the dog who bundled himself into a snickering Jace.

CHAPTER 19

The orange hue from the rays of the morning sun warmly sought to vitalize the face of anyone who came into contact with it. Especially in the area of East Legon, where the home of Manuela Boateng was buzzing with untold excitement. She moved all around her home packing and awaiting the arrival of her friends for the buoyant weekend ahead. Ignorant to her was the couple who now stood outside her home with one sulking.

"The entire weekend?" An anxious Jace questioned even though he had known about the plans the girls had about a week ago. He couldn't tell why the idea of Millicent being away for those days irked him.

Millicent faced him and saw the almost invisible pout lurking on the bottom of his face. She stood up on her tiptoes and grabbed his face between both of her hands while his hands automatically settled on her hips. They had gotten so comfortable with each other that the previous rule had become all but empty words. Jace's face settled with a smile when she pushed some of his curly hair away from his face when he failed to style them back.

"I'm going to be back before you know it on Sunday. Take care of the house hm." She tapped his face in an affectionate way which caused that discomfort in Jace's heart - the same that he had grown used to and craved. He was not unaware of the current situation which was that he was growing a liking for the lady in front of him, but no matter how hard he tried to desist from the feelings that plagued him, they never left. They seemed to be growing faster and stronger by day. He gulped thickly as his eyes drifted from her wide, bright, excited eyes to her perk nose and then her plump full lips. Even in that daze he responded to her statement.

Millicent felt the hands that held her hips tighten, and she watched in amusement when he responded, "You trust me with your kitchen." Jace whispered, pulling her closer causing her heart and body that was not immune to him to thrum in excitement. She was trying to understand his thick and lush eyelashes when they swept each time he searched her face.

"You avoid that place like it was a plague." They both chuckled, still lost in the bubble that their proximity had created. Each could feel the other's breath fanning an area of their face. She felt his eyes lower to her lips again while she was engrossed in his addictive smell- a little forest and woody smell bumped with some notes of sweet spice.

"Can I kiss you?" His dense, husky voice breathily questioned. Millicent's chest rose and fell in angry successions when she noticed where his eyes were focused, and her eyes caught off-guard widened at the request.

"No touching, remember?"

"We've gone beyond that rule, little M." He squeezed her waist and his lips broadened at her expense when she had no response alongside her abashed face.

"Well, enjoy your weekend which could have been even more fun with me." Before she could respond, he had dipped his head, anchored her head with one hand and planted his lips at the corner of her lips. It was not an actual kiss, but it still sent her body heat and her heart in an overdrive.

When Jace lifted his head, he chuckled under his breath at her flustered look. Gently placing his hand on the supple skin of her cheek, his eyes found her disgruntled ones, but they still shone with an intrigued look.

A pup barked from their car, startling Millicent and letting her jump apart from the enticing man in front of her. She cleared her throat and then croaked in an uncertain and coy voice, "Yeah, take care of mi - um the pup too." Jace was tempted to laugh at her inability to use her name to refer to the little dog, but he held himself back.

They walked to the house unconsciously holding onto each other's hands.

"Mimi!" Manuela called when her friend entered. Her eyes shifted to her cousin who held her. She was not surprised at the development between the two but that did not mean that she was not wary of him because he was a man.

"Your stuff is in the guest room, Kwaku." When he pulled away to walk, Millicent tightened her hold on him. She smiled when he offered her a sweet smile as he looked at her. Both of them were confused at the desires of their heart and how they could not seem to let the other go. Manuela sighed in resignation and stalked to the kitchen leaving them to sort their problem.

"Aren't you forgetting something?" Jace cocked his brow, and his eyes were clouded in confusion till she opened her arms.

"I knew you couldn't live without me." He pulled her by her waist just as she sucked air through her teeth but spotted her lovely smile. His arms wound around her form and she rested her head on the chest that was gradually becoming more than a comfort for her. She was scared- scared that her heart had gone ahead and fallen in love with someone who probably did not belong to her. He once said that he was never going to fall in love with her and even in that moment when she embraced him, she felt her heart break. The weekend was the best way to disintegrate her entire self from him, hopefully.

After they broke apart with a last affectionate look from Jace, he went into the guest room and came out with a bunch of wrapped goods, one long one and another four to five were rectangular and flat. Millicent only looked on as he loaded them in the car with curiosity. He did not tell her what they were and only gave her another hug with a full-blown smile that showed his white pearly teeth and then he went back.

About ten minutes after Jace left, a trio arrived at Manuela's residence.

"Mimi, the girls are here! Please get the door for them - I'm packing the last box of snacks." To them, snacks were not chips and the like. Any food, complete or not, that failed to satiate their hunger fully was a snack. So, one could imagine what had been packed.

Upon hearing her friend's call, she moved to the door and opened it to see three beaming faces.

"Mimi!" The lady in blond knotless braids that reached her butt with her copper-colored irises set in her twinkling cat-shaped eyes screamed, stretching out her round lips and the beauty mark on its left side. Before long, the smooth espresso skin of Shirley Tetteh's hands bundled Millicent in an excited hug with her baby pink top highlighting her appearance. Millicent couldn't help but laugh at her bubbly friend's excitement.

Someone pushed Shirley aside further into the room, and the medium and tan face of another chaotic person in their group stood before her glinting in joy. Mawusi closed the gap between them as soon as Millicent's hands opened. "My girl!! It's been forever!" Her strong voice, deeper than most females, bustled Millicent's tender ears.

"I know, girl, I know." Millicent's wistful voice responded before her friend's black locs swept across her face as she stepped back. Mawusi tilted her head to the side, still holding onto her arms, just scanning her friend. Her intelligent almond shaped maroon eyes squinted and she pursed her bottom heavy lips before nodding in appreciation.

"Looking good as usual, Mimi. Let me know the secret to your hair."

"I've told you, Mawusi, you'll even be disappointed by the shampoo I use." She giggled when her friend frowned. However, a sweet voice spoke from behind Mawusi, revealing the last of the trio that just arrived.

"Genes are so unfair." Asantewaa grumbled and came to hug her friend. The other two had already moved to the kitchen chattering away. Asantewaa had installed straight brown frontal hair which accentuated her dark honey skin which itself looked very milky.

"I've missed you, love."

"I've missed you too." While Shirley and Mawusi were always bubbling with energy, Millicent, Manuela and Asantewaa had a calmer front which hid their inner tendencies to be as tumultuous as their friends.

"Where's Ella?" Asantewaa screamed into the rowdy house and as if summoned, the black beauty strutted out with packages of food in her hand.

Manuela stood still for a theatrical effect with all her friends following suit. In an instant all the chatting ceased, allowing her to perform their ritual.

"Ready to bomb the boring months?" As soon as she shouted, the ladies roared in mirth with indistinct words as they stepped out. Coincidentally, they all wore high-waisted jeans of different shades with different colored tops which lit up their friendly bond even more.

Manuela was putting the items for their trip in her car when a land cruiser parked right outside her house. The girls stopped talking to observe the new addition. As the door behind the passenger's opened, a pale leg in a black knee-high boot stepped out. The auburn hair of the supposed fiancée of Jace caused a crossed look to take over Millicent's face and she turned to give an imploring look to Manuela who looked just as confused at the new addition. Gwen in her knee-length yellow dress had sunglasses shielding her eyes, and taking them off, she snobbishly regarded her surroundings.

"Whose child is this?" Shirley whispered in an intrigued voice from where they all hovered around each other. Manuela stepped forward toward the car as the driver also alighted, bringing out a suitcase.

"Manuela's cousin's friend." Millicent responded offhandedly to the astonishment of her friends. Millicent paid attention to the interaction between Manuela and the new woman.

When the lean young man appeared in front of her, ignoring the scar that ran down his neck, Manuela asked in their local language while smiling slightly at Gwen who looked like she would be anywhere other than with Millicent, "Yaya, why is she here?"

The young man grimaced but replied saying, "Madam said she can't deal with her so you should take her along with you." Manuela would have laughed at her aunt being peeved by someone if she was not impressed with the woman who had managed to cause that.

"But my car is full!"

"Ah, you see, madam said I can take you if that was the case." Just as Manuela wanted to scream in frustration, Millicent was burning in anger as Gwen gave her an unimpressed look. Her friends were curious about the atmosphere but decided to keep quiet and see how the situation progressed. Manuela pinched and rubbed her forehead but turned to smile brightly at Gwen, the woman who did more than damage her cousin. She had no idea why her uncle was being 'stupid for money' as if he didn't have millions himself.

"Hi, Gwen, I'm Manuela. Jace's cousin." At the mention of her relationship with Jace, the woman's face surprisingly diffused from contempt to a smile.

"She's a fake." Mawusi whispered among her friends for one of them to shush her.

In the end the girls settled in Josephine's car with the group taking the last two seats while they left the first seat for Gwen who the ever kind Asantewaa tried to engage only to be thrown aback by her pompous nature. She stopped all attempts to engage with her after five monotonous answers from the auburn haired girl and turned her attention to her friends who were ever boisterous.

Arriving at the lodge by the beach where they had booked to stay for the weekend, Millicent was troubled with her inability to sleep as they decided to sleep for the remainder of the morning. The fiancée of Jace being a strong contribution in addition to her separation from the said man. Her thoughts lingered on their nights and the novel they were reading. How his smooth voice would express the gravest emotions in a controlled manner. She sighed at the silence in their space, smiling softly when she remembered how she had screamed in the car during the entire ride to a barbie playlist they had made much to the vexation of the rich heiress who was with them. Her phone's vibration on the bed in the suite she shared with her friends had her sitting up and trembling at the name that was displayed.

"Hi!" Jace chuckled from the other side elated to hear her voice.

"Little M, how am I supposed to sleep?"

"I should be asking that. Your fiancée is here." Quickly his voice turned hard.

"I don't have one unless you are talking about yourself." An image flashed before her eyes, and she saw herself in a white gown which sent her heart into an overdrive.

Deciding to test the waters, she asked, "Would you prefer that?"

"Very much so." He answered without missing a beat, planting a smile on her face.

They spoke much about everything mundane in hushed whispers, treading safely along the edges of their hearts till darkness racked their eyelids and the sun reappeared burning brighter in the day reminding the ladies of the adventure that lay ahead of them.

Chapter 20

"Didn't anyone tell madam 'moke' that we are climbing a walkway that is forty meters high?" Shirley's amused voice commented from where the five of them walked behind Gwen who surprisingly wore cargo pants with her ankle length boots. The sun's rays were obscured by the thicket of canopy formed by the trees and as a result there was a refreshing coolness that surrounded them as they walked through the greenery of the Kakum National Park led by their tour guide. Manuela had also invited her aunt's driver who tagged behind them in his usual black articles.

"I did inform her royal highness but as the queen of fashion she chose to ignore it." Manuela looked at the woman who walked with her head held high away from them. Gwen seemed genuinely intrigued by the information the tour guide was relaying but she disregarded her company and left them to their plans which immensely gratified even the ones who had just come to meet her. Millicent felt her chest burn whenever she saw the woman because she always remembered her parting words from the Elrod's mansion. Yet, she felt compelled to let the woman know about the plight that she was going to face in a few moments. Even the young man in the green assigned clothes for the guides was apprehensive as Gwen trudged through the roots that formed the soil beneath them in her heels.

"I think I should let her know." All the girls turned to Millicent with a demanding gaze. The three- Mawusi, Shirley and Asantewaa- who did not know the relationship she had with Jace were still concerned as they felt the underlying antipathy with which Gwen avoided her. Manuela had the most dubious looks among them but Millicent only smiled at them. They all had their hairs up in a bun and paired their jeans with white sneakers. None could utter another word as their friend stalked toward the red-haired woman.

"Gwen." Millicent called after the guide was done speaking. She looked up and was met with the icy eyes of Gwen.

"What? Did you finally realize that you are not good for him?" Her thin, high-pitched voice sneered, and she crossed her arms in front of her chest. Millicent only calmly raised her lined eyebrow, unsurprised at the entitled heiress' outburst. Behind them, her friends were questioning Manuela on how her cousin seemed to have selected one of the worst people to call a friend.

"With your social class, you're not worth a quarter of his riches. So, leave him to the status he belongs." Her arched brow on her powdered pale face challenged Millicent. If there was one thing that Millicent despised, it was prejudice and judging someone by a bank statement.

She stood upright, a stance that all who were close to her knew of, and so her friends' gait slowed as they anxiously held themselves back from interfering in whatever was going on. Gwen, oblivious to her behavior, turned her designer bag to emphasize her statement and dusted it slightly with her pink neatly manicured nails. Millicent stepped closer to her and even though Gwen stood taller than her by a few inches, her straightened figure startled the latter and almost caused her to stumble on a root. The forest was now silent as everyone, including their driver and the guide, stood warily away from the two women.

"A tiger and a lioness. I wonder who wins." Yaya, the driver, slipped up causing the girls in front of him to snicker. The statement was even more hilariously funny with the way he spoke in their home language.

"I wonder which who is." Asantewaa quipped in humor.

"Now you listen here Gwen. My worth is not measurable by riches, a bank statement or a man. I work to get my own money and I squander none from my family. If you ever felt that gratification of being remunerated, you'd know that one's value is not determined by money. Whether I'm enough for him, is Jace's own decision. Who are you to speak, when my husband hasn't?" No one heard what ensued but they judged from the hardened face of Millicent that it was a deep matter Gwen flushed as she looked at her rival, a little in mortification and indignation. Millicent, satisfied with the muted woman, calmly apologized to the guide and walked back to her friends.

"Uh, so did you tell her?" Mawusi questioned when they moved up.

"Suffering is the best medicine for a fool." She simply stated, still outraged by the interaction she just had. Manuela comfortingly patted her shoulder and urged her to enjoy the trip, silently berating her aunt who had called to ask about the trip earlier during their rest.

"We've been here more than three times, Ella. Why are you still scared of them?" Shirley asked as they prepared to cross the first level of the canopy walkway whose wooden bridges had been secured to the trees they were bracketed by the over sixty meters tall trees.

"Excuse you. I'm sorry you don't fear heights." Manuela shivered, guiding her eyes from looking down. From the corner of her eyes she saw the great Gwen Dumas tremble a little as she placed her heel on the edge of the bridge.

"We'll be with you Ella; just don't look down." You could hear the birds of all kinds chirp, some from below with their very distant songs and some from above. The first group that just finished the first level had one person screaming and Millicent knew that was going to be her friend in a few moments which plastered a smile on her face. That was the thrill of being so high up in the air and swinging on wooden walkways.

When the guide gestured for them to go, they all waited patiently with occasional snickers when Gwen though poised to walk in heels, struggled in maintaining a secure posture. The canopy could be scarier for people who held to just one side which created the illusion that it was tipping over. After ten minutes when she made it across the first stage, the girls hopped on too. Manuela in the presence of her friends dispensed her fears and even taunted their driver.

"Come on, Yaya. You can do it." It was all playful with warm smiles, warming the man's heart and allowing him to join in the excitement with them.

On the third level, Mawusi casually spoke saying, "You girls know the little girl in junior high school that my mom brought from our hometown, right?"

"Fafa?" Shirley questioned, trying to maintain her balance as the bridge swung with more force as compared to the last two. It was higher in height as well.

"Yes, that's her. She's pregnant." A series of collective gasps fell from the girls who tried to hush the conversation so that the group behind them or ahead of them did not hear. They could still see trails of Gwen who seemed to be slowing down in her walk.

"How?" Manuela asked in a genuinely astounded voice.

"Instead of her going to school as expected, we found that there is a barber on the street to her school. It's not like we did not provide for the little girl; apparently, she was cajoled by his gifts and sweet words. She's just fifteen for goodness' sake! I felt like killing the guy."

"I think if she wasn't forced, her own interest led her there. Curiosity does kill the cat." Millicent responded lamenting for the child who might have to have a hiatus in her education. There were a lot of stigmatizing words for young girls in such circumstances in their schools.

"What does your mother want to do?"

"She wanted to send her back to the village, but she feels guilty and wants to be responsible for her till the end. We placed the stupid guy behind bars." Shirley sighed and Asantewaa also laid down her woes.

"I don't know which is worse between a father who married before divorcing his wife for sexual satisfaction and a teen who is pregnant."

"Urgh, we were supposed to be having fun. No more thoughts about all this depressing stuff. We can talk about them tomorrow." With the words of Manuela being agreed to, they bounced their way across the remaining three walkways. They went through the cultural stores and got souvenirs where Millicent was left pondering on what to get for the man who never left her conscious thoughts.

"Did you see the elephant and the monkeys?" Shirley's excited shriek implored as they walked through people in the stalls. Millicent was surprised to see that Gwen was lost in her own sightseeing. She managed not to break her legs but alas, she purchased slippers in exchange for the heels.

"I thought she would last longer." Manuela whispered among them just as Millicent picked up the beaded bracelet that she thought would fit Jace.

"Tell me about it." Asantewaa's calm voice bewitchingly floated around them as they continued to stare at the heiress who walked around in awe.

At night, when they returned to their lodge, the girls decided to have their fun on the beachfront of the resort. As they played in the water, Asantewaa argued that they should invite the red-haired woman who regarded everyone as below her, immediately getting reluctant responses from the rest.

"Oh, oh! Look at that! A proposal!" They turned to see glittering lights and a woman in a bodycon short white dress with tulle and flowers. One of them squealed in excitement.

"Are you thinking what I'm thinking?" They mischievously held their gazes with grins that displayed their teeth in the dark starry night at Millicent's words.

"Let's go crash it!" Their exclamation was followed with giggles and haphazard running till they got to the spot where the teary-eyed woman stood in the heart shaped lighted candles and the man knelt on one knee. Immediately she responded in affirmation and was locked in her fiancé's embrace, the girls hollered and called out joyous shouts, louder than the family and friends who were gathered around.

When their fatigue caught up with them, they heavily dragged their feet to their suite. Millicent, who was the last to enter, was disconcerted at the looming figure at the next door. Her hand grabbed onto her chest and her eyes wildly regarded the woman drinking wine. Her auburn hair in its waves identified her. She was going to enter the room when Gwen suddenly spoke.

"We dated, you know?" Her brows scrunched up in confusion at the words Gwen uttered. She faced her to find that her attention was on the glass and its content that she was swirling.

"Jace and I; almost two years." Millicent felt a pang of discomfort when she realized the man she liked had decided to omit another truth. Her face pressed in lines harder than initially.

"Which is why, I cannot believe that he likes you or married you. Two years is a lot. I'm going to get him back." With those words, she swayed to her feet and disappeared behind the doors. Millicent could not get an ounce of sleep with the new information that tormented her brain. All she could do was toss and turn as well as reject the five calls of Jace.

The morning of the next day was the same and by afternoon when they had to depart, Manuela who had caught onto her foul mood dragged her to the beach where the crashing waves soothed the shores close to them.

"Okay, Mimi. What's going on?" When Millicent's attention focused, she could only stare wide-eyed at her friend. "Don't give me that look. I know something is up. I mean everyone noticed."

"They dated."

"Huh?" Manuela's perplexed voice forced out.

"Gwen and Jace." Manuela, though not privy to this information, could tell her friend's heart could be damaged if she did not comfort her. She embraced her friend.

"Oh, Mimi. I don't know the entire story but what I do know is that you like that buffoon."

"I do. I like him so much that I feel like scratching that girl's eyes out." Millicent heaved out in concern.

"Ha! He's got a handful with you. So, can you let him go?" At this point they were seated on the golden, gritty sand, facing each other.

"I- I don't think so." She frowned and picked at the sand beneath her. When she felt Manuela's warm hand on hers, she looked up with that cloud of worry still casted over her countenance.

"Then you have your answer." She really did.

The trip back was uneventful and only filled with more chaotic babbling among the friends, less so from Millicent who decided to ignore Gwen.

It was night when she was dropped home. As soon as she opened the door, she was crushed into the familiar embrace of woody and spicy smell. After basking in it, she solemnly stepped back and gazed into his jolly eyes.

"Let's stop what we are doing."

CHAPTER 21

"What did you say?" Jace took a forceful step forward and his initially warm face contorted into an intensely dissatisfied look. Millicent on the other hand, looked pertinacious and only took that little step, having her back attached to the wall to accommodate some space between his impressive build.

Looking into his meteor gray-blue eyes she emphasized saying, "This marriage fiasco, I'm ending it." She saw the angry lines appear at the corners of his eyes that were blazing even with the red shirt that he wore. He thumped his full hand on the wall above her head, still intensely gazing into her eyes and becoming confused at the resolution he found in them.

"No, I don't agree. Are you even ready to let your family know that this is a lie?" He bent down his head letting his nose touch hers in a whispering movement.

"I just needed my mother to leave me and she has since she met you." Millicent's heavy, and breathy voice replied, bending away from his touch. The tense atmosphere was heating up their breaths which fell through their nostrils. "I can pay you."

She sucked in a sharp breath when his warm hand slid down the wall and pushed up her neck, crawling to her nape and into her hair that was let loose to curtain her face. Her skin heated as her lips parted, turning her eyes misty in her struggle to hold the devouring gaze he had. The gray had completely shadowed the blue in his eyes. She felt her chest struggle to be confined in the top she wore as she searched his tan face down to the beard he was currently sporting.

"Why can't I accept this sudden change? Why can't I seem to want to let you go?" His gravely, tremulous tone challenged. She was having a difficult time keeping up with the conversation and his closeness, so before she thought it through, both her hands had pressed on his perky chest and pushed him back with an average strength. Jace stumbled back in surprise which caused his eyes to open exceeding their normal range and his hand that grasped her neck to fall.

"Well, you have to! You see, I found someone I like." Millicent screamed before she stalked toward him in the hallway where their bedrooms were located. Her step caused Jace to shuffle back till he was almost glued to the wall behind him. His eyes slithered and his thoughts turned chaotic at her confession.

"Wh-"

"And I hate it when other women claim to like that man." Millicent continued, her eyes never leaving him even when she stopped in front of him. Her piercing brown eyes tormentingly drilled his own which were immensely perplexed. His pink lips separated in his muddled state as he searched for the words to let her know that her statements pierced his heart.

"I hate it when they want to own him." She shot out harshly with her burning eyes willing him to understand but he was at sea. Millicent snaked her hands up to his shoulders and roughly pulled his tall frame down and all he could do was follow the command of the woman. "Tell me Jace, why does my chest burn in fury when another woman claims ownership of you?"

At her declaration, his eyelids drew up to allow him to inspect her face and confirm the words she just spoke. He could see the anguish and the desire in the depths of those brown pools. Everything around them was silent except for the occasional chirping of the crickets outside and the hot pants of expiration that jarringly escaped their lungs.

"You." Jace whispered before suddenly shutting his eyes and shaking his head. "Oh, to hell with it. My chest smolders, wanting to explode at the thoughts of you in arms that are not mine." His raspy, abrasive voice, passionately relayed and was thrilled to see her eyes flare darkly at his own confession.

"Help me." Millicent's heart quickened at the vulnerable, pleading voice that croaked in her ears. Jace, who was still being held down, swooped his eyes down to her slightly puckered lips and groaned, "I've tried to hold back more than I could."

Millicent, in their frenzied state, did not capture when his lips descended on hers nor when she broke every rule of morality she knew, being compelled by her attraction and temptation which ended her in his bed with their bare flesh attached to each other.

The morning rays crept through the tiny openings of the dark curtains in Jace's room but it failed to reach the two who were tangled under the duvet. Millicent sighed in her sleep and stretched out herself, to find her skin brushing up another that seemed more prickly. Overlooking it to be her other leg, she tried to turn to a more comfortable array. However, her brows pushed together, creating folds on her eyelids and her lips pursed from where her face was pressed to Jace's bare chest when she realized that a heavy arm on her waist restricted her movement as well as the leg that had just lifted to trap hers. With a startled gasp she opened her eyes, disheveled while waiting for her vision to regain clarity and yet again she let out a more audible dreadful gasp when she felt the stir and beheld Jace's manly face. With a forceful push, she shot up into a sitting position which aroused Jace from his sleep.

Millicent roamed her eyes around the room she was accustomed to and felt herself shiver when a cool breeze brushed past her arm. There was a difference with how she felt. Her eyes opened further when she took in her bare upper body.

"No, no, no, no..." She chanted picking up the duvet and noticing both of their undignified states. Jace's eyes fluttered open when he caught her voice but sat up in distress when he saw that her hands were covering her face as her shoulders lifted. "What have I done?"

"Little M?" He gently called at her wailing, ignoring the intimacy of their heated bodies. Immediately he touched her, she scooted away as though she had been scorched with fire. He glowered in concern watching as she dropped her hand and clutched the duvet to her naked chest. "Tell me what happened, baby." He stared as her wild eyes snapped to meet his and he itched to get her hand when she grabbed onto a fistful of her hair.

"I shouldn't have done this, Jace. It goes against my faith and principles as a Christian. I was supposed to only have sex with my husband. What am I going to do?" When what she said registered with him, he felt the guilt bud in his heart's crevices.

Reaching her and drawing her closer by the waist he said, "I'm so sorry to put you in this situation. I should have held myself back." Millicent shook her head and her eyes glazed.

"I am to be as blamed as you are. None of us was inebriated and if anything, you had my consent. I just feel so disappointed in myself - Afterall, He has spoken to me so there is no excuse for this sin. Who knew I could be so easily tempted?" She sighed when Jace pulled her into his embrace.

"No one will know unless we tell them."

"Keep deluding yourself. Have you met an African mother's eyes before? They see into your most private affairs. Let's keep away from them for now." She felt him sigh. Of course he knew. His mother was one.

"I'm sorry, little M. But I plan on making this official." She was pushed back and saw the smile that lit his morning face. "I like you, Millicent. Will you be my girlfriend?" Millicent frowned which made him wary.

"Now that sounds even more horrible. We did it before a title." When she saw his face, she lightly chuckled and gave the answer they both wanted to hear. "Yes, I will."

"Good!" Jace simply said before he planted his lips on hers for a chaste kiss. Once they separated, a mortified Millicent sought to find her clothes and flee from him but her eyes caught herself smiling, frowning, sending food to her mouth with a wicked glint in her eyes, all of which were on canvases. Canvases of paintings, four of them in his room. She stopped to see what felt so familiar about them and then she thought about his home in LA. All of them looked as real as she did in these ones.

"What is this?" Jace was still admiring her and was surprised at the question. Following her line of sight, he found the paintings he had made of the woman he was obsessed with; so obsessed that he completed four of them in a day and a half.

"You're an artist?" Her incredulous tone had him gulping and rushing forward to explain to her. He had kept out the details of his profession for no reason. Maybe he didn't want her running or being one of those to take advantage of him when they discovered that he was one of the greatest artists in the states and a painting of his was worth millions.

"Yes. It's what I do." He thought she was going to be angry, but Millicent bounced in excitement, her eyes shining as she turned to view the paintings again.

"So, the ones in LA?" He adjusted the covers to obscure her body when they slid down, and he nodded to confirm that those were made by him. When the covers shimmied down once more, a mundane desire blossomed in him which kept his eyes on her body.

"They're so good." Millicent said under her breath, turning to praise him to see his dark eyes unwavering on her. "What happened?" She quickly picked up the covers and noticed his throat bob in a painful manner.

Jace's dark orb weakly looked at her hesitantly. "I suddenly have a very ridiculous thought." Her tousled brows lifted in query. "I want to paint you." And she gulped when his hooded eyes slowly dragged down the covers where her body was hidden. Jace reached out his light skinned hand to pick hers. It baffled her how they still sat in the bed as if nothing happened the previous night, but she was even more taken aback when she realized his request.

"You mean..." her index finger dragged down from her head, and she met his stiff nod. She knew that would be throwing caution out of the wind and breaking down all her moral defense. Yet, one look in his eyes proved that she would also do it because she trusted him and her attraction to him made her even crazier.

"I'm doing all the wrong things with you." She smiled when the dazzling smile took over his face.

"Do it with only me then. It's just going to be between us." And they did. He painted her au naturel. They turned it toward the wall though her face was not revealed. he painted her so she was looking through a window which concealed her face and instead showed her voluminous, tightly coiled, long black hair.

About two in the afternoon when they had come out of their fantasy, the doorbell sounded, and Millicent moved from her spot on the couch to check but came rushing back which caused the little pup to bark.

"We're both going to be killed today if you don't shut up." Jace lifted an inquisitive brow on his amused face, coming to a stop in front of her. The bell rang again.

"You didn't open the door." He stated as he settled his hand on her waist in her agitated state. Millicent pushed his hands away and paced in the same way the pup was shuffling.

She raised her head to him as mimi continued to back with an inscrutable look and worriedly spoke who the dreaded person was and even Jace blanked.

"My mother is here."

CHAPTER 22

"Kwaku, my son. How are you?" Millicent winced at the sweet tangy voice of her mother. She was now tucked in bed playing the sick, but they had agreed not to voice her presence in the home until her mother asked.

Regina smiled kindly when the handsome young man allowed her in and took the items she was carrying. Looking at his muscular build, fair and well groomed skin, his eyes and finally his hair, she was certain that he could be the one for her daughter. She just wanted to find out what he did for a living and that would bolster her decision. Her mouth broadened when he set the bag on the counter after they entered the kitchen.

"Ah, Kwaku, I'm sure that child forgot to make you food. Let me get you something." Her eyes gleamed when she noticed his anxious face and somewhere in her bed, Millicent only grumbled at her mother downplaying her importance in the kitchen.

Jace, being highly amused and also nervous of the older version of the woman he liked, responded, "I'm the one who cannot be trusted in the kitchen, auntie." He awkwardly rubbed the back of his neck when the scrutinizing gaze of Regina intensified on his face.

Regina was only taking time to comprehend the words that were clouded in his accent. Once she comprehended, she clapped her hands together and clicked her tongue. She walked around to where he stood with a very satisfied look.

"Love always defends." She gently patted his back and craned her neck to see him. Regina was tall but over the years a little stoutness had taken over her body which made her seem shorter than she was. She was content with the young man who was yet to marry her daughter.

"No haste, my son but when is the family going to be introduced?" Millicent sat up suddenly and stiffly after hearing those words. Her door was cracked open so she could hear their faint voices. The older woman lightly laughed, oblivious to the reddening ears of the young man and the compromising situation. When Jace failed to answer but only stared back at her with wide eyes, she added, "You see, we have to be certain and settled to ward off other men when they ask of her but because you've not come formally..." Her sage eyes lit with the knowledge that only she was cognizant of after her lowered voice informed him. She leaned behind the counter as he stood tall in front of her.

If possible, Jace stood even taller - his way of possessing the bond between him and Millicent - and without dithering, responded in a firm way, "It will happen soon." He hadn't known he liked the woman so much that his mind could not materialize her with any other person.

Regina nodded when she assessed the conviction on the now hard features of his face. "Okay. Now, let me make you some good home food. I hope you can eat it." With an expectant look she moved around to start her preparation.

"Yes please. My mother taught me to eat all our delicacies." Jace spoke, stepping to the side and allowing her to work. He remembered something that unsettled him. "I'm so sorry, would you like anything to drink?" Regina smiled inwardly, impressed by the man's reception to culture.

"That's alright. I'll make this and go clear out that busy child's room. By the way..." She was cut off by his rushed voice.

"Oh, she's home. She wasn't feeling well today." Millicent puffed in relief at the timely answer.

"Sick?" She heard the usual heavy footsteps of her mother when she was concerned, rushing to her room. Her door opened and the woman badged in with Jace in tow. Regina had creases of worry on her forehead and around her eyes. Jace hid a snicker behind the back of his hand when she squeezed her face in pseudo pain and looking right at her he could detect the little glare in the depth of her squinted brown eyes.

Millicent quickly picked out the thermometer that Jace placed in the hot water under her bed and placed it in her armpit. She signaled with her eyes for her man to get moving in the act they were portraying.

"Oh, the thermometer!" Jace said and rushed forward to draw it out while Regina sat on her bed with her intelligent eyes scanning her daughter. "My! Thirty-eight degrees!"

Regina's eyes widened and she sent her hand to Millicent's forehead where a hot towel rested until seconds ago. The shock of the heat made her snatch back her hands.

"Aba, why are you so hot? What happened?" Regina turned in search of Jace but the latter was coming out with a bowl of water and a towel. What a caring man. Her eyes squinted as she thought of the most effective way to let such a man be enticed by her stubborn daughter. Her thoughts reinforced the anxiety for her sick daughter. She inspected her face and seemed to notice something. The look caused Millicent to cower, shrinking into the bed and her wide eyes signaled Jace.

"There's something about your face though, Aba." The older woman continued to pry.

"What mama?" Millicent forced her voice into a croak which alarmed Regina.

"Eh, auntie, let me cool her a bit." Jace offered in an eager way which sounded too good to be real. But the mother taking it to be a sign of adoration stepped up.

"Sure, go ahead, dear. I'll make some light soup and food for you." She addressed both of them to see her daughter painfully try to nod. "Or we can go to the hospital."

"No!" Millicent's strong voice surprised her. "I mean no, ma, I want Jace to take care of me." She said weakly and gazed at the man with loving eyes causing him to flood with emotions that the older one should not see. He sent her a warning look as he put the cool towel on her. Regina smiled.

With another long look at the weird glow on her daughter, Regina answered, "Okay. I'll be in the kitchen."

As soon as she vacated the room, the couple burst out in breathy laughter and Jace threw down the towel. He grabbed her face gently with his starry blue-gray eyes twinkling and dropped a long kiss on her forehead making her fall further into him. She focused her eyes on his when he pulled back with a grin while chuckling.

"You did good, babe."

"What can I say? We make a good team." Millicent also grinned but suddenly glowered. "She almost caught me. I told you their eyes are not human." She felt Jace rub her neck to soothe her.

Another ring of their doorbell caused the two to break apart. The little pup barked, and they heard her mother exclaim.

"So, this is where that boy brought you?" Both Millicent and Jace chuckled but were curious who the new person could be.

"Why did everyone decide to come today?" They strained their ears to hear the conversation after Jace opened the door. Because the house was silent, it was easy for the voices to bounce off the walls, echo and get to them.

"Good afternoon. I'm looking for Jace." A well-known voice to them spoke in their local dialect. An alarmed Jace wide-eyed looked at Millicent's comical ones.

"Did she say she was coming?" He shook his head in a daze.

"Ah! My in-law?" She heard her mother's excited voice confirm their suspicion of the identity of the new person. The mothers themselves have gone ahead with an intuitive initiation of the family introduction.

"Ei, our in-law oh!" They heard the two women excitedly chatting.

"Jace, hot towel, now." He cocked his head to the side but put it on her head, nonetheless. His white shirt spanned across his pectorals.

"You think she's going to come?"

"Aba is sick, so he's taking care of her." She heard her mother's voice again.

"You mean Millicent?" Regina nodded in affirmation.

"Oh no. Can I see her?" Millicent's eyes spoke the knowledge she had to Jace who took off the hot towel and pushed it under the bed while beginning to clean her with the other.

"My dear, I hear you're not well." Josephine said as soon as she entered, and Millicent lightly groaned to indicate her pain. Jace gave way for his mother who soon spotted the same scrutinizing eyes that Millicent's mother initially had.

"Are you sure it's just sickness." Millicent searched for Jace with the eyes. He stood behind his mother, and she made sure her eyes conveyed her thoughts. What did I tell you? Jace cringed with a sheepish look. She tried to hide her mortification as she looked at Josephine.

"Uh, I don't know what's wrong auntie, but I could barely get up today." The woman sympathetically rubbed her arm.

"Hm, I hope it gets better, especially with Kwaku taking care of you." She teased, cupping Millicent's face with a motherly hand. She stood and gestured for her son to sit.

"I'll help your mother cook, so get all the rest you need."

The two mothers prepared the food and spoke of the prospect of the union of the two families, both gratified with the other's child.

They took care of the sick lady and stayed with them for a while before finally allowing Millicent to stand from her pretense when they left.

Before she left, Josephine caught hold of her son.

"Your father is trying to end that arranged marriage he inadvertently made with the Dumas group, but the girl is still holding on. I can tell you like Millicent and I like her too. It would be up to you to dissuade Gwen from entertaining thoughts of any future marriage." She expressed, holding her son's hands in hers. "He can't just throw the group away. Though Anthony can sustain his group even without them, I told him he would never know when he would need a man. Hm?"

"Yes, mom. I understand." Josephine affectionately rubbed his cheek.

"I don't know why that girl is seeking to destroy you twice, but I will not allow her. And I really like Millicent; her mother likes you as well so you're in the right with her family." Jace stared at his mother with the same fierce and power-filled look as they stood by her car. Gwen Dumas had succeeded in shattering him once, but he was not going to allow her to destroy this chance with Millicent, the only other woman his heart currently beat for.

Chapter 23

J ace's hand reached out to brush out Millicent's hair which was flying in the wind. They sat on high stools in an ice cream parlor. There was a bit of perspiration on her face as it had just been a few minutes since they got out of the furious heat of the sun.

"So, you're not going to sleep in my room anymore?" He grumbled, a little displeased about the turn of events. Ever since the night they were intimate, Millicent had avoided his room like a plague. She only stepped in once in a while to admire his artwork. At her subsequent nod, his lips set into a firm line, but Jace understood because every time he saw her sauntering around the house, his thoughts would drift to them.

"What about Anna?"

Millicent grinned and swooped her eyes down to follow the direction of the spoon she held to her mouth. Once the sweetness melted, she regarded the man in front of her. He had cut his hair in the course of the week and now it was a medium crop cut that allowed for his curls to still abound in their soft mass. The cut emphasized his jaw lines and allowed more light to reach his eyes.

His light shave stubble enhanced the entire look. His neck bore a thin golden chain that disappeared beneath the black shirt he wore.

"I'll read it myself." She grinned when his mouth moved in another grumbling session. However, a thought that flashed through her memory, pulled her lips down and her eyes dimmed as she scooped and dropped the scoop of ice cream back in the pretty cup. Jace noticed the change in mood and placed his hand on her cheek that was next to him. Customers walked in and out and sat all around them in the music filled room.

"Hey." He said softly and gained her attention. When Millicent saw his elegant right brow lift, she smiled. He was able to lift any brow as he pleased.

"I was just thinking..." Jace dropped his hand, lifted himself and pulled his chair closer before settling that arm around her seat, oblivious to the awed looks young girls were discreetly peeping at, at their intimate display.

"I told you my ears are always available." He smiled when her eyes glinted. The smile that she only saw when he was with her.

"About Gwen." Millicent looked worried when the man beside her stiffened at the name. His face contorted to a hard look and the hand around her tightened their hold. It was the same steely, disdainful face he made the first time she met Gwen. "She said you two dated." The statement came out like a shy question.

Jace snapped his hard eyes to her and inhaled sharply. He felt Millicent's soft palm straightening out the frown lines and rubbing them. After a moment of that contact his features softened.

"Why do you hate her?"

"I don't. That would mean I care about her, and I don't have that emotion for her." He was startled when a quick kiss was dropped to the corner of his mouth. He turned to the bronze-skinned woman and chuckled when she quickly looked around them.

"Good!"

"Do I get that every time I stay away from other women?" But she refused to talk, only hiding a smile. Jace sighed after a minute deciding to lay bare what she should have known when they made the false marriage deal.

"We dated about three years ago - the first girl I ever loved. I thought she loved me the same way. In our second year, I was preparing for an exhibition, a very important one. She was like a backbone especially when I went blank. I painted a series of landscapes. The morning of the exhibition I was called to be told that my artwork never arrived at the gallery. I made two copies of three of my favorite ones that captured the different spheres of nature - ocean, forest, city. Sent those to the gallery only to be accused of plagiarism - that's a huge thing anywhere but in the art world, it's deadly. Dad investigated and found that Gwen stole my work and gave it to her notorious brother who is also an artist." When he heard Millicent's gasp, the dark cloud cleared from his eyes, and she saw the horrific face she made. He ruefully smiled.

"It was a hard couple of months after that. Critics arose audaciously, and my credibility almost went downhill, and my heart was trampled on."

"And Gwen?" Millicent dubiously asked of the horrendous woman.

"She traveled to somewhere in Europe. I lost my inspiration to work. What was the use if it was going to be stolen? My manager after five months got frustrated with my unproductivity and I came here." He looked up to see Millicent's confused expression. "I'm guessing you're wondering about the arranged marriage. Her dad thought to clear both families' names, we could marry and give a press release stating that it was a mutual collaboration and what not."

"That's stupid." The emotion that dripped along with her words caused him to laugh.

"I wish you could tell my dad. I think it was more of Gwen's decision to come for me, but she ended it herself when she left without dignity or integrity."

"I'm so sorry about that. But..." Millicent's voice bubbled in excitement. "We're here to rectify that and find inspiration for you. It's going to be rowdy, crowded and a little dirty because this is Accra."

They were in the heart of Accra where hawkers lingered, traders called for customers and thieves worked like no man's business. When they got out of the parlor and walked into the multitude of people who walked about, dangerously engaging in their own activities, Jace felt his soul come alive. This was the kind of thriving community he had yet to see in the US. Different colors of people bustling together, sweat, toil and smiles amidst laughter alike. It was a vibrant collection of expressions in different settings. The scents and colors around them hypnotized him. He saw the young kids play and his heart broke for those who took shelter under the stairs of stores. He stood in the center of a trade market where people carried goods, on the heads of women and on the shoulders of men. Millicent stopped them from one station to the other, clothes, food, street food, shoes, bags all strewn around shops and mats on the ground.

Millicent saw the way Jace's awareness reflected in his curious eyes which lingered from one person to the other, not in a rude way. His visage was brightened under the illumination of the sun. Whenever her hand dragged down to pick his hand and lead him to another spot, her hand would brush on the beads of the bracelet she bought from Cape Coast and a ghost smile would touch her lips. They squeezed between people, getting food at the places she usually stopped at.

"Are they fighting?" Jace asked when he heard screaming even in the midst of the throng of people they trudged through. Millicent strained her ear to hear and discovered they were speaking another language of their country.

"They're speaking Ga. It could just be casual talk, or they could be fighting. From the insults I'd bet they're fighting." Millicent wistfully smiled but was stopped when Jace pulled on her hand which was in his. He had an expectant face.

"Can we go, and see?" She tilted her head in astonishment.

"You want to go and see women and men in an argument?" The manner of eagerness with which the tanned man nodded made her chortle. "Alright, come on."

A lot of things happened on the streets of Accra and arguments were not a new occurrence. Jace gasped when a bigger woman grabbed onto a bulky man screaming in his face. The cloth around her fell and she stood back down as the man also charged at her with his own words. After she readjusted the cloth, she resumed screaming and a group of men and women tried to separate them.

"Crazy, I suddenly want to call Sean. What are they saying?"

"I suddenly want to slap the awe off your face. We recently got a new phone. This place is no different." He pointed to her bag, which he held, to indicate that the phone was already there.

At another shout he reiterated his question, "What did she just say?" He assumed though this was not Twi, Millicent understood because she laughed from time to time and cringed at others.

"Oh, um she insulted his mother." Jace's eyes widened. "Yeah, crude, I know." Her eyes narrowed when he grinned.

"Interesting." Jace watched the crowd increase and the group tried to separate the two. He was intrigued at how feisty the woman was. In that moment he felt an opening in his mind.

"Little M." He called and looked down at her and away from the ruckus. "I've got it."

"Told you!"

The next few days, more of his supplies were delivered at their home. Jace was locked up in his room as he usually did when he gained his inspiration. His morning jogs, phone calls and even some of his meals were forfeited.

"Jace Kwaku Asante Elrod!" His heart thumped and the paint brush fell out of his hands at the frightening tone with which his girlfriend mentioned his name. He listened closely for her footsteps from where he sat on his stool in front of the canvas, another part of his collection. When his door banged open he quickly stood from the chair and faced the open hallway waiting for the attractive woman to step in, her eyes roaming till they shortly settled on him and those brown orbs flared. Her lips turned downward and her brows drew together. He knew what was happening. The tray in her hands was evidence enough.

"Listen here mister man, you're going to take that apron off, wash your hands, eat and then you can do whatever you like. I've left you for the entire week but I can't stand another moment of this." After her rambling, she marched to the table in his room and set down the food. She respected his work ethics but there is only so much the body can take and she could see it on his haggardly energized face.

She straightened when she felt his shadow loom over her and swiveled to meet his broad chest right in her face. Her head traveled up to see him mirroring a very amused face and her arms settled on her hips. Jace leaned in till his face was right in front of hers.

"Admit it, little M, you miss me." She startled and gulped at the truth she tried to conceal. She didn't sleep in his room as she did previously and she didn't want to bother him when he worked, so she barely saw him after work too.

Deciding to be truthful of her emotions like she promised herself, if she ever started a relationship, she sighed and said, "I do miss you. I don't even get my morning hugs."

"But I do hug you."

"Well, it's not as warm and cozy." Millicent whined in an accusing voice but smiled when he bopped his nose to hers.

"I didn't know you could whine and be so needy. Don't worry, I missed you like crazy too." Jace dropped a sweet kiss on her cheek which warmed her fluttering chest. She turned in demureness and her eyes caught his painting.

"I thought you'd be done. I can barely see what is going on behind the colors, but they look so real." Jace stood and followed her sight.

"I take a while on projects I'm passionate about, ironically."

Millicent's vibrating phone stole her attention and she grinned when she saw the name.

"Sean!" Jace's eyes narrowed, and Millicent placed the call on speaker.

"Hi Mimi. What's popping?" His voice sounded strange.

"I'm good and you're on speaker."

Jace decided that was a great point to interrogate his friend. "Buddy, why are you calling my girl?"

"If you picked up your phone - but I guess you're working- I would still call her." Millicent giggled at the lively man.

"Something's up." They both frowned when Sean gravely spoke that. "There's an article about you and Gwen. Why didn't you say she was getting back and you're getting married?" This time Millicent stilled in confusion and fury, blankly looking at Jace who walked to pick his phone. That woman was set on destroying her love. "The press is looking for you in the city. Wait, you said I'm on speaker. Is Mimi...?"

Jace walked back to pull Millicent with him to the bed seeing her troubled look and he shook his head to assuage her worry.

"She knows. You didn't know about Gwen because I have not proposed to anyone." When he saw the headline, a picture of him and Gwen, declaring an engagement he had no idea about, he lifted the phone and stood up in outrage, ready to smash the device.

Millicent, catching on to what he was going to do, quickly stood and grabbed onto his hand.

"The phone did nothing wrong."

"I'll destroy Gwen Dumas." She hugged him when a chill passed through her at his tone.

"And I'll have a coffin ready." Both their shoulders shook after Sean declared but that fierce look overtook Jace's features as he tightened his hold on Millicent.

CHAPTER 24

Millicent calmly situated herself on Jace's bed, sitting beside him after the call with Sean. He picked his laptop from somewhere on the other side of the bed still entertaining a frown on his face. She sat crossed legged in front of him, settling herself softly on her heels and she faced him when he opened it and began to type.

"What are you doing?" She asked and he looked up from his furious typing to tenderly gaze into her calm and intrigued eyes.

"I'm sending an email to a friend - a journalist. I have evidence of my stolen work." Millicent's visage altered to a confused look.

"I thought you held no resentment for her." He set the laptop to his side and turned to face her, following her manner of sitting.

"Little M, I won't let her sabotage what I have with you." She could see that he was really desperate to preserve what was happening between them and so was she. She scooted forward till she could grab him and pull his lost face to hers.

"She has no authority over the relationship we share, Jace. We found ourselves and decided to like each other. Yes, you need to prove your innocence but I don't want you doing it as pettily as she did. That would make you look as immature as she is, hmm?" A small smile took over his features when he saw the conviction shining in her eyes which reflected in his own.

Jace snaked his arms around her waist while hers remained on his face. "Thank you, that brought my sanity back. I don't want you to get the wrong idea because for some reason, the thought of you doubting or hurting because of me succumbs my heart to pain."

"If you want to know how I'm feeling, just ask. I'm not going to hide them. No one knows me more than me. You'll get the truth anytime you ask and all I ask is your honesty as well." She smiled when he dropped his head in the crook of her shoulder, and she felt him sigh.

"I fear sometimes you'll run before we can talk." Millicent ran her hand through his hair and stroked his scalp to feel him relax further. It made her ask how many times he had experienced that. His relationship with the heiress might have made him insecure.

"I mean sometimes I need to be away sometimes to keep my emotions in check, but I don't run easily. If anything, you'll be stopping me from breaking your neck." When he pulled back laughing, she was overwhelmed by the adoration that shone in his eyes. She had not seen him give such a look to anyone else, and she could have sworn that she had finally met the man who was made for just her.

"How did I find such an awesome woman?" Millicent giggled when he groaned and faced up to the ceiling. "And why can't I kiss you?"

"Because I already broke my morality code with you after a kiss. I still feel guilty."

"I'm sorry. I'll bear that guilt." But she just shook her head with a smile and let him hug her. Somehow the man seemed too good to be true. Afterall, she got him after starting on a false journey with him.

"Can I kiss your cheek then?" Millicent chortled at how he could not seem to keep himself away from her. She turned her cheek to him and almost mollified with how sweet the action was.

"I still want to confront Gwen. I'm not going to be able to work until I get it straight with the woman." He grinned when she kissed his cheek as well. Seems I have to settle for pecks.

"I'll come with you after church." Her eyes lit when his own glinted at the mention of her weekly endeavor. He went with her the previous week and everyone fell in love with him. From the pastors to every single woman, she knew in the auditorium, but all she could do was hover around him because she did not want outsiders prying into their relationship at its early stage and none knew of their fake marriage allegiance either.

"Stay away from the other women." She giggled again when he playfully like a soldier saluted her in obedience.

In the moody atmosphere of that Sunday afternoon which usually induced people to sleep by the sheer grayness of the rain pregnant clouds, Millicent's hand what interlocked with her boyfriend's in an intimate hold and from time to time he brushed his fingers over her hand, and they would turn to the other with a smile whenever it happened.

As soon as the door to the Elrod's mansion opened, Jace was pushed aside, and Millicent was embraced in the arms of the sweet smell of ambrosia.

"Aunt Josephine! How are you?" Millicent was thrilled to see the older woman again looking as splendorous as she always did. Once she stepped back, Jace moved to be in step with her and curled his arm around her waist, eyeing his mom with mischief.

"Don't you know your favorite son anymore?"

They both chuckled when Josephine said, "You're my only son, meaning I see your face too often. Let me welcome my new daughter. And I'm so sorry about the article, dear; you should know it wasn't us. Anthony likes you greatly though he was unable to rectify his mistake."

"I know." Millicent answered truthfully.

"About that. Where's Gwen?" Both mother and son had similar fierce and annoyed looks when Jace mentioned the woman's name.

"She's upstairs in the guest room on the right. I'm looking for ways to send her over the ocean." Millicent gulped, discovering that the intimidating personality of Jace which he exuded on others was not only acquired from his father but his mother also.

Jace pulled Millicent closer just as Josephine excused herself in fear of burning her food and he leaned down to whisper, "I'll be right back, baby."

She placed her palms flat on his chest, not ignoring the endearment that had over the weeks become part of his vocabulary and gave him a meaningful look. "Behave." His head dipped in a nod, and he smiled, dropping a quick peck on her right cheek. Standing back up, every trace of emotion faded from his face, and she felt that domineering aura take over the sweetness she was used to. Others probably suffer from his rich boy attitude. He stalked up the stairs and she went to the kitchen to help Josephine.

Jace waited for a minute after knocking. He heard a little shuffling behind the door and the red-haired woman appeared before him. His tongue squeezed in distaste when he remembered that in their years of dating that hair used to be a dull orange color not far from her natural blond. Her olive eyes widened in mirth when she saw him and she jutted her hip out, sweeping her currently straight hair to one shoulder before screeching on an uncomfortably whiny voice, "Jacey!"

"Finally, you came to see me. I've been so bored because your mother will always be out with your father, and I'd just spend the day roaming around with a driver. A driver!" Jace lifted a brow at the scornful tone with which she referred to the nice man. He rubbed one ear with his hand and addressed her soporifically.

"Can I come in?"

"Yes, yes. I'm so glad you came. Your father took down the marriage post, darling."

"That's because the stupid arranged marriage was only ever your idea and not mine!" Unable to control the onslaught of emotions, he forcefully pushed out the words while cornering Gwen to the wall after a massive step.

"You use me, dump me and then come back to oblige me into marriage. Does that make sense? What do you want from me, Gwen?" At his scream she timorously lowered herself away from his imposing body, never seeing him so ruffled. She sank away when he hit the wall above her with his hand. Her eyes had become misty. Jace sighed when he remembered Millicent's warning words before he came up. He pinched the bridge of his nose while descending from his furious pants, wanting to get out of the room.

"Look, Gwen, I don't love you. Not anymore. My family has always preferred peace and quiet which is why they tolerated you and your family. You know my father has the power to rip everything away from you but my mother is a level-headed person. She acknowledges that we are children. I'm going to prove my innocence now that I'm outside wallowing in self-pity. Please venerate yourself to keep the last bit of dignity I see in you." He looked at her yet again impassively, searching his feelings but finding none for the woman who was now squatting in defenseless manner with her pleading tearful eyes staring at his legs.

When Jace turned to leave, he was grabbed by a wailing and shrieking Gwen.

"No! It's all because of that new woman. Jacey, you love me, and you will know once she is out of your life." Her words blinded him in rage, and he pirouetted and grabbed onto her arms roughly, almost shaking her. His burning eyes captured her frail ones while she cried.

"If you do anything to Millicent, Gwen, I swear that I'll destroy all that you hold dear to you. Stay away from us and it'll be good if you just go back home." He didn't stay a minute after that. He was beginning to feel suffocated in the room.

"I love you!" He heard as he held the door open, but this time, he did not turn to look at her when he spoke.

"No, Gwen, you don't love me. You're obsessed with the idea of us both from the guilt you feel for what you did and from the outlooks of superiority and hierarchy that runs through your mind." He stepped out and shut the door after that. As he got to the end of the hallway, he heard a piercing scream followed by the loud crashing of a glass artifact. His mother was going to throw a fit at whatever was broken. She had never appreciated his association with Gwen to begin with.

Millicent, who was seated on a stool cutting vegetables and laughing at Josephine's jokes as they cooked, shot up from her seat which stumbled when they heard the scream and the crash. She looked at Josephine who seemed just as alarmed, holding the ladle in her hand. They dropped the utensils and rushed out of the kitchen, meeting Anthony who was coming out from some part of the house, equally looking taken aback.

"I heard a crash." He said looking at the two women in question. Millicent, who was gradually worrying about her man, was about to step out to climb the stairs when he appeared at the landing. His jaw was clenched but he also looked relieved.

"Jace!" She called when he did not descend causing the man to snap his head up. His parents looked worried, and his dad had a massive appearance hoarding an unspoken guilt. Seeing that made him smile to appease the man. When he looked down the stairs, Millicent had already rushed up and soon pummeled into his body. Her hands started roaming everywhere on him.

"Are you okay? She didn't do anything to you, did she?" Jace shook his head, but she was still rattled by the noise, fretfully scanning him. Holding onto her shoulders, she stopped her movement, refocused on him and exhaled in relief.

"Oh thank–" Before she could complete her sentence, she had tipped back, falling over with her eyes over the roof. She saw an orange dress to the thigh of the person who wore it and dashed by her. Gwen had knocked into her.

"Millicent!" Two voices she recognized called out in devastation.

"Little M!" The anguished voice of Jace which she hoped she never heard again, because it tore at her heart, was the last she heard before she lost hold of reality.

Chapter 25

"Little M. There, I've got you. I've got you." Jace's reflexes had been fast enough to grab onto Millicent's flailing arms before she toppled over and down the stairs. Nonetheless, his arms were trembling as he sat on the landing with Millicent curled to him, whose eyes were shut in fright, and he reassured himself through rugged breaths and a loud heart beat that she was okay and in his arms. His forehead scrunched up as he softly rubbed her cheeks to get her to respond and open her eyes and after a minute, he saw those brown eyes that never failed to calm him.

Anthony and Josephine, who had rushed up and hovered around the couple with deep lines of worry etched onto their faces, both exhaled in relief when they saw her eyes open. Anthony felt his wife wobble into him and he grabbed onto her, curling his arm around her and sending another worried look to her whom he now held in his hands. Seeing that she was looking at Millicent with a glad face with one hand still on her chest from the panic, he leaned down to kiss her forehead in assurance.

Millicent traced her eyes to the anxious meteor gray-blue ones that gripped her to her soul. She tried to smile to calm him but she could tell he had been unhinged by the incident just like she had been. Her heart rate increased when she comprehended how crazy Gwen could be. She had actually wanted to push her down the stairs and even though they were not a long flight, they had been molded to be steep enough to support any kind of feet. She felt Jace's firm arms tighten their hold, and he moved to stand while still holding her in his arms.

Once they were on their feet, he was turning her in all directions. "You're okay." He kept murmuring and his parents surrounded her, giving her allayed smiles. She grabbed onto Jace who wouldn't stop inspecting her. When her hands settled flat against his cheeks, he stood still and finally held her gaze. When she smiled, he immediately pushed her against him in a hug.

"I'm fine." Her voice tickled the hair of his neck where she was cradled.

She was pushed back gently, and he took a minute to scan her from her head to her toe and then looking at her, he said, "She's lucky. Stay here with mom, I need to find Gwen." That intimidating look was back in place, and he looked above her to where his quiet parents were and he found his mom's eyes, who nodded and stepped closer to them to take Millicent in her arms.

"I'll come with you, son." Jace nodded at the meaningful look his father gave him.

They rushed out of the house and walked around to find Gwen, pacing around the swimming pool in a frenzied manner. The duo of the father and son, in a similar fashion strode toward the woman who had still not realized their presence. She turned around in terror, though her face betrayed none of those emotions, when the overwhelming presence of the two men emerged over her.

"What the hell was that, Gwen?" The calm voice of Jace impaled her where she stood at the edge of the shallow pool. His furious eyes were a vast contrast to his impassive face and placid tone.

"What are you talking about, Jacey?" She widened her eyes which hid the orange eyeshadow she had luxuriously applied.

"What am I talking about? You almost knocked Millicent down the stairs." There was a subtle twitch of displeasure in her eyes when Jace exclaimed that the woman had not fallen.

Anthony placed a calming hand on his son's shoulder and firmly grasped it so that he could quell his displeasure. Turning to face the daughter of a business partner he had regretted forming an alliance with after all the events that had taken place the past few weeks. He saw her eyes still had their innocent disposition.

"Now Miss Dumas, even a car feels aftershock after it crashes into something." After his statement he saw that the heiress was evidently stunned. She had never truly witnessed his aristocratic nature beyond their house.

"And I'll let you know that I do not simply allow people to hurt my family, which you have done twice now. I thought a business negotiation with your father would be enough to dissuade you from further harassment, but it seemed I thought too much of the matter."

"But Mr. Elrod..." Anthony held up a suave hand to halt her words, an action that gradually increased the vexation of the woman who searched with her eyes to find Jace. He was staring away across the expanse of the pool with his back to his father's side profile.

"Millicent is family, and I do not appreciate you trying to harm her. From your actions, I doubt I can continue to work with your family. This is the end of my commitment with you and your family. Consider returning home as well." Jace inhaled harshly. His father was finally acknowledging that the Dumas were not the best people to work with. Both children were as destructive as they came. He considered helping their company because their in-house design team was struggling with a new concept as the team leader had been poached away. Anthony had been exclusively asked to aid them because their release date had been announced before the team went awry.

"Don't try to mess with my family because I won't want to lift a finger otherwise, you'll lose your wealthy family." With a final fierce look, he patted his son's back and swaggered away leaving an incredibly disconcerted Gwen by the pool.

After Millicent was soothed, the couple decided to return to their home. Seeing Gwen sitting at the edge of the pool in the sunset, she left a persuaded Jace in the car and approached the red hair.

"I don't know what you tried to prove today but I hope you begin to understand what no and a rejection mean." She received no answer from the woman who began to pull her hair, so she returned leaving her as she was.

In the course of the week, Jace had gotten back to working on his art. With the days that drifted, he was engrossed in that until he felt he was missing a part of him, which would be the only reason for his to step out and that reason was Millicent. This was the justification for why the two sat across each other on a Wednesday night at the junction where they last had kebab.

Millicent giggled, the sound which curled Jace's pink lips upward in adoration. When her brown eyes found his orbs which twinkled in the twilight after drinking her soda, he raised a brow in curiosity.

"This was where our fake marriage plans began." His eyes shone in mirth.

"And would you look at us now." Their eyes lingered on each other's mirroring the same adoring look.

"Why does your family call you Aba?" Millicent couldn't contain the robust laughter that ruptured from her chest.

"God, I like how you call that, but let's stick to the ones we have. We'll work on this later." She was glad to catch his chuckle. "Aba is the same as Kwaku for you."

"So, it signifies the day on which you were born? But I know all those names and I've never heard Aba."

"That makes sense. What you probably know is the Asante names. As you know, the Akan is an ethnic group and within that ethnic group, there are different subgroups like the Asante, Akuapem, Akyem." When Jace nodded that he was following with the intrigued look on his face she continued, "My family is Fanti, so the names are a little different. Aba is our name for a girl born on Thursday, which for you is..."

"Yaa." Millicent bobbed her head in excitement that he actually did know and pronounced it quite well. "That's really interesting."

"Mhm. Max is Kobina but my mom usually calls him by the normal Twi name Kwabena."

"So, what will I be called?" His leg under the table grabbed onto hers causing to almost choke on her meat. Her wide eyes regarded his own mischievous ones as she wiped her lips with a tissue.

"Funny enough, it's the same pronunciation, though the 'a' in Kwaku is an 'e' for us." Their legs swayed under the table as the aroma carrying smoke drifted around them. All kinds of people were walking around.

"Wow. I never knew about the different subgroups."

"Yeah. Unless you live here it can be difficult to understand the dynamics."

"What was it like growing up for you?" He smiled when he saw her lips broaden in the reminiscent smile.

"It was entertaining whether in school, outside or at home. I mean you can see it now." They looked around them. "I was a little naughty but not your kind of naughty." Jace chuckled.

"I had good friends, who were my partners in crime, and my brothers were like my fathers. We do go to boarding school for senior high school and that was a blast."

"Sounds crazy amazing. I wish I was there to see you."

"Ha! No thank you. See me in this refined form." Jace shook his head in disagreement.

"I want to see all of you: good, bad, refined, crazy. They are all you." Her soft smile was enough to tell that he spoke the right words. "You're really close to your brothers huh."

"I am. They are the best. I really love them. Anyways, how was growing up in the states?" Another twenty minutes was dedicated to mindless laughter when Jace opened up a can of worms about being part of a wealthy community and entitled socialites. About thirty minutes into their laughing fit, Jace's phone rang, and he groaned when he saw the caller ID.

"Cole." Millicent simpered and shrugged, noticing his displeasure at the man who she had come to know as his manager.

"I mean he's just doing his job. He might just have a little problem in his math faculty at calculating time." Chuckling, Jace gestured to go answer the call away from the music and chatter that was going on.

Ten minutes as she ate and drank while waiting for her companion whose eyes were on her the whole time, she saw the shadow of another person over her. Lifting her head, she saw a man who looked to be in his early thirties. He had a really low cut, his eyes were a little dull, his nose a little crooked and wide lips adorned his face. His skin was flaky and the black outfit he wore in the dark night almost passed as a second skin. Millicent lifted a questioning brow in an authoritative manner at the new addition.

"Beauty. Are you alone? I entered and saw your glowing face and knew right away we could hit it off as friends." Millicent tried her best not to laugh at the interesting look he was giving her. She slyly turned to see Jace frowning from where he was watching them. His lips were moving really quickly now. Her eyes traveled back to the stranger who spoke again.

"So, can I have your number?" She gave him a daring smile and decided to indulge him. This always happened, men approaching women with the weirdest lines.

"Sure." She proceeded to give a random number which he called to get no response.

"Oh, it might be because my boyfriend is using the phone." The stranger startled and followed her eyes to see an imposing Jace sauntering to them.

As soon as Jace got there, he placed his phone in her purse that she offered him and sat next to her instead of across he, wounding his arms around her waist.

Kissing her cheek, he asked, "Who is this babe?"

Seeing the man's disoriented look, she decided she had had enough fun and waved him off. She turned to Jace after the man scampered away and spoke.

"No one. He thought I was alone, but I played some prank on him."

"Did you now? I wonder what my innocent little M can do." He grinned as they got lost in their eyes again.

"Have I told you that I love you? I love you, Millicent." She felt her heart skip and beat out of its range. But looking into those meteor-gray blue eyes that easily made her smile and happy, she knew her answer. Millicent didn't know how it happened, but it just had.

"I love you, Jace." Respecting her boundaries, he crashed her into his chest in a hug in the dark lit space under the twinkling stars of the sky, a witness to the new discovered emotions.

Chapter 26

The blaring of horns could be heard from the main road beyond the street of the Arthurs where Millicent was walking. She greeted the older woman who sold porridge in front of her home three houses away from the home of her infancy. The man whose candy shop was previously a stationary shop when she was in middle school greeted her warmly. The morning of Saturday was especially exciting for school children who had just a few chores to complete before they could call it their rest day.

When she reached her family's home, she could hear the bustling inside. She herself was excited at what she was to discover after her mother had called her. She wanted to see the woman who had managed to capture her eldest brother's heart.

"Mama!" She screamed as soon as she entered. However, the response she got was a familiar little girl's body crashing into hers with joyous giggles. She had no doubt her aunt had also come in to hear and see the promising rumor concerning her nephew.

"Bridget!" She lifted the little child, who seemed to have accumulated a good amount of weight over the past months, in her arms. Her slender arms circled her cousin's neck, sniggering.

"Aba, you came!" Millicent looked amused when her chocolate eyes similar to her skin's tone searched around them and seeing no one she beckoned Millicent's ears and asked, "Did you bring toffee?"

She tenderly rubbed her index knuckle on Bridget's button nose. "I didn't." The little girl's face deflated even after being admonished by her mother to stay away from candies. "But I brought you something better." Her eyes widened in expectation and Millicent marveled at how easily children could be pleased.

Picking through her bag, she found the pack of grapes she purchased before coming. She handed it to her cousin and asked to be directed to both their mothers and she was not surprised to know that the two women were in the backyard, probably eating their breakfast. Their backyard was paved and there were wooden chairs assembled under a mango tree.

"Ah, where is the man of the moment?" She questioned as soon as her presence was made known to the women who sat next to the wall.

"Ei Aba you're here." No, I'm not. Yet, she held her tongue in fear of disrespecting her aunt and smiled warmly to keep the sassiness away.

"Bridget Efua Wilberforce! What are you eating? Didn't I say no more toffee because your tooth is loose?" Millicent looked down at her little cousin who spotted a small frown that pushed her dark, bushy brows together.

"It's just grapes, auntie."

"Ah okay." She chuckled when she again looked down and saw her cousin's tongue poke out at her mother.

"I say, Aba, your brother will be coming later in the morning. I went to give him food and saw a woman there. She even offered me water. Now who does that unless they are usually in the house?" Regina was pleased when her daughter's eyes widened just as her sister who sat by her was surprised to hear the news. It was thought that Josh would always be focused on his path as a lawyer that he was blind to women.

Millicent shuffled closer to squat before her mother and aunt to indulge in the confabulation. "Really?" Her bright eyes demanded. "Did she know that you were his mother?" Her eyes darted to her aunt who responded to the question.

"She didn't."

"Wow."

As they continued to speak with Millicent drawing a chair closer to the older women to hear the new developments in her brother's life, she heard the undeniable mirthful interaction between Bridget and none other than Max.

"I always knew Max would be crowned the king of tattling." Millicent mumbled and stood up from her seat. They had long finished breakfast and were awaiting the arrival of the man of interest.

"Little bubble, where's everyone?" He bustled through the back-door second after that question.

Max's eyes scanned the entire vicinity after he acknowledged his mom and aunt. "Wait, where are they?" His expectant eyes drifted from his mother to his sister who cheekily smiled at him.

"Too bad, you missed them. They just left." His comical face left everyone laughing.

A few minutes after the arrival of Max, Joshua Arthur made himself known with a woman next to him. She had medium tan skin, the lightest shade of brown eyes she had yet to see and a very pleasant air and radiant smile. She also held a box in her hands while she nervously looked around all the curious smiling faces. Max stepped forward and began introductions in a very mature air. Her name was Elsie but that was not what astonished Millicent.

When the woman stepped closer to her to hug her, she whispered a forgotten wish that caused the entire family to begin their celebration.

"Happy birthday!" She had been utterly surprised especially as she had forgotten that it was really the twelfth of July, the day she was born.

"You always forget." Josh said from where he sat next to her after being ambushed with curious questions about the first woman he had ever brought home. Elsie related well with his family and was now chatting animatedly with everyone except Millicent who he was speaking to.

"Correction, my calendar forgot to remind me." She grinned but deflated inwardly when she realized that Jace had not remembered either. "You like her." She said to her brother to escape her thoughts.

Her smile turned warmer when her brother's gaze traveled to Elsie, and he watched her with a soft look. "I do."

"I'm happy for you. She looks really genial." She thought about how her brothers were always considering her needs first before theirs and was inclined to believe that her brother had stayed away from publicly declaring interest in this woman to make sure she was not left alone if he got married before her. The thought became more probable when she analyzed that he had brought her out when Jace appeared. However, she had never met the woman once in her visits to her brother. She looked sadly at Max and thought he was also harboring the same ideas.

Turning to Josh, she asked, "JJ, how did you guys not throw a fit when I introduced Jace?" When his brow lifted she added, "I mean you did but it was not as much as I thought it would be." There was clinking of cutlery and giggles as Bridget ate the cake that Max fed her. It was a little feast for Millicent.

"Because that was the first time you had willingly brought a man, kk. You always refused when mom suggested marriage even if she approached it the wrong way. So, seeing you with someone you had chosen, we had to discard our protectiveness and respect that you had made your choice. We are happy to see you happy, in as much as we don't appreciate the way you approached it. I was inclined to think it was a hoax to stop ma." Millicent felt her heart stop at the declaration. Her brother was one of the best young lawyers for a reason.

When it was midday, she decided to return home. Walking down the street to her own home after denying rides from both her brothers, she remembered the exchange she had with her mother.

"Aba, the son of sister Daisy came to ask of you. See how men are interested in my beautiful daughter." Her eyes squinted in intrigue. The woman was their neighbor, and that son was her childhood friend whom she had grown up with. Her feelings were no other than platonic for the man.

"And?"

"I told him that he unfortunately came in late." She chuckled and embraced her mother, lauding her for the words she used. She never knew that Peter was interested in her.

When she reached her home, she was stunned to see how uncharacteristically dark and silent the house was. Normally, if Jace was at home there would be music floating through the entire space. She walked into the center of the sitting room trying to figure out what felt wrong in the moment. Before she could delve deeper into the situation, her eyes flashed at colored lights that blinked around her and the appearance of the faces of her friends and finally Jace walked out of the kitchen. She chuckled when she saw he held a tray of chicken with a lit candle in the middle.

They sang in her celebration when Jace reached her. So, he didn't forget. Her pleased smile caused him to grin as if he knew what she was thinking as she blew out the candle. She laughed at the sight of the chicken.

"We thought you had cake at home so we're having a lunch party. Happy birthday little M." She mouthed a thank you with misty eyes.

"Happy birthday, Mimi." She felt the arms of Manuela circle her.

"I'm still annoyed that I'm discovering your relationship status like this, Mimi." She heard Shirley say from behind Manuela. With her attention on Jace, she had failed to acknowledge that her close friends were all present.

"I know!" Mawusi wiggled her brows when she stepped closer to hug her. Jace and Manuela arranged the chicken and soda they had gotten, one of Millicent's favorites.

She was hugged by Asantewaa as well and just then her doorbell rang.

"I'll get it!" Manuela stood to receive the caller. Millicent heard a familiar male voice which made Jace frown while shifting closer to where Millicent sat.

"What's he doing here?" She jabbed her elbow to his side which made his scowl disappear, but his mood was still sour.

"I thought you made the guest list. Aseda is a nice person." She showed him her glittering white teeth in a teasing manner, causing the crease lines of his frown to return while he grumbled.

"I'm nice too." She smirked and got up to address the new person just like the girls who had not seen their friend in a long while. She was given a boxed gift from Aseda who seemed to hover around Manuela more than typical.

They ate and celebrated, and she stayed in the arms of Jace who still did not seem to appreciate Aseda as he stayed a little too close to his cousin. Millicent, like her friends, only looked at the two with intrigue. They were even more curious at Millicent and her boyfriend who they interrogated with increased fascination.

Hours later into the late afternoon, they were startled out of their party when the doorbell rang. Millicent's questioning eyes found her friends.

"Who else?" But they just shrugged in confusion.

She moved to get the door but stepped back in shock at the person who stood in front of her. Her red hair was curled, and she wore a strange look. Her practiced equanimous posture unnerved a perplexed Millicent.

"Gwen." She said flatly with a tinge of bewilderment. Jace was by her side as soon as he heard the name she had called. He stood tall and proud exuding that dominant aura, which he set aside for her friends' sake, yet again.

"Uh, I'm here to apologize to the both of you." Millicent's wondrous eyes sought for Jace who stood with an emotionless face as he did whenever Gwen or anyone other than his family was concerned. Her pitchy voice was anything but apologetic.

"I'm sorry that you almost fell when I descended the stairs." Millicent almost chuckled at how uncomfortable and wrong the words of her justification sounded but deciding to be the civil one she nodded desperate to be rid of the young heiress who seemed to always want to destroy something of hers. Somewhere from the room a scoff that sounded much like Manuela's voice was heard.

"Jace, uhm, can I speak to you alone?" She faced the man after condescendingly apologizing and getting a favorable response. She wished to do something to get into the good graces of her ex. Millicent tapped Jace who remained unmoving and tipped her head subtly toward the woman who scorned inwardly after witnessing the exchange. Though the woman was still overbearing even in the moment, she had to be given a final opportunity to redeem herself. Jace sighed, looking at his kind girlfriend and gave in.

"Follow me." He led Gwen to his bedroom away from the party and curious eyes. Naturally, they were all wary of the woman who had just arrived due to her contemptuous display of superiority. "Now what is it Gwen?"

"I just wanted to apologize, Jacey. And since we have a history, I was thinking I could at least get a parting gift as a souvenir?" Jace raised a brow at the audacity of the woman who seemed to be ignorant of the concept of apologies.

"What do you mean? Don't you think you have enough of that in your possession?" Her heels clicked forward and she raised her hand to touch him which he sidestepped. He missed the clenching of her hands, a habit she had when she was irked. Looking around and seeing that he had packed all his work and the art that remained were doodles he had done, he decided to offer that and get the cunning woman out of the house.

"There are paintings here. Pick one and meet me outside." He did not wait for a response and hastily left the room, waiting outside where Millicent approached him trying to dispel his vexed atmosphere.

Gwen pursed her lips in distaste when she looked around. She had come to try to persuade the man, but he barely looked at her. All the art she grabbed looked different from his usual work. When she turned to observe another one of the paintings of a backyard he had made, her eyes rolled in displeasure at its roughness. From the corner of her eye, she saw a canvas peeking out of his closet that was partly opened. With light clicks of her heels she bent and pulled out the art piece and what she saw caused her eyes to widen in embellishment. She brought her hand to her mouth as she watched the nude art of the woman she despised. Though her face was not present, she was the only one she had met with the hair Jace painted. Grabbing her phone, she took a shot before she stood in conspiracy.

Her lips curled up while she stood tall, grabbing a random canvas before strutting away.

"Jace Elrod, I'm going to make you regret rejecting me."

CHAPTER 27

"Why? Tell me why you had to wake me up at seven in the morning on the one day I do not have to go to work. I'm sorry you have a peaceful summer vacation with no work but some of us need our beauty sleep. And what? To dance because you found an exciting song? And to go on a jog with you while dancing. Gosh, I love you but I'm rethinking. And now God knows where you're stealing me to." Jace bit his lip to hold himself back from laughing at his sulking girlfriend. His eyes slid to his phone to check the GPS route he was driving on before crawling his hand to her thigh to smooth it. He knew it was an important day and he did not want to do anything to wreck his plans.

"Little M, I didn't think you could be this grumpy in the morning. I really thought you were a morning person." She slipped her hand into his hand that was on her thigh and from the corner of her eye she saw the ghost smile grace his lips.

"How did you come to that conclusion?" Jace quickly turned to look at her so that she could see his raised brows. He turned to maneuver the car through a bend.

"Babe, you wake me up as early as six to get me to do devotion with you so that you don't fall back asleep." Millicent's lips twitched as she acknowledged the fact. He squeezed her hand letting her know that he got her. "Which has effectively stopped my morning jogs."

"But you conveniently moved it to the night. And see, even you know the reason is so that I don't sleep."

Jace shook his head at the ease with which she gets him to do whatever she desires.

"But you do want me to do it with you." At the red light, he leaned back to watch her, who had managed to seize his heart even when he promised himself not to fall in love.

"I do. Don't you just love devotions?"

"I need to find a way to unwrap myself from your finger." He spurred the car to move and grinned when Millicent playfully tugged his hand.

"Do you even want to?" Her voice dropped lower to accommodate her suggestive tone which caused him to toss his head back and roar in laughter. He could hear her sniggering.

"Oh gosh! I love you, baby." He simply responded.

Gwen had left about three weeks ago, and his own vacation was dreadfully coming to an end. He had officially finished his art series two days ago and had wrapped and shipped them to his gallery the previous day to an anxiously awaiting manager.

"Come on, little M." Jace held her door open, and she grasped onto his hand as they approached the building, he had brought them to. "It's an art and cocktail studio."

"I never knew places like this existed here."

"Because you don't necessarily involve yourself in artwork."

"So, what are we doing here?" They stepped into the coolness of the room before he answered.

"I'm here to purchase an art set."

Jace got the set he purchased, and they returned home for Millicent to discover that he had already set up the backyard garden for a paint session he arranged for them as a couple. Now they sat at the opposite end of a rectangular wooden table facing each other trying to paint each other on the small canvas Jace had gotten. Max's little pup, which he had failed to retrieve after a month, played and yipped around the garden. Millicent believed that he did not want to spend or suffer to train it in its infancy. They had sat for about twenty minutes in the shaded part of the garden painting, but she realized that Jace had not once lifted his head to look at her and he appeared on edge.

"Are you sure you're painting? You've not even looked at me once." Her eyes playfully narrowed, and she hoisted a brow when he finally raised his head. He seemed startled to hear her voice.

"I can paint you in my sleep, little M. I know every detail of your face." She suddenly turned bashful at his words and her reticent smile drew him out of his present apprehensiveness.

"Well, Mr. Artist we have-" She turned her phone over and continued, "twenty minutes more courtesy to my poor art skills."

The timer bellowed and they both looked up with similar grins on their faces. Millicent held her work close, setting aside her paint brush. She looked down at her complete work and fell into a fit of giggles; looking back up at the man seated on the other side of her, she found his shoulders shaking. She saw mimi curled up by his feet while she leaned her head on her hands which held the canvas erect on the table.

"Should I even see what you did?"

Millicent pouted, "Hey, you brought this whole date idea up." The Bluetooth speaker they brought out filled the backyard with ranging pop tunes.

"Okay; you go first." She grinned and jumped up to her feet basking in the silly painting she was about to show. Her hair was held up and the apron Jace had sweetly put on her was weighed down with most of the paint that spilled.

"Okay, drum roll." She frowned when he tilted his head but then again there was nothing the smitten man would not do for his love. His beat on the table caused the puppy next to him to wince before resettling in a more comfortable position.

Jace's hands stopped and laid still on the table. His now thinned lips quivered continuously as he stared at what was presented to him. He acknowledged that she got the colors right but the shape, especially of his head, was just terrible. Unable to restrain himself any longer as her own gleeful brown orbs were dancing with laughter, his shoulder shook with force and he had to bend his body over the table to humor his rambunctious guffaws. Millicent, happy to have achieved the purpose of her silly work, joined him, gratified that she could loosen him up after he spent weeks working indoors.

"Ah, I'm quite the man in your eyes." He finally spoke after another twenty minutes of occasional pauses to admire the work and spontaneous bouts of howling afterwards. Millicent shrugged, wiping her moist eyes.

"I want to see yours. You draw so beautifully; it's going to put mine to shame."

She noticed the abrupt change in his demeanor as his blue gray eyes locked with her brown eyes with an unknown emotion lingering in them. It looked almost like anticipation. He stood up from his seat with the canvas turned to him while she waited patiently in both delirium and worry.

Then he ultimately turned it over.

Jace searched her face anxiously as she squinted her eyes. His right foot was rhythmically tapping the grass beneath it.

"That's not my face. What is that?" Millicent stepped around the table but froze midway to him when she resolved the art he had made. Her doe eyes widened and her colored hand shot up to cover her mouth while she stared at Jace in disbelief. The man walked from his side to meet her, holding up the painting to her and got down on one knee after she grabbed it with her trembling hands.

"Millicent, I found you and saw how true it is to say what we call the beginning is often the end. And the end is to make a beginning. The end is where we start from - I thought my life had ended till I found you. Yes, it is only with the heart that one can see rightly; what is essential is invisible to the eyes - when I saw you, I thought I knew you but when my heart began to beat in tandem with yours, when I began to love you, I saw the face of God. I know I am not going to be afraid of storms, not because I am learning how to sail my ship but because you will be present in that ship with me, in this ship called life. You have ravished my heart and given me courage with a single glance of your eyes. So, will you give me the pleasure of waking up to see you lying next to me and by my feet from this day forth? Will you marry me, my love?"

Millicent's teary eyes found his earnest orbs patiently looking up into hers. "What— I mean—" She dropped herself in front of him when her mouth betrayed the words she wanted to say on account of her tears. Jace wrapped his arm around her and let out a shaky breath.

"Is that a yes, little M?" She nodded and sniffled, grabbing onto his body.

"You should be sued by those classic writers for taking their phrases and making them sound beyond romantic." Both their bodies shook in their laughter as Millicent pulled back and presented her hand to the man who she had no doubt in her heart to be the one for her even in the short time span.

"What can I say? I'm talented in many departments." He grinned when Millicent shook her head in wonder.

Helping her up, he heard her say, "Incorrigible."

Two weeks later, Millicent was in her family's home together with her brothers and her father's brother, as well as her uncle Seth Fiifi Wilberforce, Anita's husband. Josh sat beside her nursing a cup of tea just as she was, under the mango tree of their backyard. The door to the backyard from their home opened, revealing the last of the trio, Max, who came in holding a mug himself.

"So, Jace said he proposed to you again."

"How-" Millicent trailed off, trying to avoid the intelligent eyes of her brother. For them to avoid suspicion, she was sure Jace had not told anyone of his proposal except Manuela who knew their fake marriage scheme.

"He came to ask us for your hand." She looked between her two brothers who shared a knowing look.

"We approved because he did it right this time. You didn't even know he came to us, so we can tell it's sincere." Max added fondly and they continued to chat until they heard the knock on their front door causing Millicent to beam and shoot up.

"Woah, slow down kk. We know they're here for you." Josh rubbed his sister's head affectionately as Max snickered causing her to puff out air.

When they entered their home, the Elrod family, all in burgundy kaftan wear entered with Josephine in a similar color of straight dashiki wear. Millicent sat around in the area designated for her family. This was the knocking ceremony and the family introduction for the couple who intended to get married. Her eyes were glued to the aristocratic-looking Jace whose eyes sought for her in the room. When they met, his blue-gray eyes shone in pleasant recognition just like hers.

She had lost track of the entire conversation when her uncle, Terry, her father's brother, asked for the Elrods to state their purpose. She was locked in a hearty staring contest with Jace, occasionally tuning in. She sat up when Anthony Elrod dropped the drinks they brought and spoke.

"I have been sent by my son to ask for the hand of your daughter." Her eyes drifted to Jace's hands on his lap. I miss you. That was a code tap they had developed, and she reciprocated the action causing both lips to curl.

At the end of the ordeal, her uncle Terry who was the linguist responded, "As per culture, we will need to ask our daughter if she agrees, and once she replies we would send you a word."

Millicent grinned as everyone chuckled when Jace groaned after hearing the last words. His ears warmed as he had not expected the sound to be audible. Millicent walked up to him with a teasing smile. One that indicated that this was one of the many customs he had to succumb to before they were officially married.

Chapter 28

Millicent's brows were scrunched up and the lines on her face which made their presence known whenever she was angry had appeared. She stomped down the stairs from the master bedroom in her work outfit, a suit dress, and the slippers she wore furiously slapped the stairs with her gait.

When she reached the lower level, she found Max eating the food their mother had prepared earlier, also arriving earlier from work and lounging on the couch.

"Maxwell." He turned to face her with an expressionless scowl coupled with an expectant look, holding his bowl of food in place.

"Max." Millicent corrected and could only shake her head when he grinned and tipped his head up.

"What's up Mimi?"

"Where's ma?" He stretched out his hand and extended his index finger toward the back door. Millicent, not wasting another minute, trailed to the backyard.

When she stepped out, she found her mother grooming whatever plants they had in the back and taking a breath in she spoke,

"Ma, why did Uncle Terry ask for a television, he even specified the dimension, an air-conditioner, and a car? Isn't that exploitation and why does he need all that?" In her exasperation, she shot one leg forward and cocked her head to the side.

"Aba, hmm, that father of yours is so different from your actual father. He thinks he is smart. I just invited them out of courtesy to honor your father and he wants to swindle through your marriage list to furnish that house of his that he never completed." Her mother's eyes blazed indignantly which surprised her because the woman had remained silent when all the unreasonable demands of her uncle were being made. She had even seen Josephine's countenance change which greatly mortified her.

"Josh and I felt so demeaned." Millicent's hand shot up to her chest when her brother showed out of nowhere. She turned back to see her mother sitting on one of the seats under the tree with a thoughtful look and she moved to sit next to her. The house was quiet meaning, Ewurama and Juanita, their cousins, who stayed with their mother were out on errands.

"But why didn't you say anything, mama?" Max pulled another chair as they huddled around their mother.

"There are some things that you need wisdom in dealing with. I didn't want our family to be unnecessarily blamed for disrespect, so I already communicated with ma Josephine in the room." She turned to Max whose head had just turned to her. The women spoke nothing about the issue with the lingering presence of their uncle, so both siblings were mystified. There was a look in their mother's eyes when they looked back at her which made them confirm that the women probably spoke with their eyes.

"I spoke to her yesterday. Your uncle will be in for a surprise if he thinks he's going to get all that."

"But mama, did you see that her fiancé did not even care. If it was up to him maybe, he'll give Uncle Terry an entire mansion that has been furnished just to marry Aba." Their teasing laughs made a smiling Millicent coy.

"You're enjoying her love. You, Kobina, when are you getting married?" Millicent snickered watching her brother be a sputtering mess.

"Ma, do you want any kind of woman? Patience. Like I say, I'm a ghost." With that he bid hastened goodbyes and escaped to his home. Millicent shook her head with a chuckle. Her brother was undoubtedly the clown of good humor among them, a trait which he had gotten from their father even though Josh was most like him.

Millicent dove past her friend's house, and Manuela offered to go home with her to chat and watch a movie together.

"It makes sense that my crazy cousin might even agree to buy a house for your uncle." Manuela giggled in answer to the information her friend had passed onto her concerning her traditional marriage list. "And you know I'd be more than happy to be your maid-of-honor. See, I could tell from long ago that we were destined sisters." This made Millicent smile ruefully as she made the turn to her street.

"But you wouldn't believe what happened to me today, Mimi!" Millicent moved her eyes to question her friend, raising a perfect brow.

"What?" The concern dripping from her voice was palpable as she moved to park her car.

"So, my colleagues and I went out to eat lunch. After we came out of the eatery, there was a man on the side of the street next to the shop after the eatery. He was dressed, like well dressed; okay, maybe not the shoes that were mismatched and his hair that was cut irregularly but it took me a while to notice those. Anyways, he was singing, 'girl, girl, pretty girl'. I thought it was funny because he was singing behind a group of women and you know how my giggles cannot be contained. One second my friends are next to me and the next they all disappear. I look behind and this man has started running with an angry face, shouting who knows what and began to chase me. Oh my God, Mimi you know I was not born for the tracks but you should have seen my Usain Bolt come out of me." Millicent could not hold her laughter at the point at the expense of her pitiful friend who had unfortunately been pursued by a mad person. It seemed the siblings had a knack for being chased.

"I know it's funny, trust me, I was laughing after a few tears. The man ran after me all around the neighborhood till a woman in her shop came and pulled me in before sending him off. It was so embarrassing." Manuela groaned thinking of how her heels were even missing after the scenario.

"Oh, Ella." Millicent cackled a little more at the expense of her friend. "Sorry, sorry." She said when she received a scowl. "I blame your great storytelling prowess. But were you alright afterwards?" The concern in her made its presence known as they sat in the car parked in front of her house. Her friend sighed and nodded. "But what would have happened if the man got you?"

"I don't know, and I wasn't waiting to find out. No one ever does." Her friend moaned in distress. "How am I supposed to face my colleagues?"

"Honey, if anything they're the ones who should be embarrassed for leaving you in such a situation alone." Millicent asserted and after a while of giving her friend an assuring look, she felt vindicated and reassured. "Come, let's go in."

When she opened her door, she was not prepared for the sight in front of her and neither was her friend. Manuela quickly took out her phone and snickered behind her hand at Jace who was dressed in a medieval costume. The feather on the cap took her out. She never knew her cousin could be so humorous till he met Millicent. He had yet to see her as she hid behind Millicent, who had stilled in stupor and amazement.

Millicent didn't know what reaction to give to her fiancé when he thrust the lit screen of his phone in her face saying, "Little M, look what's here, the portrait of a blinking idiot." It looked like his manager.

Millicent choked and heard her friend chortle lowly behind her. The deep, fake English accent and the stupefied frown on Jace's face added to the fact that she had a love-hate relationship with Shakespeare - hating all his readings in high school - caused her hand to shoot to her belly as a deep laugh bubbled within. She always thought Shakespeare was a funny guy and that was the reason why she was currently doubled over in laughter squatting and slapping her thigh. Manuela had obscured herself by attaching her shaking form to the wall.

Jace, thinking he was doing right, went on with his theater. Millicent had shared before that those lines were so funny to her for no special reason.

"In sooth, I know not why I am so annoyed. It wearies me; I know it'll weary you. But how Cole thought it, planned it, decided it without my knowledge, what stuff his brain is made of, I am to learn; I have much ado to know him better." He grinned when he saw Millicent rolling in laughter. There was a chortle close by that had his neck snapping to the side of the wall, exasperated to see his cousin with a phone in her hand.

"Manu! Tell me it's not recorded. Give me the phone."

"Oh gosh! This is gold. I- I can't. Mimi, what did you do to my cool cousin? He's become cooler."

Millicent's cackling subsided and she stood to grab him. "Wait, what did Cole do?" She asked, trying to contain another onslaught of chortles.

Jace glared at his cousin one last time before turning to the golden beauty behind him. He took off the absurd hat, grinning when he caught sight of her giggling but still peeved at the new information that his manager had sent him earlier in the morning.

Recognizing her question, his smile dissipated and Millicent catching on to the change in mood also sobered up.

"Cole apparently decided and started planning my opening solo exhibition for the end of the year. He has even sent invites, and the man decided to tell me today that it'll be held next week."

"What? But that's not how things are supposed to be done. Isn't that guy normally afraid of you?" Manuela put her phone away and frowned at the news. He had told her that he was planning to finish the traditional marriage before he left to work.

"Trust me, he is considering his actions as we speak and has been calling since that call. His head!" Millicent chuckled and Manuela snickered at the last statement. He had caught on to a lot of local parlances. He even discarded his accent when he spoke such words.

"Next week? When are you leaving?" Millicent spoke with a sour taste in her mouth as she thought of being separated from him. Jace took her in his arms and Manuela left the couple, venturing into the living room.

"I'm leaving with my parents this weekend." He fumbled with her fingers, pulling and playing with them. Something she noticed he did whenever he was nervous, so she gripped it to stop the movement. He lifted his head when that could no longer be done and a pair of anticipating blue-gray eyes stared into her brown ones. She smiled encouragingly and heard him ask, "I was wondering if you'd like to come with me. It's my first exhibition this year and the only one as well and you were my inspiration."

She frowned. "I was?"

"Babe, you were the first opening to my focus even the first time I met you. So..." He had an expectant look.

"I'd love to. I've yet to see you in your element."

"Jace, ma said she didn't know you could be a comedian." Millicent snickered when he almost fell, sauntering in pursuit of his cousin.

"Manu, you sent it to the group chat?" His tired voice called out while Manuela sneered.

"And Millicent, she is disappointed that you've not visited to let her know that 'her child is becoming her niece'." Millicent flushed in shame walking to see the siblings fighting.

Friday afternoon trickled in with Millicent busily trying to put her work in order before her departure. She was silently laughing at the video Manuela had earlier sent her of Jace in his costume and lamenting earlier in the week. It was apparent that his little drama was more to reassure himself: she had seen over the past days that he looked nervous whenever the upcoming exhibition was brought up. His past experience had taken a toll on him and even the almighty Jace withered at the thought of reentering his career after being in hiding. She tried to be next to him and assure him as much as she could.

A call came in from her boss to meet him in his office. She was ushered in by the secretary and was stunned to see Jace's dad in the middle of a handshake with her middle-aged boss. They both turned to acknowledge her, and she saw the stern look of Anthony dissolve into curved lips when his eyes fell on her.

"Millicent!" Anthony's excited voice rang through the room which caused her boss, Mr. Darko to reel back in surprise at the change of the imposing man's disposition and he looked at his employee in curiosity wondering how she was affiliated with the aristocratic business magnate.

"Uncle Anthony?" Her melodic voice questioned, her brows pulling together to frame her squinted eyes as she stepped further into the room. The older version of Jace wrapped a warm arm around.

"Is it okay if Millicent clocks out now?" His accent was thickened in the room's atmosphere. Mr. Darko nodded after a minute already knowledgeable of the leave she had taken for the following week and her request to leave earlier.

The two walked out chatting and going to pick up Millicent's stuff.

"Jace said you left your car and so I'm here to pick you up." Millicent shook her head with a smile at how Jace was always fussy over her and her safety. She allowed the older man to send her to the airport where they met the rest of the family - Manuela decided to support her cousin as well - and in the best of condition they flew across the Atlantic Ocean.

Chapter 29

The shoes of passers-by hit the pavement mostly in light steps and heads unconsciously turned when the two figures passed by them. One of glorious golden brown skin and the other of a beautiful tan. Their shades covered their eyes in the afternoon sun and the uncharacteristically long, kinky hair balanced out the short, wavy smooth hair. Their white shoes matched their equal strides on the sidewalk. The woman's gray slim fit high split maxi dress matched the gray polo shirt of the man and all in all they were striking to whoever they passed by.

Warmth seeped into Millicent's body traveling from Jace's hands which was entwined in hers. The confidence her companion exuded augmented her poised and elegant form that matched his. She was captivated by his warm smile that only she could put on his face as they laughed off some mundane stories they shared.

It was Tuesday, the day before his exhibition. She had offered to accompany Jace to scout the gallery and get an overview of the space which he undoubtedly knew. However, Jace was sure the series he had made needed unique attention in positioning them just the right way so that he got his message across.

"So, what is the theme for the showcase?" Millicent's honey-coated voice dripped into his ears as he steered her to the street where the gallery was. They had parked a bit away from the FloShay gallery because Millicent desired to walk and get some steps in which he easily obliged.

"Hm, I asked you this once. Life in color or the color in life?" He saw Millicent's head bob slowly with their leisurely pace. "I was wondering which to use." She rounded her mouth at the revelation which ignited a smile on his face and his thumb rubbed the skin of her hand affectionately. "You said life in color was a little bland because it sounded like life being put in color, literally. The color in life, like you beautifully put it, sometimes it's hard to find light in darkness and it is only in the light that we can have color. Through the struggles if you discover the end of that tunnel and allow light to flow into your darkest states, you'd find that you missed the tiny hopes of colors that could be seen which could beautify the dull life because you were initially drowning in the despair of darkness. That - it just made sense and settled in my heart. Yes, that's the theme." He added when he saw the familiar twinkle in her eyes.

"We are troubled on every side, yet not distressed; we are perplexed, but not in despair. It reminds me of this scripture that says there's always hope for us in Christ. It may seem far but there's hope." Millicent said wistfully following Jace who stopped in front of a grand building. It was a neutral mix of paint in sea blue, white and olive on the exterior. She relaxed further when she was brought into the well-known snugness of Jace's arms. His chin rested on her head.

"And if you feel like giving up, hope even harder; hope does not add or subtract from life, but it gives you a leverage to keep fighting, you know. I've seen that if people or a situation tries to crush you, it seeks to steal that expectancy away because they know that rising out of the ashes makes you even greater. So, don't be scared to rise." She dropped a kiss on his exposed neck.

"Thank you." He mumbled from above her. "For being that hope for me." She felt his hand tighten once more before he let go of her, stepped back and smirked so that his teeth glinted in the sunlight. Her eyes were adoring as they tried to make out what color stood out the most in his eyes. Before she could examine further, he turned around and faced the building they had halted in front of. Jace pulled on her hand and stepped in front of the glass doors which slid open upon detecting their shadow.

As soon as they stepped in, a somewhat skittish but bulky man approached them with an anxious look. His brown hair was gelled back in a prim manner and his dark eyes scanned them nervously; he had a strong jaw but still held some fleshy muscles in his cheeks, and he was tall but not as much as Jace was - the same height as Millicent. He had an averagely toned build and was un-doubtedly good-looking. Millicent recognized him as the manager, Cole. She peeped up and saw that that mask of indifference had taken over Jace's features but the tenderness of his hold proved that he was still her Jace.

"Cole." He flatly stated and she saw the older male flinch at the iciness of his superior tone.

"Jace! Isn't it amazing to be back? I've seen the work and it's going to blow up the industry - it's such a new breath, eye opening in diversity." The man's light tone sang off, preventing Jace from speaking in fear of actually losing his job. He quickly turned to Millicent who had a ghost smile dancing on her lips when she figured out what he was trying to do. She saw Cole's eyes widen when they fell on her.

"You must be his muse. You look even better than the cover." Millicent's brow rose in question, but the man continued speaking as Jace drew her closer to him by her waist, his sharp eyes on his manager who refused to meet his gaze. "Cole Hardy, his very expedient manager." This staking of claim made the chuckles fall from Millicent's lips. She grabbed his outstretched hand, which was quickly broken by her fiancé, who took hold of her hand after a second.

"Millicent Arthur."

"Cole, how is the array?" Surprisingly, the man altered into a severe business atmosphere at Jace's question, and he led them around the gallery, describing and discussing with Jace where they wanted the pieces to be put.

Millicent tugged Jace's hand that was still in her hold and the man bent down to listen to her as other staff and people walked by them. "Why haven't they put up your work?"

Jace's answering murmuring voice matched her own. "These guys like money, so instead of closing the museum like normal people would, they work and then set up at night when normal people are sleeping." Millicent sniggered breathily at his attempt to covertly slur the gallery.

Again, being lost in themselves, they were unobservant to the occasional prolonged and wondering glance that Cole gave Millicent and the couple. He was fascinated by the woman who had unhinged the invisible Jace Elrod.

A young woman and man approached the couple after Jace finished walking through the details with Cole and his staff. The woman was short with shoulder length curly black hair, purple at the ends and the man beside her was a tall brunette, almost as tall as Jace and just a little taller than Millicent. Jace assessed them to be college students.

"Excuse me. Jace Elrod?" The baritone voice of the man called out and Jace gave a curt but polite nod to see a mighty grin override both of their features. "Told you!" He said to the woman next to her whose eyes were glowing on the man.

Millicent observed with interest as they pulled out notepads with pens looking back at Jace with an expectant look.

"Could we get an autograph, please?" She felt the anxious rumble of Jace as he grabbed their pen with a small smile. It had been long since he had been approached.

"Our art professor loves you and we love your works too! We discuss them almost every time we meet. My favorite is mystic worlds." The young lady rambled in excitement as the man bobbed his head enthusiastically.

She thought that was the limit to his fame but was proven wrong when she made her way with Manuela and the rest of the Elrods into the venue. There were flashing cameras everywhere, especially as soon as Anthony Elrod stepped out of his car, people with cameras and devices were hovering all around them. Manuela and Millicent plinked uncomfortably with their hands linked together, inching away but the mass of reporters was too much to escape. Anthony and Josephine stood tall, and she saw Josephine's eyes wander to find the two girls. She grimaced when she saw them, but she looked up and smiled and turning to them she had that reassuring smile.

Someone pulled Millicent and Manuela through the crowd causing them to shriek but once they reached the side door, the person threw down the hoodie and a recognizable mop of blond hair and blue eyes greeted them.

"Sean!"

"Mimi, hi!" He bundled her into his arms for a bear hug, and a delightful grin was evident on his face.

"Hi Manu." Manuela was startled, impressed that he recognized her. The last time they met was about six years ago when he escaped the US to follow Jace for a short vacation in Ghana.

"You recognize me?" The man only gave her a humorous look before pulling her in for a hug and ushering them inside the building and out of the prying eyes. The hallway leading to the art pieces had been red zoned for Jace's speech and would be opened later.

They were led to a conference room where chairs had been set up, a multitude already had filled those seats, and a podium was raised at the one end. Her eyes scanned around for the shiny, waves of black her on a handsome and tall tanned-skin man but she was disappointed not to see him. The feeling was short-lived when strong arms snaked around her body and a lingering kiss was dropped on the back of her neck. They had all decided to wear African print outfits to highlight the exhibition and when Sean walked back out after going to take out the hoodie he wore, she saw that he was in similar wear.

"You're going to do great." She smoothed the lines of worry from Jace's forehead as he was called to make his speech.

"Hi, thank you all for being here today. We weren't expecting a massive turn out in light of previous happenings. Firstly, I would like to thank my family for the never ending support, and the love of my life for appearing at this time. I appreciate my manager, the staff and FloShay gallery for making this possible. I won't bore you with a long speech but know that this showcase is the color in life. I hope that it clears all darkness, introduces light and brings clarity that opens a hope to see colors in life so that you embrace them as I have. Thank you and enjoy." The applause was resounding as Jace sought to find the woman who had captivated him and brought color to his life, but he was swarmed by a group of art enthusiasts seeking him.

Millicent decided to explore first. Her heels clicked on the marbled floor and her smile expanded when she saw the exhibit scheme. If there was a painting of the marketplace, there were props around to bring it to life. She saw the scene of the man and woman who were arguing, and a laugh bubbled in her throat. She had seen all these, but the vibrant imagery Jace created never failed to amaze her.

She was staring at one painting with other people around it when the anxious voice of Manuela called close to her. She turned to her friend who had a weird look in her eyes. "Mimi-" Manuela anxiously scanned the perimeter, and her friend worried, calmly placing an arm on her.

"I don't know what is going on, but you have to see this." She said in a frenzy and strutted forward leading them to the end of the last pieces at the end of the hallway.

Millicent stopped midway in her tracks before they even reached what Manuela was desperate to show her. Her mouth was agape and her heart thumped and throbbed loudly in her own ears. Because she could recognize that piece from anywhere. Her hands slumped beside her, her heart clenching at the thought of the person she loved lying to her and breaking her trust. Manuela's mouth was moving in front of her but she couldn't make out her voice; everything was loud in her ears, the ringing, and the breaking of her heart. Her eyes drifted around and she found the eyes of men looking at her in a strange way and their grins looked evil; even the women. She spiraled, stumbled and almost fell but a slender arm grabbed onto her. A tear she didn't know was making its way out fell and her eyes landed on that red-haired woman who was grinning in triumph standing by her nude painting that Jace made but this time her face was right there, and everyone could tell it was her. Even in her tear- blurred eyes, she could tell it was her.

A broken and pained gasp escaped her, and she turned on her heels escaping the looks that made her skin crawl. They looked at her like they could see every layer of her.

"How could he? He promised." She whispered in pain as she stumbled out but right there, the media stood with knowing looks.

"Are you Mr. Elrod's muse?" Her hand tightly gripped her head to shield herself and escape the flashing lights. Somehow, she pushed her way through and stumbled on the streets.

Blur took over her tear-filled eyes, and she was inattentive to the car that was rushing forward and trying to skid to a stop. But it was too late when the screech reached her ears causing her to lurch to the side.

Chapter 30

Manuela rushed through the space in search of her cousin. She was torn between directly following her friend and informing her cousin of the mishap. She didn't know what had just happened but she knew from a glance from the presence of the red-haired heiress that she was involved in whatever was happening. When she finally found her cousin, she found that he was still thronged with people. Her present scowl hardened, and her eyebrows attached to each other.

Her eyes scanned the people and her cousin in their midst; she raised her hand to get his attention but even in his tall frame, all his attention was on the people chatting him up, but she could tell by the slight tremble in his hands that he was anxious to get out of there. She saw his eyes dart around but they barely found her. Manuela was anxious because an increasing waste in time meant she was missing her friend. Her legs shook and her eyes scanned the perimeter stressfully for another opening. Her eyes met blue orbs in an African print shirt, and she exhaled in relief, waving at Sean and started to move toward him.

"Sean, Millicent, something is wrong." Sean's face contorted in worry, and he shifted his eyes momentarily to Jace, who he knew was looking for a way out to see her. He grabbed onto Manuela's shoulders and his eyes bore into hers. He had to bend down to do that.

"What happened to Millicent?" She gulped in confusion herself.

"There's a painting of her in the last hallway; Gwen was there and when Mimi saw it, I don't know Sean, she rushed out. I have to go find her. Get Jace; let him get that thing off." She was speaking so quickly that he had to focus to make them out.

Sean did not wait to comprehend whatever she had said. He pushed through the crowd and placed a heavy hand on his friend's shoulder. Jace stopped his words and turned to see Sean's face and he instantly sobered from the chatty atmosphere. When he heard the words that his friend spoke his gray eyes shot to Manuela who was already turning away. He strained himself out of the crowd, Sean following close and walked directly to the end of the display. His jaw clenched, his meteor gray-blue eyes had an enraged fire as he looked at the painting he had never done. Every angle and stroke showed that it was not a work of his hand. His heavy footsteps echoed in the hall among the people and he wasted no time in yanking off the art.

Cole stood next to his daunting presence searching around with a nervous pair of eyes as people's surprised eyes probed the scene. He saw Sean with his own lips set in a thin line and hard eyes on the spot where the piece had previously been. The material was thrusted into his hands in an angry fashion, and he could barely stand in position when the harsh glare of Jace fell on him.

"Get rid of it." Jace was already running out of the venue before any remarks could be made.

He found Manuela pacing feverishly in front of the entrance, held back by the many flashing lights and just like Sean had grabbed onto her, he held her shoulders in fear.

"Where is she, Manu?" His cousin's eyes were just as fearful.

"I don't know. But this is bad. I don't know what is going on but to Mimi right now, that would be like her dignity being ripped off. We were once exploited sexually as a country and so most of us never expose ourselves like that. She's probably breaking." She watched him pull the roots of his hair like Sean who ran a hand through his blond locks.

"Let's split. I'll go with Manu and Jace, go to the next street where there are less people. Do you know where she could be? What she does when she is in a bad mood." Sean asked equally distraught about his friend.

"I need to find her. I don't want her getting hurt. I'm going round." Jace's long legs had already carried him out and he ran through the press.

Jace's feet beat the paved sidewalks of the streets of LA with his neck straining from left to right for the kinky curled that was in a gorgeous up do and her flawless face. He ran his hand through his head when he made the turn to the third street with no sign of Millicent. His jaw hardened and his eyes were fiery as he searched the streets with numerous shops and people walking around their daily life. Raising his phone that was clutched in his hand, he dialed Sean as he continued to run through the street.

"Did you find her?" His anxious voice called out and he stood still turning all around him to do a double take.

"No man. She doesn't know these streets and it's hard to point out where she would be." Another second later, Manuela's voice tumbled through. "Kwaku, look into cafes; she likes calming drinks when she is disturbed." Jace cussed when he recognized the verity in her words. Dashing through the fourth street, this time surveilling the shops well, he still found nothing of Millicent. His heart stamped his ribcage in complete anguish. Again he called the other pair that was searching but they had not gotten any luck. He had momentarily forgotten that he was supposed to be holding a showcase but Cole's continual calls, which he declined each time, managed to remind him every time.

Right after Jace got off the phone the second time, he turned to look behind him, a screen glass wall separating the people inside from himself. The ground echoed with the music from inside and people sat in getting their fill of refreshing drinks while others worked on their computers. However, what had stolen his attention was not any of those events but the burly man with possible long black hair that had been held in a ponytail who sat in the middle of the shop. His light beige Latino skin was apparent and there were a few ink-lines poking themselves out of the tight shirt he wore. This said man sat next to no other than Millicent who was laughing at something the man said. Another look at the crinkling corners of the man's eyes had Jace propelling into the cafe.

They were so engaged in whatever they were discussing that Millicent did not notice him until he stopped in front of their table. Her eyes widened when she saw him but they narrowed in displeasure after a minute. The man next to her met Jace's eyes and there was a knowing grin on his face. He turned his mischievous dark chocolate eyes with hooded lids to Millicent and his clean-cut beard rustled a little as he smiled.

"This must be the luckiest unlucky man." Jace frowned when his fiancée giggled but was grateful for the distraction that seemed to occupy her rather than anger. The stranger picked up his cup and stood up, sending an impressed look to Jace who stood staring at the woman whose eyes were looking anywhere but at him.

"Well, MJ, it was nice to meet you even with this circumstance." Jace's eyes slithered at the nickname wondering who the man was. She received that name when he found out she had the same name as his older sister. So, the J stood for junior.

"Likewise; and thank you for everything Ignacio." She raised a bruised hand that was covered in a band aid, which had Jace rushing to her side ignoring the man who winked and stepped out of the cafe.

His entire body was tense with worry about both her safety and what was going through her mind concerning the event that had just taken place.

"What happened, baby?" Millicent didn't know she was rigid with anger and disappointment till his touch on her head and hand that was bruised offered the safety for her to unwind. His tender voice, one he used whenever he thought she was in danger almost made her cry, but she remained expressionless much to his dismay even when she debunked his question with a head shake.

"Just some unfortunate accident." She pulled her hand out of his hold and saw the pained expression on his face. Ignoring it, she spoke in the usual composed voice of hers asking, "What was that Jace? You promised that was going to be something only the two of us knew of." She turned her neck around the coffee house, feeling the creeping discomfort on her skin as if there were stares piercing her. She had felt insulted when she saw herself up there with men watching her like a commodity - so disrespected that she couldn't feel any anger.

Jace, still squatting at her side, grabbed both her hands earnestly and said, "I don't know little M, but you know I would never ever dare to disrespect you that way. I love you too much to do that." Their conversation was low and hidden by the music that gently bounced off the walls.

"How did it get there?"

"I heard you saw Gwen there, though I didn't find her around. My best guess is that she is the culprit." Millicent's eyes rolled, an action she rarely indulged in. It made Jace wary of her at the moment.

"Of course it's her." She blinked and looked at Jace's agitated blue-gray eyes. "My question is how did she get it and how is my face on it?" In the course of finishing her tea and speaking to the amiable stranger, Ignacio, whose car she had almost run into, they had analyzed all the possible scenarios but still could not find how it happened.

Jace's brows knitted together and after a minute he blinked in realization. Millicent squeezed his hand when she found the change in his eyes to which he refocused saying, "I think it was the day she came to apologize. But I had hidden your painting in the closet, unless she snooped through my stuff. What the hell is wrong with her?" He stumbled back slightly.

"I'm so sorry little M."

"Don't be. I'm sorry for you who decided to date an idiot - I apologize for the word." This made his lip twitch in humor. "How did you even decide to date such a person?"

Jace rubbed the tip of his ear - another thing he did when he was abashed. "I mean I thought she was pretty but that's not the case now." He quickly added when she shot him a look.

"Oh, she is pretty." She smiled at his confused look. It's okay if I say it, you just can't. She grinned as if he could read her thoughts. She was frustrated and just wanted to get rid of the nuisance called Gwen.

Jace's phone rang, and he sighed at the ID. Bringing the phone to his ears he spoke, "yes, I've found her." He stopped and looked round. "Drinklicious or something like that. I didn't check the street name. Okay." He put the phone away and focused on Millicent.

"I know this looks bad, little M. Believe me I would never do this to you." She spoke nothing, turning to look at the table and then back at him. His hope rose when she gently rubbed his hand with her thumb.

"So, are we good?" He gulped at the blank stare he received. Receiving no answer, he tried to eradicate his fear by asking, "You're not going to cancel our marriage, will you?"

He was frightened when she still remained silent and slowly dragged her hand from his. However, what made his heart rate resemble that of a dying person almost giving up the ghost was the fact that he neither felt nor saw the engagement ring on her finger. His heart shattered when he looked up and saw that torn look in her warm brown orbs.

Chapter 31

Millicent gazed at him with conflicting emotions for a hard long minute, and being unable to hold herself she dropped down to a squat like him and cornered him so that he was almost backed under the table. His expectant disappointed look was in place as she leaned forward, traced her hand behind his head and smacked him, hard.

"Ouch?" Jace's eyes widened at the slap to his head, and he looked at his love in wonder. Her lips were in a neutral position and her eyes were filled with chagrin. He noticed a pair of feet in black flats, and he glanced around her to see a barista peering down at them in amusement.

"Oh, I'm sorry. We saw you guys under the table and wanted to check if you needed anything." Millicent, hearing the voice of the new person, swiftly scrambled backward barely missing the chair behind her and the woman stepped forward to support her. Millicent thanked her with a low voice and took her seat.

They watched Jace elegantly unfold himself from beneath the table and sat next to her. Millicent smiled at the barista and asked if she could get a chamomile tea.

"Sure. And don't worry, I'll bring it to you." She grimaced with a sheepish smile when she winked and walked away.

She heard Jace clear his throat, and his deep voice proceeded to ask, "So, why did you knock my head off?"

Her blazing eyes found his eyes with a grim face. "You think I agreed to marry you as a joke? That I think so lightly of our marriage that a stupid conspiracy will cause me to call it off?" His eyes gleamed at her statement. "I feel like slapping you. If I considered marriage so flippantly, I would have married anyone that came my way. I wouldn't have agreed to marry you if I was not certain."

"Little M-" Jace moved to grab her, but she raised her hand to stop him. The only person who had ever so abruptly halted him that did not move a bone of fury in him. So, he obediently settled back down.

"No, hold up! Are you thinking of divorcing me in the future? Oh, then let's stop this right now, mister. I'm not going to get my heart broken in the middle of a union. I'm not entertaining roadblocks after my life is enmeshed with yours."

"What? No, little M. Never." The fire in her eyes smoked out at his answer and she relaxed in her seat, smiling a little when she saw his lips curve.

"How many times did you break up with Gwen in your relationship? No questions, I'm curious." She added when he opened his mouth to speak something.

"Maybe every three months or so. Gwen is a difficult person as you have seen." She hummed.

"Well, I've told you this again and yet again - I'm not Gwen. I like to talk about things before I get to a conclusion. So, speak to me. Next time something like this happens don't assume I'm leaving you; just ask how I'm doing - that's enough for me." She said in her sweet melodic voice, encouraging him to understand how seriously she thought of him. His heart swelled as he leaned to pull her into a hug.

"I'm sorry little M. I'm supposed to be comforting you but I'm basking in yours." He pulled back, and his blue-gray eyes were filled with admiration for the woman who was understanding beyond his comprehension. A shadow was cast over them and the kind server had brought over her tea.

"Thank you!"

"You're welcome. That's on the house - your eyes share your love, and we wanted to honor that." Millicent gave a coy smile as she retreated.

"But where's your ring, little M?"

"That ring is so shiny that I'm scared of losing it, so I placed it here." She pulled out a necklace he had not seen her wear from under her dress and he saw her ring dangling off it. He released a breath and stretched out his hand to cup her cheek staring at her grinning face in wonder.

"What am I to do with you?"

"Simple - love me."

"Mimi!" The feminine voice of Manuela called out and she turned away from the love bubble to see her friend rushing toward her with Sean behind them. Jace's phone rang again to see Cole's name and this time he decided to pick it up.

Millicent was soon in the bone crushing hug of her friend and as soon as she let her go, she fell into the warm hands of Sean.

"You got us worried there, little Mimi." She scowled at the description Sean had started to use about a month ago. He only ruffled her hair with a grin and moved to sit next to Jace while Manuela sat next to her.

"Are you okay?" Millicent smiled and nodded.

"I'm okay now, Ella. Sorry for worrying you. I'm not sure how to feel after that."

Manuela's eyes shifted from understanding to confusion and then to questioning. She looked between her cousin and her friend. "So, did you make that painting?"

Millicent coughed out on the choked tea she had in her mouth, looking around the table after she peeked at Jace from under the table with gaping doe eyes. Manuela gasped in understanding.

"You did!" She turned an accusing eye to her cousin. "What did you do?"

"He didn't do anything, Ella. If anything, it was I who allowed him." Seeing her friend's shameful gaze lowered to the cup of tea she had in hand, Manuela only glared at her cousin once more and at Sean who whistled mischievously. She placed a comforting hand on her friend's back.

"It's okay. You're still Mimi." Millicent shook her head and brokenly glanced at her friend.

"But it's... I..."

"You're still my Mimi. I can tell from your face that it wasn't meant to happen." She relished in the presence of her friend. Her heart was still heavy from having sex with Jace and that was a result of the principles she carried. Under any other circumstance she would have been excited to have been intimate in that way with him.

"But I assure you, that painting that was there was not done by me. I don't paint little M like that. Each stroke felt wrong." Jace asserted and he saw Millicent turn to him with a meaningful expression.

"I know, I've seen you paint my face and that looked nothing like it. Your art always feels like you see me." She grabbed his hand under the table and naturally their lips broadened as they turned upward.

"Gwen!" Manuela murmured in an enraged voice, cursing the woman who was hurting her best friend in such a demeaning way.

"What are you going to do about it?" Sean's question drew a menacing smile and fire from Jace's eyes.

"I just spoke to Cole. There're a few hours before it closes for the day. I want people to come watch the art with a new perspective in the coming weeks, so I decided to hold a press conference." Sean bounced in his seat, taking the girls by surprise.

"Finally, bro!" The quizzical faces of the women forced him to expound on his earlier statement. "He finally decided to clear his name. That was the initial plan, but Jace was a little under to do it and his dad did not want to make him feel worse by forcefully clearing his name."

Millicent turned to him to find his eyes already probing for hers. "I'm proud of you." She murmured for him only to see a light shade of pink tinge his cheeks causing her to grin.

"I'm going to go right now." They all stood with the exception of Millicent and Jace bent down to cup her face with his hands.

"I think I'll stay here. I know I've nothing to be ashamed of but I'm too tired of the day." Jace had an understanding look, and he dropped a tender kiss on her forehead before stepping back and searching for Manuela who was already nodding in agreement to the unspoken request.

Just as the two men stepped out, he saw his father's name on his vibrating phone.

"Dad, yeah, I'm doing the press conference." He paused and smirked at something his father said as they walked down the street. "Yeah, I know dad. It's long overdue. She tried to hurt Millicent too." Jace frowned and unconsciously halted his steps in the middle of the street they were crossing. "What?" Sean pulled him away when he refused to move in his stupor. "Of course! I'll be happy to help. It's our redemption." When he dropped the phone, he looked at his friend with a hard look.

"Apparently, I'm not the only person Gwen has done this to. She has successfully destroyed two artists' careers both from abroad and Zane Black as well. She was dating those abroad as she dated me all for her twin brother."

Sean who was normally unperturbed by issues now held a disgusted look, stupefied by the effrontery of Gwen Dumas. "That is bloody, freaking disgusting. What the hell man!"

Everything that Gwen had ever been to him was a lie. She was exploiting him to buttress her brother's fame as she had done to those three artists. When she broke up with him, she was with another. Dwelling on these instances just heightened the anger he had.

They got to the gallery and found that there were no reporters outside. Jace knew that Cole had directed them inside already. He was a man shivering in apprehension to keep his job. Jace walked in, head held high, and the aura of unmistakable importance dwindled slightly when his mother pulled him into her embrace. She had warned him when he got involved with Gwen, but his desires superseded his thoughts that he disregarded his mother of many years. Now, he savored her warmth with bitter remorse.

"We're right here." She said as his father gave him an affectionate pat after distancing himself from the hug.

From the seat on the long table where he sat Jace searched for the faces of his family and friends who were around, the closest friend being Sean, and he thought about his love in the cafe as his eyes flittered over the room of flashing lights and eager storytellers of the media.

"Good afternoon, ladies and gentlemen." He finally speaks, his eyes above the heads of the information fishers with the flashing devices in their hands. "I know this was an extempore invitation and meeting, but I am here to do what should have been done months ago when I was slandered." There are a few collective gasps as his steely face casually looks around the room of confused reporters.

"Yes, slandered. Seven months ago, I was accused of having plagiarized my own work. I was pulled in a dark place unable to believe the betrayal and hence my inability to elucidate and exonerate myself. But today after a few occurrences and discoveries, I and others like me have agreed to bring these injustices and preposterous behavior of some individuals to light." He breathed in for a while before continuing.

"My artwork was stolen from my studio and handed over to an undeserving person who was given misplaced credit. To prove this, I would like you to know that unknown to you all, my signature which is now on the screen is always hidden in my canvases. All those works that were sold after they were stolen have been traced and the signatures have been confirmed. Please look up at the screen." He turned behind as mutterings took over the atmosphere of the room with comments of disbelief.

"This has not only been my story but that of Zane Black, a phenomenal icon in this world who I have invited today." A tall, lanky man in fashionable eyeglasses made his way to sit next to Jace offering him a handshake. "Derek Dubois on zoom as well as Eric Osman."

"Hello, everyone. I am Zane Black, and I represent one of whom has been destroyed through calumny." One by one these men testified to the world what cruelty had been done to them.

A reporter's hand shot up after their speeches and he was prompted to speak as others aggressively typed away.

"We can guess who the culprit is, but Mr. Elrod could you make known, beyond our assumptions, the name of this offender?" Jace turned shortly to the man with bushy brows sitting next to him. He had a determined look along with those of the small screen in front of him.

His jaw set in distaste as he prepared to make known the heartbreak, he had endured months prior to this and his eyes found his family's solemn gazes, encouraging him. "Offenders." Jace corrected. "The culprits who have worked their way into destroying the careers of us artists for their benefit are Gwen and Gary Dumas."

Chapter 32

Glasses clinked in the kitchen while Millicent sniffled lightly, rubbing her nose with the back of her hand, adjusting her back on the throw pillow behind her on the couch in which she sat. The blanket around her drifted down to her laps showing the gypsy skirt she wore as she stared at the screen in front of her. She turned her head when she heard the graceful footsteps of Jace and she tried to smile through the drops on her face when he emerged with a glass bowl. One look at her, and he was rushing to the couch and placing the bowl on a table in front of the couch in which her legs were folded, he worriedly held her face in his hands, blue gray eyes scanning her.

"Why are you crying, sweetheart?" His tender voice broke her further and he scooted forward, collecting her legs and draping them over his legs. One hand dropped around her neck and tightened its hold there, his eyes clouded, fretting and pushing her into his arms.

"You're scaring me, little M. What's going on? Did you hurt yourself?" All the questions tumbled out hastily when he didn't get a response.

"Wait, wait. I'm going to miss the rest of the episode." She wailed as she pushed a bewildered Jace backward. She turned and opened her arms, calling him to hug her again. "It's so sad. The drama my friend recommended." His thoughts snapped into place at her words. He sharply pulled back from the hug with wide eyes.

"So, you're telling me that you are in tears because of the drama?" He felt her nod as her head laid on his shoulder while she focused on the ongoing drama. Jace sighed heavily, rubbing his forehead and tightening his hold on her, picking up the bowl of strawberries in chocolate for her and feeding her one.

"Oh, that tastes nice. Is that chocolate?" He nodded only to hear her sob, sending his nerves on alert but he found her engrossed with the movie on the screen.

"What's the title?"

"Thirty-nine. I don't cry this bad normally but it's hella sad." Jace chuckled under his breath at the heartfelt comment.

"Now I want to invite Sean over. He's horrible at watching sad stuff but I don't need two bawling humans to take care of."

"Oh, call him! The more the merrier. You're not crying so might as well get someone else. Manuela is also taking a nap so I'm on my own." He was going to debunk the offer till his eyes fell on her magnificently bright doe eyes.

"Hold on." Millicent's phone pinged, and she picked it up to check. The message on the screen elicited a bubbly laugh from her which caused Jace's brows to lift at the change in sentiment.

"What's making you laugh?" He watched as she typed away.

"Ah, it's Ignacio. He's wondering if you were unluckily out of the picture." She looked up to see him scowling and simply dropped a kiss on his sulking face.

"That guy who almost ran into you. Why is he texting you? Sean's going to be here in twenty."

"Great! Let me restart this. And I'm the one who was saved by Ignacio - I walked into his car." He chucked one strawberry into his mouth to stop the grumbles leaving Millicent in a fit of giggles.

They were still sitting in the couch entangled in their arms with the drama paused, and they fed each other till the last of the strawberries in the bowl disappeared. Exactly twenty minutes later, his doorbell went off and Jace got up to receive the caller. Sean burst through with bright blue eyes shining in exuberance and he rushed toward Millicent who was unfurling herself from the couch, bloodshot eyes still in place, as she crashed into the broad chest of her blond-haired friend.

"Mimi! I heard there's a drama marathon tonight!" He spun her around through her chuckles.

Jace was facing them as he reached to shut the door but a foot that jutted to the narrow space stopped him from closing it. His head snapped up and from the milky-white skin of the orange painted toes of the foot in the wedge shoe, he traveled his eyes up from the green floral dress to the airy, wavy, shoulder-length, chestnut hair and then he stumbled back in fright at his cousin's face.

"Tamara?" The woman had a wide smirk plastered on her face when she saw Jace's wide eyes.

"My, Jay! I would think I'd be the first person you would share the good news of finally discarding that Dumas family with. I had to hear it from the Siberian husky you grew up with." She poked her chin in the direction of Sean and she glamorously sauntered in, but her eyes narrowed at the woman who held Sean's gaze. Her skin shone like the bronze her father got from mining different ores and she had a radiance behind her that was hard to miss.

"It had to be done." She raised a suggestive side of her lip and the edge of the right side of her face raised, watching him as he finally managed to rip his adoring eyes from the said woman to shut the door.

Of course, she's here to rub it in and say, "I told you so." She indeed spoke them. Tamara never held back her teasing, and she may have been the only person to urge Jace out of his comfort zone when he was a child and taught him self-worth as well. One of the reasons she was able to reject Gwen outwardly upon first meeting her. He tried to prevent her from exerting the force of intimidating pressure on Millicent which was the reason he had not introduced them. She smiled and shrewdly blinked away her scrutiny and teasing as she took in Millicent's form again.

"I see there's another person."

"Don't mess around, Tammy." Tamara's eyes grew open at the demand and the authority underneath and Sean looked at the two powerhouses in anxiety. Millicent, though inquisitive, calmly awaited the introduction after Sean had whispered their relation-ship to her.

Tamara walked in and stood still before Millicent, with no ex-pression while the latter's tranquility projected into the room. When Tamara lifted a daring brow, she allowed her own brow to slightly shoot up and maintained a challenging eye with her. Milli-cent was hardly imposed by authoritative presences. She accorded respect and politeness when necessary but she never allowed anyone's status to belittle hers - this was how she had always protected herself. Jace was just about to step in to dissolve the issue when his cousin surprisingly smiled.

"I like you!" Tamara suddenly declared much to Sean's relief. She was the only woman who had the capacity to daunt him because she carried out her threats without leniency, a ruthless businesswoman. Millicent beamed in response to the woman and searched for Jace who moved next to her to place an assuring arm around her.

"Little M, this is Tamara. She's my cousin and daughter of my father's older sister. Tammy, Millicent." As the two got acquainted, a well-rested Manuela emerged from one of the rooms and was startled to see the house filled.

"What's all the noise?" She shrieked when Sean grabbed her from behind and pulled her to the center of the room.

"Jay, I thought I taught you better? You leave one and now you have two?" Tamara's bold voice echoed through the room from the couch where she sat with her legs propped on a table. Her eyes looked lazy, but the fire and curiosity directed at Manuela was unmistakable.

Jace was emerging from the kitchen but stopped in his tracks as he sibilated. "What- what the hell are you saying? This is Manu, mom's sister's daughter!" Millicent cackled at the stupefied look on all their faces and before long everyone was doing so as well.

They had proceeded to settle on the couch and the ground, surrounded by snacks, engulfed in blankets and huddled together. Millicent sat with her back to Jace's chest and her legs across Manuela's while Tamara and Sean preferred the ground where they relaxed against the couch and tipped their heads back so that someone on the couch could feed them without them being disturbed. Before long, after a good few episodes were done, there was a snuffle. Jace blinked and searched around. It wasn't Millicent though she did have a lone tear leaking from her eye. Manuela was invested but her eyes were pooled at the bottom and glittered in the dark room. Tamara looked hardly moved but even she was wavering and he turned to Sean to see his shoulders quake. Millicent lovingly patted his shoulder in comfort.

Minutes later, the main lead was wailing on the ground, heart aching for her friend.

"Shit!" A thick voice sounding like Tamara's, whispered and she sniffled. "Sorry, that's freaking sad."

"Tamara Vaughn, are you crying?" Jace asked with a laugh to receive a muted but firm response.

"Shut it!"

Millicent pulled away from him and launched herself into Manuela's awaiting arms and they were the first in the party to cause the raging dam to break. Their loud cries drew out the rain cloud from Sean's eyes and he hopped onto the couch huddling close to them. Tamara jumped up, pulled Jace out of the couch and broke too.

Jace stood warily in the middle of the room, watching all of them cry but he really could not take Millicent's cries. They broke him. She was seriously considering the drama and crying. He could tease everyone in the room but not her.

"She has cancer." He heard his friend's baritone voice speak in his sobs.

"I know."

"They spent most of their life together. Imagine what it'll be like to see her die."

"They wrote such a sensitive topic so well."

"How is she going to tell her friends?"

"Let's just watch." The conversation amidst the cries continued and Jace sighed, walking into the kitchen to prepare hot chocolate for them.

"Does he have tissues? My nose is blotchy from all this crying." Millicent passed the box she had to Manuela.

"Need some too."

As they distributed it round Manuela questioned her friend. "Who recommended this?"

"Francis Aryeetey. He knows I don't do romcoms or Korean dramas in general, but he persuaded me and said this was good."

"The guy who lived opposite us in Uni?" Millicent nodded.

"Don't know who this guy is but appreciate his sense of reality." Tamara chipped in, wiping her tears away.

Jace returned and set the mugs down for them and they each wordlessly took it with their eyes glued to the screen. He shook his head in wonder and sat directly beneath Millicent who dropped a kiss on his cheek in gratitude. He turned back with a sweet grin and turned his other cheek to her.

Another sob and bawling.

"It really is a difficult decision to make."

"She decided to spend her final moments in pain with her family and friends rather than a deteriorating state."

"Jace, you don't cry." Millicent spoke but everyone else in the room knew what the man was like.

"This stone figure from the ice age can't melt." Sean supplied.

"You're just a crybaby, Sean." And again, they were bantering.

"Let's pray. I don't want to go through this with any of you." All pairs of eyes turned to Millicent in wonder and humor. "What? I'm not sure how people deal with cancer but it's so terrifying to see a loved one go through that." And like this the banters went through the night with occasional crying and cuddling watching the drama into the night.

At midnight, Millicent was on the ground with Jace, seeking comfort in his arms and at dawn when they had cried the most after the woman finally died and left her friends, they all closed their eyes. Regardless how prepared viewers had been like the characters themselves, everyone in his house wailed like they were at a funeral.

He gently picked up his love in his arms and walked her to the room she was using. As he lowered her to the bed, Millicent shuffled, and her eyes fluttered slowly.

"Jace?" Her hoarse voice asked.

"Right here, little M." Her hand tightened around his as she snuggled into the bed.

"She died." He hummed. "But she was alive in their hearts." Another hum as he traced her hair away from her face. "I want to be alive in your heart." Jace stilled with a furious intensity.

"You're forgetting something, little M." He waited for her sleepy eyes to pop open before speaking. "We're growing old together." She had a drowsy grin as she looped her hands behind his neck and pulled him down to meet his lips with her leaving him in a stunned kiss.

CHAPTER 33

"They're currently still in custody. But their father is arguing for a forfeiture." The contours of Jace's visage hardened upon hearing his lawyer.

"He's trying to buy his way out again. See to it that it doesn't happen." His stern voice cut across the device looking through the window he stood by.

"Don't worry Mr. Elrod. With the number of artists, they have stolen from and the careers they've ruined, I can assure you that they will be detained. I'll work to see that they receive jail time."

"Good. I'm not going to be around for all that, so I trust that these matters are in your capable hands." He stuffed one hand into the pocket of the sweatpants he wore.

"Without a doubt."

"Thank you, Shay." He heard the man exhale lightly with a breathy chuckle.

"Always a pleasure." Jace took out the air pods from his ears and finally allowed his stony face to stretch when he heard the music that moderately bounced off the walls of Millicent's home.

They had returned to Ghana at the end of the week of his exhibition, one of the most massive showcases he had ever had, especially after he decided to do a mini exhibit titled 'The Redemption' for the other artists who had been conned by Gwen and her brother.

He trekked out of the room he used and walked into the kitchen to find Millicent with her hair up in a ponytail, humming and dancing to the upbeat music. Bringing his strong arms to his chest he crossed them and inclined himself to the doorpost of the kitchen, a little smile resting on his face while studying the lovely woman who had her back to him, placing a pan on the hot plate of the stove. Aprons seemed like an unnecessary addition in the homes of most Ghanaians he had been to and Millicent was in that category which made his eyes squint in concern. When she finally turned to return to her work on the counter, she shrieked at seeing him because he was dressed in black like a shadow and her hand reached up to clutch her chest.

"My God!" She screeched in her dialect and Jace's smile broadened in an apologetic manner. "Why are you standing there like that?" He didn't respond as he watched her resettle and rinse out some rice.

She felt the heat of his eyes on her and peeked through her lashes to see his unwavering eyes on her.

"Why are you looking at me like that?" Her eyelids lifted higher when she turned her attention to him who was still leaning on the wooden frame of the door with accusing eyes on her.

"Don't you think you owe me something for taking advantage of me so easily and then throwing me out of your home?" The nasal whine in his complaint caused her to sweep away the smile lingering in her eyes with her lashes.

Jace pushed off the hard wall when he saw her coy expression and how she turned her gaze away. He sauntered forward to the counter, standing opposite her with a teasing grin. His commanding presence caused her to look up and she squeaked when she saw him so close. Her body unconsciously stepped back when the intense eyes of the man she loved gave attention to nothing but her. Jace's lashes danced with every shift of her body at his passionate stare.

"I told you I don't remember anything." Millicent stepped back to working on the food she was making.

"Maybe I should remind you." Jace spoke suggestively which made her head snap up, but he was no longer in front of her where the counter separated them, so her eyes began to scan around the kitchen, and she was stunned to turn and find him breathing hotly down her neck. She jumped back. That's all she had been able to do since that night - escaping his forwardness - because he wanted to get an answer to why she did what she did when in fact she had no reason.

"Jace!"

"Mhm?" He languidly questioned, eyeing the space she had put between them. He had enjoyed goading her. Millicent was not a shy person; she always had something to say back to him even though she said it in the sweetest and kindest way possible. This, apart from when they were getting to know each other and when they were intimate, was another time she was being demure, and he was enjoying every moment of it.

"Okay! What do you want me to do?" She threw the napkin down, placed both hands on her hips and turned to the man that was not letting her live down her actions. "I need to cook for our friends."

"If you get to take advantage of me, I should be able to do so."

"Okay, do what you want." His eyes widened and he subtly shook his head before lunging forward

Jace gently grabbed her face, his eyes intent on her brown ones that were nervously assessing him. He felt her increased rate of breathing when he sent his head closer to her face, his face beamed with love as his mouth dropped to the corner of her full lips leaving a chaste kiss there. When he stepped back, he saw her stunned look.

"That's it?" Millicent watched him a little skeptical as he straightened up, took a step back and hid both of his hands in his pockets.

"Yes, sweetheart. You don't want us kissing, and I respect that. So, when can I officially kiss you?" She giggled at how eager he looked, and she nudged him to cut the vegetables.

"After our wedding."

"Which one?"

"Hmm white? Okay the traditional one but nothing extreme." She heard the knife hit the cutting board and looked up to his star-struck face coated with an infectious grin.

"That's in two weeks!" She was tackled into his hold as he peppered kisses around her face and neck.

"Alright, alright. Let's put the same excitement into cooking. They'll be here soon." She beamed when he grumbled and gently settled her down. "All this love for kisses." She muttered but from the look he gave her, he had heard her.

At noon the house was filled with the expected visitors who sat at the table bantering, chatting and making jokes. Tamara and Sean, who had come down to join in on the upcoming wedding celebration, sat with Manuela, Jace and Millicent.

"This is good food. So, you're saying I'll move in with Ella, and they are going to Ella's house?" Tamara pointed to the two men. Millicent hummed and pinched Jace's hand that was shaking her thigh, silently telling her to rescind her decision. However, the decision had already been made and the women had brought their belongings with Sean's help.

Her eyes looked at the watch up on the wall and Millicent exclaimed in astonishment at how much time had gone by nearing the next appointment.

"What?"

"Why, what happened?"

She ignored the mixed voices of her friends and looked at Jace with her big doe eyes.

"We need to be home with my mom in thirty minutes."

"Shit! Sorry, yeah. Apparently, we are going through some details."

"Oh, I loved the piece that you chose. What did you say it's called?" Millicent turned to Tamara at her question and saw the excitement in her eyes.

"It's called a Kente. Actually, are you using the woven one or the print material?" Manuela twisted her body to look at her friend.

"Also, are we just throwing the piece around us like I've seen online?" Sean's voice looked like it had been charmed by whatever he saw which made Manuela and Millicent chuckle.

"Ella, we're using the woven one. I have to go see Auntie Mavis." She informed her friend of her intended visit to see her family to which Manuela nodded. They had been such good friends that they knew each other's families so it was no surprise that she wanted to go see her mother who even considered her a second daughter. Sometimes, Millicent's own mother would send some food over to her when she came to visit so they were both used to the deep familial ties. She never knew that those ties were going to become official through marriage.

"And yes Sean, you can decide to wear it however you men want it. Now we have to run; I'll bring this one to you at Manuela's place."

Some minutes after they bid their goodbyes, they were seated in the home of the Arthurs with Jace's parents. Her family was also around snacking and brainstorming with her much to her brothers' dismay. None of them liked events that required excessive planning.

"Mimi." Max's voice called and just as Millicent responded the little pup that had grown a bit more since she was taken back to her owner's abode barked. Millicent only took the throw pillow that was next to her and chucked it at her brother who, anticipating the attack, turned so it flew in another direction. "Aba, I told you that when you two are around, I'll call you by your soul name." His exasperated voice laced with a roguish undertone caused even Jace to snicker.

"Alright, we need a theme for you." Josephine spoke after she had her laugh and gazed up to see Regina coming in with a restock of refreshments.

"We can use how they met." It was Anthony who had surprisingly spoken, and his wife's lips stretched up sweetly.

Josh also spoke up for the first time. "Yes, how did you meet?" This was the first time he seemed genuinely interested in anything that was going on because since they entered the house, he looked to be distracted by something, and he was giving the couple very weird looks.

"Don't they know about how we met?" Jace shifted close to Millicent and whispered the question in her ears.

"They never asked that explicitly." She responded into his ear oblivious to the amused and concerned eyes awaiting their response.

"So, what's the story?"

"We never had one. We just went with the flow of things." Millicent's whisper was cut off with the loud clearing of the throat of her mother and they turned back startled, finding every pair of eyes on them.

"Tell the story baby. My mom catches me whenever I lie." Millicent's incredulous eyes fell on his own.

She shifted even closer to him and spoke in an intense whisper meant only for his ears. "Are you kidding? Don't you remember how I answered both their questions in the beginning? Don't forget about the time one. Make her believe; if anything, you are a better storyteller." Jace silently laughed at the reminder.

They both turned around after a conclusive eye contact. Jace took a breath and began his tale.

"It was a rainy day, and I was shopping when I met Millicent."

Max's brows scrunched in confusion, and he didn't hold back his muddled state as he interrupted Jace and asked, "I thought you two met online." Everyone straightened up, and Jace raised a brow discreetly at Millicent who cussed under her breath looking at him with wide eyes.

"Uh, yeah. Because it was a rainy day, I decided to remain indoors and shop online." He smiled when he remembered a scene he watched in a show. "Millicent's items were delivered to me and mine to hers which was really stupid since there is no connection between our names but yeah, that was along the lines of how we got to know each other." Impressed by the line of thought, Millicent slapped his behind in appreciation.

"Okay so I think we can let the designer make open packages with the photos popping out of them." As the older people spoke, she rested her head on her fiancé's shoulder, and he held back on his physical contact as he had learned from her to respect the elders, but the essence of their love could not be missed by anyone.

Jace's parents had departed but the couple decided to stay for a while. When they decided to finally leave, they heard Josh calling for them.

"Millicent, Jace, could you come to the study for a moment." Millicent's playful stance changed when she heard the voice of her brother. It was the same tone he used when he was taking up the father role. Jace observed this change and squeezed her hand, her change in state making her also solemn.

Their father's study had always been on the ground floor of their home, filled with numerous books because he called his children down to come do their homework in there when he was sure they would play. It suited him being a professor. They entered the dimly lit room and found Josh behind a huge stylish mahogany table which was nicely polished. He gestured to the seats in front of the table so they could sit. As soon as they sat he threw a file with its contents out on the table. His facade was calm but the manner in which the papers fell on the table caused Millicent to search up for her brother. When she found nothing there she looked on the table, feeling Jace's hand tighten around her. Realizing the information on it with their signatures, she discovered it was the fake marriage certificate; the sudden fright she had made her squeeze and search for Jace's reassuring eyes, but he was already looking at Josh with a firm look. Millicent squirmed.

"What is this I hear about the certificate being fake?" Even Jace had to gulp at the authoritative voice, and he felt Millicent tremble from their linked hands on his lap.

Chapter 34

The couple sat in the tense atmosphere of the room observing the older brother who looked to be extremely frustrated with them and the situation at hand. He had called when they were in the US to ask for the certificate to work on the one that they would be receiving in Ghana as well. Without thinking much of it she had directed him to it and this was the consequence. Millicent shifted when he ran a hand down his face and she decided to speak.

"JJ." She winced when his sharp eyes turned to her. He heavily dropped both of his hands on the table and hunched over it.

"What happened? The truth!" He added when her mouth opened to respond.

"It wasn't Jace's fault." Millicent said when she saw the hard look that her brother was giving her fiancé. "I approached him, and I asked him to help me evade mom's advances with all those men hunting. I'm sorry, Josh." She sat quietly and Jace rubbed her hand also sitting up to help her.

"I was also the one that agreed to help her. I also wanted to get out of a union, so it was mutual." The strong form of her brother stepped back and looked at the two of them with displeasure.

"So how exactly did you two meet and put that together with how this entire lie began."Jace turned to Millicent and she signaled that she would be the one to speak. She was feeling guilty toward the man that she had looked up to as a father and a brother and the expression was palpable on her face as she stared at her hand in her lap. She breathed a calming breath and trained her face back on her brother's awaiting one.

"We met almost three months ago in Ella's house. The day after mom scared me with her arrangement. I met Jace and begged him after some time to be my fake husband. He didn't want to initially, but I persuaded him."Jace saw her brother's eyes on the documents on the table.

"I took her to the states and let one of my friends make that. We signed it there and came back."

"He's good." Josh uttered in wonder.

Jace hummed and continued, "But none of the moments we shared were bound by contract. They really were genuine." Millicent's eyes pooled with tears, looking at the adoring expression he had when he spoke these.

"And so, this was going to be kept a lie and never revealed."There was a heartbreaking emotion dripping with his statement which inadvertently caused Millicent's tears to drop. None of them spoke because they had not thought about telling the truth.

Josh sighed in distress and stared particularly at his sister. "I am so disappointed in you, Aba. Couldn't we have helped you as your siblings if mom was doing that?" Her tears dropped in torrents. "You both are going to confess, and it has to be before your wedding otherwise, I'll have to be a bad person."

"But..." Her melodious voice rose in objection, but Jace pulled her hand just as Josh lifted a daring brow.

"We will do it. I'm sorry about this, Joshua."

"That's not all. You are not to see each other for the rest of the week. That's my punishment for you, Aba. You may be old now but this is disappointing and it's one for you too." He turned to Jace and there was the evidence of a smile hiding behind his stern face. Jace could tell he had long forgiven his sister, but this might have been to correct her for the entertainment of it.

"What? You can't be serious, JJ!" The dense chair barely scraped on the ground as Millicent stood.

"Do you want me to tell your crimes? I may not say it as nicely as you would, and Max may kill him." His chin jutted out to Jace who had stood up following her.

Millicent thought about what he said for a moment and had to relent her argument because her brother was not known for bluffing. She dropped her eyes and heaved a puff of air before turning to look at Jace who was silently trying to assess the situation. "I guess we'll stay apart."

"I need to have a word with her, Jace. I know you can drive. Get her keys. I'll send her back." That made Jace realize how dire the situation had turned. He subtly showed his anxious state to Millicent who was also in the same condition. They had been around each other for the past months and the thought of being away for even a day looked daunting. She grabbed onto him, and they whispered words in front of her brother.

Josh had not been joking when he said they were to stay separate. The couple had agreed to confess during the weekend and Josh had personally ensured that he took her to work so that even if Jace was waiting for her in the morning, he had to hide away and couldn't see her. If she was to be in her own home, Manuela had been tasked to chaperone and his cousin was too respectful toward the man to defy him. They were able to communicate through technology but for the last three days, her brother ensured that she was away from him. All Jace wanted was to see her and speak to her in person. The craziness of his love had led him to call his cousin for help.

Tamara sat on the bed with Sean who was laughing his head away at his friend's expense. Her shoulders shook as she took in her brooding cousin. "So, Sean forged the certificate? Of all the ways love stories begin, this was yours?"

A pillow was chucked at Sean while Jace stood at the foot of the bed unimpressed that he was having his fun.

"Wait and what's the new update, Sean?" The bed squeaked when the blond man sat up on the bed with a playful conniving grin.

"Ah, as you know, Mimi's brother has kept them away from each other. He hid in her office one early morning but the security walked in to see him dressed in all white. Thinking he was a ghost he was frightened and tased him. I was waiting in the car downstairs. Imagine how scary it is to have a twitching driver!"

"Oh my gosh! This is the first time I'm seeing you behave so stupid outside your early years." Tamara wheezed, picking up the items she brought and placing it on the vanity table where Jace sat. "Okay, let's begin."

"You know I'm really very proud of you that you put the Dumas down." Jace squinted while she worked around his eyes. Tamara's voice always dropped a tone lower when she was speaking about solemn issues.

"Why is everyone saying that?" He questioned.

"Because you do so much and so little." He heard Sean's voice from the side.

"Yes, you give your all to make sure that everyone around you is doing so well but then you tend to neglect yourself, taking all the bullshit of life for yourself. I think even Millicent knows this. You think you are not kind because you're so indifferent to outsiders but Jace, those of us you love, you'd get killed for us and as flattering as that is, know that we also want to see you happy. So, yes everyone is proud of you."

"Including me." She perked at Sean's voice which drew a silent laughter from them.

About forty minutes into endless laughter and complaints Manuela badged into the room. She stopped short at the sight in front of her.

"Ouch! Tammy, watch it." Jace whined.

Manuela turned to Sean who was recording and snickering. He saw her and grinned. "That's him?" Sean bobbed his head amused and amazed at what was happening.

"Wow, Tammy. I barely recognized him. You're a good make-up artist." The woman grinned and continued powdering a vexed Jace's face.

"Thanks. Would have been my career if my father was not against it. So, what's the plan?"

Manuela jumped on the bed next to Jace before taking out the hair she brought and responding, "Mimi is staying at home with her family today, obviously, under Josh's watch. We're going to visit with this buffoon dressed like a woman and posing as Sean's girlfriend. He sees Mimi and we come back."

"Perfect! How does your girlfriend look, Sean?" Tamara stepped away and giggled when she saw the disgusted look on their friend's face.

"Please don't say that outside of acting but you did a good job. It was as if he was supposed to be born a woman. Ah, what you do for love." Jace poked his head around the mirror marveling at his transformation.

"Wow! This is good. Let's go before night falls. Give me the wig."

Millicent greeted them when they got to her family's home. She watched the new person with interest, failing to recognize that it was her fiancé, and he smirked at her expense feeling utterly ridiculous that he had done a make-over in order to see her. He had his hand being held by a funny looking Sean. There was no one else seen when they entered the house except for the two young girls that resided there with Regina Arthur.

When Sean saw Millicent's unwavering and confused stare on Jace who watched her with just as equal interest, he introduced them, "Mimi, this is Lucy." At Jace's sharp glare, the two women in the room openly laughed, to Millicent's swelling dubiety. "My girlfriend." The declaration caused her eyebrow to rise, a habit that was becoming so ingrained after the many life surprises she kept having in the past months.

She knew that Sean was not one to go into relationships because, as she had found out, he couldn't last in a relationship for more than five months. She just thought that he was not ready to commit to anyone. He was scared of commitment but refused to admit it but she wasn't one to interfere in the lives of others without cause. Millicent was taken aback while her friends were roaring in laughter when the said girlfriend suddenly knelt in front of her and tried to reach out for her face. She jumped out of the couch to stand and there was an unmistakable look of hurt on the person's face.

"Little M." The scandalous gasp broke out of her mouth, and she tried to make sense of why the woman's voice sounded like Jace. When she put the pieces together, she watched them amused, eyes settled on the female version of Jace.

"You— You are a woman." She noticed the pink hues on his face while their friends chatted behind making fun of him. She grabbed his hand and dashed up the stairs with him to her room leaving them to do as they wished.

She stood in the center of her room quietly inspecting a visibly uncomfortable Jace.

"Wow." She simply stated and chortled under her breath. She was suddenly pulled into his arms, and she felt the familiar muscles underneath the large shirt. "You went all out, huh?" Her breathy laughing voice spoke into his chest.

"Well, I missed you. It's been three days of hell without seeing your face." Her face was pushed back, and he scanned it with at-tention while she could barely hold back her laugh at the makeup on his face, especially the rouge lipstick.

"I missed you too." She took another look at the long wig and cackled. "You should pay whoever did your face." He scowled and they settled into their usual loving atmosphere. The loud voices of their family interrogating the two young girls and Tamara meeting Max could be heard from the spot where they laid in bed in each other's arms.

Josh was working in the study and had barely been out since they had arrived, so their time was spent peacefully. When it was time for them to depart, as they descended the stairs, they were met by Josh who was climbing up. He stopped his trek and watched the suspicious way that Jace turned around and Millicent's body inclination. The squeaky voice of the new woman who stopped as Millicent wanted to greet. Millicent gulped when her brother's brow slightly danced - they had been caught.

"Good to see you here, Jace. I hope you have decided the day to tell the truth."

With that reminder and their stupefied looks, the next day they knelt before both their families with their heads bent in shame.

"We lied. I'm sorry; we're sorry. We were never married before." Jace spoke looking at his parents and Millicent's mother. There were solemn looks of displeasure on their faces one moment and the next, their laughter was bouncing through their ears. Millicent tilted her head looking as perplexed as Jace who turned to her with wide eyes.

"Oh, we knew." Josephine simply said causing both to snap their heads to them.

Chapter 35

"How?" Millicent croaked out the query.

Jace only regarded his father, knowing that if anyone could see through his willfulness it had to be him as most of his qualities compared to his. From the expression his father held as he watched him, he knew he had found out long ago; yet, what he couldn't understand was why none of them said anything.

"I thought there was something suspicious about your attitude and answers when I first met Millicent. I told Anthony and he said from a father's intuition that you had done something, so he investigated, and guess what we found." Josephine's eyes twinkled as she watched the two uncomfortable adults kneel with guilt consuming one more than the other - her son the less. They had gotten over the initial ill humor concerning the matter when they realized that their son would not engage in such a farce without having interest in the woman.

"I told Auntie Regina when I met her in your home." That would have been some months ago. Millicent would have thought that her mother would rage but she sat there with an amused grin on her face, and she had no idea how to react to that.

"Why didn't any of you say anything?" Jace was still trying to grasp their revelation and the one that their parents had shared.

"Knowing you, if you were not interested in Millicent, you would not have done that." His mother replied.

"And if this child-" Regina got up and hit her daughter on the back. "- did not like you, she wouldn't even have asked you."

"Ow!" She exclaimed as her mother raised her hand again and the older woman gave her a challenging gaze. Before her hand could hit her, Jace was in front of her, but that was not needed before her phone began to ring.

Millicent watched as her mom picked up the phone. Her face paled and her body tensed. Jace, noticing the change, moved away from Millicent and stood, helping her up to her feet as well. They had already confessed to Max who with a disappointed look stormed to his room and had not been out since. Josh left them to deal with the older people themselves.

"Eh?" Millicent stood taller and walked in front of her mother who had a disbelieving look. The intonation of this exclamation was that of impending doom. It made Josephine shoot up in her seat, throwing a concerned look to Millicent who was waiting for her mother.

Regina dropped to the couch with a lost look. Millicent squatted before her mother, grabbing onto her hands that were in her lap. "Ma?"

"Aba, grandma- grandma just passed." Her tear-filled eyes watched her daughter as she relayed the news that her mother was gone and no more. Millicent paled and fell to the ground before Jace could hold onto her, sitting. Josephine's gasp was muffled with her hand that was now covering her open mouth.

"Huh?" It took a while to comprehend what her mother had said. "Grandma? You mean your mother, grandma?" She asked brokenly, a tear falling from her eye. This was the sage woman that bathed her from her birth till she was weaned, the one whose warm laps she played, fed, and laid on, the one who gathered everyone around constantly so her house was filled with the chatter and laughter of both adults and children, the one who supported them with money when their dad was no more, the one with whom they spent almost every Christmas with in joy, the one who just made everything better. And right before her wedding.

A sob broke from her, and she choked on her words. "How? They said she was recovering well in the ICU." Regina on seeing her daughter's tears broke down herself. She didn't know how it happened. It was a tear in the esophagus which had successfully been repaired. She could not believe the news herself. Jace sat next to Millicent on the ground and cradled her in his arms and Josephine took her mother in a comforting hug.

Max and Josh came out to meet their mother and sister crying and once they became aware of the news, even they as men could not hold back their tears. The month had become a mixed period of joy and sorrow. Mourning had taken over.

After a while of basking in the solemn air, Jace spoke, "We can shift the wedding to a later date."

"Yes, I agree with Jace. You don't have to endure any pain. We're also your family now." Josephine said calmly rubbing Regina's arms in sadness.

"No, she wanted you to have the wedding this month. It's like she knew she was leaving and wanted to leave remembering this last happiness." Regina croaked. She had cried even more when her siblings called, especially Anita who worked in the hospital where their mother was being treated.

"I have to leave now to help with things back home, but we will all be here next week to celebrate your union in memory of her." Regina said and was sent together with Anthony and Josephine who wanted to ensure that she reached there safely. None of her children were in the capacity to drive.

"I'm so sorry for your loss." Josephine hugged Millicent who still could barely believe the news. Anthony also offered his condolences and with an engaging look to his son, he left with his wife.

After they left, the siblings broke the dam of tears again.

"She was the best." Millicent said.

"She was."

"She really was."

At night, when she returned back home, Manuela and Tamara kept watch of her with Jace's instruction and under their own disquietude. The night was spent with her in the middle of the sitting room where they had prepped makeshift beds while they all shared stories of their grandmothers whom they knew.

"Though she gave up the ghost, she wants to leave us with happiness, so we'll do as she wishes."

One week later, she was in her family home in her room, smiling wistfully at her face that Tamara had done a while ago. She dragged her hand down the ombre blue and gold woven Kente dress. It was an off shoulder whose sleeves were designed in a curly flowery fashion; it moderately plunged down to her chest barely giving a view of her breasts but leaving the imagination wild, and a brown body net covered the plunge up to fit as a round neck. The bodice was a light corset that comfortably did not reveal its nature with a cross tie at the back. Its color ranged in gradient fills of aqua blue, pink and gold with blue and gold pearls lining the upper body. The rest of the Kente pattern was left as a trail behind her - not too long. She looked nothing short of regal and beautiful.

Millicent felt dizzy for a short while and when she refocused, her friends were around her all wearing their blue and gold glittering dresses. They were all about ten, including Tamara who had agreed to be part of the party on a short notice.

"You look so beautiful our ayeforo." Asantewaa wrapped an arm around her friend and beamed at her beauty.

"Of course, my daughter is as beautiful as the sun." She turned around and saw her mother dressed and her eyes welling. Regina was happy that her daughter had been given to a man worthy of her.

"Let me speak blessings over you, Aba." She took the hands of her daughter who was smiling in hers as her friends gathered around in agreement. Laying hands around each other, they prayed for their friend who had found a new path to her life, some hoping that they would be the next and others sharing their happiness that they had found through their own marriage. Tamara was not used to such an audience around a bride during a wedding, but she was genuinely warmed by their presence.

"Are you ready?" Manuela asked after her mother stepped out to make their arrival known.

"I think so. I'm so nervous. What if I trip and fall?" The girls snickered.

"We'll be right behind you and will even fake a fall to make it look like there was something that caused it." She chuckled at Mawusi's words, but the truth was she had been feeling sick since the previous day and was having a few dizzy spells. Nonetheless, she picked up her gold fan and made her way out with her bridal procession.

The music buzzed through as she danced her way through the crowd of people who were seated around with excitement, wearing contagious smiles while she trudged through to find her soon to be husband. And there he sat, his feet tapping the ground anxiously, wrapped in a similar color of cloth with the rest of the family next to him. When he raised his head he saw her dancing majestically to him and her beauty and radiance carried him to his feet and his eyes stayed glued to hers which were glittering even from a distance, her pearly teeth describing her ecstasy.

Millicent felt energized as soon as he raised his meteor gray-blue eyes to her. His pink lips stretched and she could feel the titillation run through the length of his magnificent body as he dragged his eyes down her entire body. When she reached him, they were hardly able to keep their eyes off each other, barely hearing what transpired till they were officially engaged.

After the ceremony, they went inside to eat the food that had been prepared but Millicent felt even more frail and tired. Jace noticed and carefully held her, leaning in to inquire.

"What's wrong baby?"

"I feel a little uncomfortable, but I think it is from the stress and wedding jitters." His eyes narrowed in worry, and he rubbed her hand which she held gently.

"Are you sure?" She smiled timidly and nodded. He watched her a little longer, unconvinced.

"How do you feel after finally paying the dowry?" She beamed when she felt his excitement.

"Like I own the freaking entire world." Millicent giggled when he brushed a kiss on her cheek and peppered it discreetly along her face and to her covered neck. He had indirectly called her his world.

When the food was placed on the table in front of them, she felt herself being appalled by the aroma. Jace picked up the food and tried to feed her but she lurched subtly, feeling nauseous. She brought the fan to her mouth and shook her head at the food Jace was bringing.

"Little M, you have to eat."

Millicent stilled, going silent and blocking out all the noise from the room when it dawned on her what she could be facing. She couldn't believe it.

"It can't be!" She whispered in disbelief looking at Jace with wide eyes and he only sat watching inquisitively.

CHAPTER 36

Jace's eyelids squeezed together when he saw her frightened state and her lips silently moving. He reached out to grab her shoulders and her slightly hooded eyes widened when he closed his fingers around it. His own face showed a little anguish at the way she was disoriented next to him. He gently cupped her face with one hand as the music and dance continued to ensue around them.

"What's wrong, baby?" Millicent blinked at the question and took in a rugged breath before forcing out a smile. She was going to enjoy the day before thinking about all the possible scenarios that were currently running through her head.

She smiled and spoke sweetly, the usual shine in her eyes currently dimming which Jace could see. "Nothing. I just thought of something silly." He did not want to push her into speaking what she was not ready to.

Millicent denying everything, made sure to enjoy her last moments as a spinster in bliss but as the minutes trickled down and the day was nearing its, the disquietude her previous discovery brought spiked in the pit of her stomach. Manuela caught her gaze as she left final regards to the guests who were leaving and she could immediately tell there was something wrong with her friend.

And if anything could further sour her mood, Jace was not going to be around her for the rest of the night. The said man himself was extremely displeased as he held her in his arms and she basked in his smell and warmth that surrounded her.

"I can't believe they are separating us for this long." He grumbled holding her delicately while still being able to feel all the right dips of her body in the glamorous dress.

"I know. I already miss you." Jace mischievously leaned back and eyed her with twinkling eyes. He was happy to see her good humor back and yet the fact remained that she was not totally alright.

"I knew that you couldn't resist my charm!" Millicent scoffed playfully.

"Considering that you are literally begging for me to be walking down an aisle in a gown right now, I would say it is the opposite way." They both grinned and unable to contain herself, she leaned forward to drop a rather intimate and suggestive kiss at the corner of his mouth. She heard his sharp intake of breath and felt his hand that was curled around her waist tighten. She pulled back after a minute and smirked at his dumbfounded look.

"I'll see you tomorrow, darling." He was brought out of his delightfully stupefied state when a knock resounded in her room. Manuela and Sean stepped in both laughing and still swaying to the music.

"Okay, man. Time for you to be separated. I'm loving this culture. They make both of you suffer before the wedding." Manuela slapped him on the back of his head as Millicent shook hers at Sean.

"Technically, they can meet but he cannot see her in her gown. Except now none of us can trust them as they are the definition of pranks and fake plans." The couple grinned as they both discreetly looked at each other with thoughts of their journey flanking their minds.

Sean was able to pull a reluctant Jace out and Millicent collapsed on her bed placing her head in both hands. She felt the presence of Manuela in front of her and she looked up to see her friend's worried gaze. Manuela gently clasped Millicent's hands in hers, waiting patiently till the latter had the courage to speak.

"Ella, I think I may need a pregnancy test kit." There was no judgment in her friend's eyes as she smiled at her. For such a religious home as theirs, Millicent thought it was going to be difficult to tell her friend the truth. However, since university, the girl had been her partner in crime. She opened her eyes when she felt her hair being smoothed.

Manuela smiled.

"I'm right here and thankfully so is that crazy cousin of mine." A bubbling laughter burst out from Millicent's chest just as her friend giggled and she threw her hands around her in a hug.

"Thank you, Ella."

"Do you want to let Auntie Regina know?" Millicent shook her head in denial. "Okay, stay here and I'll go get the kit. I'm sure they'll come up to check on you soon so I'll text when I'm coming."

True to Manuela's guess, about five minutes after she left Regina and Josephine were in her room to check on her. They had a joyous contagious air around them because as far as they knew, their children were already married with all the customary rites being fulfilled, yet as Christians, they needed the approval of their churches to bless the matrimony. Once they were satisfied that nothing was amiss with their daughter, they left with a final promise.

"Aba, I'll bring you food. I know you didn't eat out there." With that Regina marched out.

Twenty minutes later, she was hiding her face in the curve of Manuela's neck as they awaited the results.

"It's time, Mimi."

"No, check it first." Millicent's eyes were closed as she spoke these words. She heard Manuela sigh and the next second her mouth dropped open with uncontrollable laughter as her friend tickled her. Once she opened her eyes, the test kit was right in front of her and what she saw caused her to draw in a sharp breath. Her eyes found Manuela's twinkling eyes as hers pooled with tears.

"I'm going to be a mother." Her friend's head bobbed in excitement.

"Yes, and I'm going to be an aunt - the coolest of all time." Manuela smugly proclaimed. Millicent's sob took her by surprise and she turned to find the disbelief on her face.

"There's a new life from me and Jace inside me, Ella. What do I do?" Her wide doe eyes were on her friend.

"First, you're going to have to calm down babe and you're going to take a calming bath. After that, we can think of the next steps.

Ensuring that her friend was calm, they moved to refresh themselves and were soon settled in her bed.

"I don't know how Jace is going to react." Millicent whispered from her place under the sheets where she was lying in a similar fashion on her side facing Manuela.

"He likes kids and I hate to raise his ego but you two are going to make the cutest children that I can spoil." Millicent lightly giggled and Manuela was pleased to see the change in her disposition.

"It's going to be another wedding gift for him, don't worry. And I'm sure Auntie Regi is going to be supportive. She may seem tough but she loves you immensely which is why we were chased out of the cooking area."

"Thank you, Ella, really." Manuela smiled at Millicent's solemn voice. She knew that if the roles were reversed her friend would have done much more than she was doing for her.

"You're my sister." She simply said. "Now sleep; you need to look good for the D-day tomorrow." Just then Millicent's phone rung and she checked the caller to see it was her soon to be husband. And she answered and they spoke late into the night, talking about sweet nothings till Manuela roused from her light sleep and grabbed the phone from her friend.

"Go away Jace. If you want your bride to be present for your wedding, go to bed." Millicent slowly chuckled and turned silent when the line shut and her friend bid her goodnight. Unbeknownst to Manuela, she was jittery, shameful and fearing what was to come the following day. She didn't know whether to carry her pregnancy as a secret or tell the truth and she was not feeling right to wear the snowy wedding gown that was meant to symbolize purity. She almost jumped when her friend's hand circled her.

"Sleep, Mimi." And with that command, she allowed herself to finally succumb to the darkness.

Somewhere in the early morning of the following day, there was chaos ensuing in the room where Millicent was getting ready. Regina was already heading to the room to check on her daughter when the commotion began. She increased her pace and just when she was on the landing, she saw a concerned Josephine with hastened steps rushing to the same place. Josephine decided to remain with her so that they could take care of the young girls together as the men were in her home.

"What's happening?" Josephine questioned looking at Regina.

"My sister, I have no idea. These children want to damage my ears before I am ready." She pushed the door open and gasped at the scene.

Millicent sat on a chair crying, pushing away the wedding gown she was to wear.

"No, I don't think this fits me. It's too white and I don't deserve to wear it." Everyone in the room was confused as she repeated the words again. Manuela tried to hold her still but her friend was drifting away with the jitters and the weight of their new discovery from yesterday. And it didn't help that she had awoken from some sort of nightmare somewhere within the night.

"Aba! Aba, what is wrong?" Her daughter whipped her face to the highly distressed mother and she fled into her mother's arms.

"Ma, it's too white, I can't wear it." And somehow, those words made the perfect sense to Regina and when she turned to look at Josephine, she found the same understanding on her face. That whiteness of a wedding gown symbolized the purity of a woman who had not yet been intimate with a man and if Millicent was freaking out because of that then there was only one explanation.

Josephine ushered the entourage in the room out and left the mother with her daughter.

"What happened Aba?" Regina's soft voice questioned as she tried to wipe the spilling tears away.

Millicent had already decided to confide in her mother as the guilt of her immorality as per customs and her faith dragged her into a sinking hole. She took a staggering breath and tried to keep her eyes on her mother as she brokenly whispered the truth.

"I'm pregnant."

It was silent for a while before her mother spoke. "And so what?"

Millicent's head shot up with incredulity to look at her mother.

"Aba and so what? I can see that you never meant for this to happen. I myself permitted you to stay with a man before verifying your marriage status. If anyone is to blame then it is me. You have been one of the purest souls I know and this did not in any way take that away. You've always been obedient, loving the Lord and His will and I know even He does not hate you. No one despises you. You are not less of a woman than you were when you were not pregnant. Yes, it was not right but you know that now. We're not ashamed of this new addition and we consider him as a gift so wear that gown with pride and walk to your husband."

Millicent released a sob and hung onto every word her mother had uttered. She had just felt how unworthy some women felt after they felt they had wronged every entity out there. It was a bitter feeling that she wished no one felt, especially to single mothers. This was how some mothers began to despise their children and she was glad she had the best people around to slap wisdom into her.

So she got dressed with a jollier sense and was bursting in anticipation as she sat in the backseat of the decorated car with her best friend.

"I can't believe you are getting married before me."

"Oh stop that. I can smell yours from the corner of the road and don't bother denying what is happening with Aseda!" Millicent was waiting for Manuela to divulge the news but it seemed she had stepped on it first. Manuela shyly turned her gaze from her dazzling friend. The make up looked so natural on her and her bronze skin looked shiny and polished in the luxurious white wedding gown.

"Today is about you, Mimi." Millicent was going to answer when a harsh break of their car almost jostled both girls forward causing their heads to bump into the air in front of them. There was a curse from the driver's seat and a quick apology.

She felt Manuela grab onto her right hand tightly. She tried to crane her neck around but only saw multiple cars with tall, intimidating men in black ahead of them.

CHAPTER 37

There was an anxious air around the men dressed in neat suits as they slowly took their spots. Jace was accompanied by Sean into the building of the church and his father walked up to him as they took their position in front of the church waiting for the bride to arrive. He smiled when his father stepped down as if walking to his seat but then turned momentarily to his son and placed an affectionate hand on his son's shoulder. Sean looked around the interior of the building and at the numerous people gathered in the vicinity dressed in ostentatious outfits with a merry buzz among them as they awaited the highlight of the ceremony.

"I never thought I'd see the day you would willingly settle down." One side of Jace's lip twitched, an action that hid a lot of nervous energy while Sean tuned in to the conversation and grinned knowingly in response.

"Trust me dad, I never knew this day would come." His eyes glinted and they turned to gaze at the entrance longingly.

"Never knew someone could snug him, Anthony." The men smiled reminiscing the old days and with an encouraging tap, Anthony conveyed his acceptance through his eyes making his son's smile broaden.

"I'm sorry I ever thought of Gwen as an option." Jace's jaw clenched a little as people from their seats looked at the group in curiosity especially with handsome white men that some women thought they would have a chance befriending. His eyes dashed to the entrance that had been decorated again and he heaved out an impatient breath.

"They'll be here soon." Anthony teased his son and threw a meaningful gaze at Sean before stepping into his seat in the congregation.

Just as he sat, he felt his phone vibrate from within his suit's pocket. Jace watched as his father frowned and abruptly stood. His heart rate spiked and he watched the concerned look take over Sean's face. They both knew that nothing took Anthony Elrod by surprise unless it was absolutely alarming. His face composed the look he had as he threw a quick glance at the men who were up and waiting for the arrival of the bridal team which was due about five minutes ago and walked back and out of the exit of the church. Jace panicked but looked at the people who were smiling and waiting and reminded himself that Millicent was coming with her brothers.

"I'm sure they are fine and are going to arrive soon. I never knew you could get jitters too." Sean tried to alleviate both their worries as his blue eyes darkened and shot a hot and disturbed look at the entrance himself. He forced his hand down when it tried to run through his neatly styled hair in worry.

Jace was just about to step off his place when a calm looking Anthony walked back in with his communicative gaze trained on his son. The look caused both men to relax in understanding as it screamed one thing. It's okay. Whatever happened is under control. It's going to be a good day.

"That was such a weird encounter and it has made us a little late." Manuela commented from Millicent's side as she also pondered on the strange event that took place just a few minutes ago. Those men looked like bodyguards but no one was allowed to leave the car as instructed by their driver who had looked to be on edge. He worked for Anthony and Millicent tended to listen to the father of her husband to be as his knowledge she had come to know surpassed theirs in ways beyond comprehension. Her mother and brothers who were driving behind her had been alarmed by the incident and were getting antsy they had been held back by Josephine who was in there with them.

She turned to her friend and spoke through her eyes turning them to the driver. "Hey Travis, what was that about back there?"

The man looked up through the mirror in front of him with a grim look. "It was nothing, miss, there was just some nuisance who didn't seem to know how to drive. Some of Mr. Elrod's guards cleared the road."

The girls turned to each other with raised brows. "Oh, I see." Millicent responded and eased her mind from all the nerves that threatened to drown her. She felt Manuela's hand rub her hand. She couldn't help but think that she saw someone being grabbed by some of the men like he was being arrested.

"Did you see?" Manuela's face which was tight with apprehension turned to her friend who had whispered to her but smiled when she caught her eyes.

"I think whatever it was is under control. You'll be walking down the aisle soon." The reminder caused Millicent's breath to stutter as Manuela also tried to put her friend's mind to ease - at the moment any kind of stress was certain to be detrimental to her health. As a matter of fact, Millicent was excited and at the same time a bundle of wrecked nerves awaiting without decorum to see his face. Jace. A shy smile took over her features.

"Oh gosh, look at that." Manuela teased as she admired how the white gown radiated her beauty even more. She doubted her cousin would be fine as a man when he set his eyes on his bride. "I still can't believe that he stayed up with you last night just to read you a book."

Millicent coyly watched her carefully manicured nails at the discovery Manuela had made when she had snatched her phone from her hand to hear Jace's voice from his end continuing the chapter of Anna Karenina as they religiously did.

"It's not just any book." She murmured which her friend could not hear. She cast a quick glance to see the gleam on their driver's face as he got a glimpse of the love life between his boss and his love. Before they could expand on the topic, they had already pulled into the premises of the church. Millicent's eyes turned wide and she looked at her friend in panic.

"Mimi, darling, we're right here. The man you love is impatiently waiting for you but just let us know whenever you are ready and we'll go with you. You are such a beautiful bride." Their eyes turned glossy and they hugged. They heard the voices of her family as they flunked the decorated expensive car.

"Just don't take too long which could cause Pastor Francis to use us in his preaching next week." They laughed at the thought of the older man and sure enough he had walked out to poke his head around the bridal entourage.

"Speak of the devil." Manuela turned and dropped the veil over her face, properly hiding it from view now.

Just like that she had stepped out in her carefully made dress, her best friend beside her and was hugged by her mother and Josephine who stood around to make sure that she was okay and in safe hands before making their way in. Soon Asantewaa, Shirley and Mawusi who were a part of her bridesmaids stepped out in their tailored dresses to arrange themselves behind their friend. The excitement was tangible among them.

Beside her, Max and Josh flanked her. Their solemn promise was to walk her to the altar where her husband would be waiting because they were without a doubt her fathers. She tried to quell the emotions that were increasingly attacking her.

"You've grown well, Aba. I'm sure dad is proud wherever he is watching you from." Millicent, finally unable to hold back, lightly choked on her tears. She heard a slap and turned back to see Manuela looking at Josh with an annoyed expression.

"You were not supposed to make her cry." He lifted his hands in surrender and they all chuckled in humor.

Millicent whined when Max decided to pinch her cheeks with the veil. When she glared at him he only smiled sweetly.

"Max! Go get a woman and stop worrying me." he scrunched his face in distaste but she knew it would take a while before she would see Max settled. He was obsessed with making sure that his wife was in the best condition with him so he wanted to be maximally prepared before starting a family. She inwardly smiled at the thought.

"What? This might be the last time that I can worry you like this." She watched him with a deadpan look, reminding him that he was just pulling both their legs. Millicent said it so that he knew that she was privy to the knowledge.

"We both know that that is a lie. You love torturing me."

"Who me? Whichever ghost disturbs your beauty sleep?" They both grinned. Max's gaze took on a solemn front as he stared at his sister. He could hardly believe that she was going to start her own family when he had seen her young and continue to grow up.

"Your obsession with ghosts is questionable." He still looked on with his calmed face. "I'm going to be right here, Max. Maybe across the continent for sometime but still here." Max smiled and threw his arm lightly around her shoulder. Her brothers had always been openly affectionate with her. They were broken apart by the music from the church.

"Come on kids, it's time." Josh smiled when he caught the offended look on both their faces.

When they crossed the threshold of the entrance, Millicent's heart skipped slightly looking at the heartachingly handsome man who was waiting for her. Jace sucked in a sharp breath, his eyes glued on the magnificently glorious woman who seemed to be walking in the midst of a regal host of protectors toward him. She looked enchanting, so snowy in the gown that accentuated every part of her which was able to leave your imagination wild and restless like he was. He felt that he could finally breathe properly after seeing her. Though her face was shielded from his, he saw it as her lips stretched upon seeing him. He felt his hands shake as she neared. His eyes could not leave her. His little M. It felt too surreal for him to even smile well and finally she was a hair's breadth from him.

"Wow." Was the only word the only breathy sentence he could speak when her brothers entrusted her to him. His eyes never strayed as they continued with the entire ceremony, not when he said his vows nor when he put the ring on her finger finally claiming her and neither did her eyes.

They danced; they were merry in their actions and in their hearts but neither could wait to be alone where they wished to be.

When they finally stood alone at night in their bedroom, in a house he had surprisingly gotten, he watched her with dark, hooded eyes which made her squirm in awareness and her grinned in pride. Taking a step forward, Jace saw Millicent's chest in her new dress expand and fall heavily as she watched him in a daze. He stopped directly in front of her and watched his wife struggle to contain herself from the wild emotions he was evoking. He could watch her for a lifetime and never get tired. He dragged his eyes from the sole of her feet and when he reached her eyes, he saw them burning with the flames he had trailed on her skin.

"What are you thinking?" Millicent's small voice squeaked in nervousness. She saw his throat move heavily as he gulped. He was just as nervous if not more. His eyes dragged down to her skin and the material that clung to her.

"That I want to rip this dress off you right now and act on my thoughts." Millicent swayed at the admission. She had a firm sultry look as she responded with no inhibition.

"It's your right as my husband and my acceptance of you." When he caught her words, he wasted no time and caused all that covered them to fly around the room as they got entangled with the bedsheets.

He loved her like he was meant to.

Chapter 38

Millicent sat up in the bed where the warmth of her husband huddled around her. Her eyes pushed together for a while and she turned to see Jace on his stomach, his hand still possessively holding her even though they had slipped as she sat up. He was dressed just as she was because they had woken up earlier and he had surprisingly made a good breakfast for them. Now as she was awoken from her slumber, her mind slipped back to the task at hand. How to reveal what she had discovered.

Her hand unconsciously slipped toward his mop of hair that she had suddenly come to love. They looked so unruly when they were untamed and especially after she had abused them a little too much. She smiled as his nose twitched when she pushed the hair that covered his face. With another last glance she got out of the bed when a plan formulated in her mind. Millicent walked to the bathroom and retrieved whatever she needed before coming back and settling next to Jace trying her best to seek as much of the safety and warmth he provided her.

"Where did you go?" Her heart stuttered at his rough voice. Her eyes traveled to him but his eyes were still closed. The hand tightening on her waist reminded her of the question she had failed to reply as she got lost in him again.

"Hm, to the restroom." As she spoke, his blue-gray eyes that looked like the midnight skies glittering with stars after he woke up were revealed and focused on her bright brown ones. Her breath hitched as some memories flashed through her making her body heat up. It was no help when he traced his hand up to grab her neck, angle it and then latch his mouth in the open space he had created.

Jace pulled back to see her still held in the contentment of being showered with his love. "You left me all alone." He turned to check the time. "Wow, it's almost noon." He faced her to see that she was looking a little disturbed.

'What's wrong, sweetheart?"

Millicent lifted her eyes so that she could meet him and she greedily breathed in a calming breath, sitting up on the bed and smiled slightly when he did the same. For some reason, his movements were always in tune with hers and she had no idea whether it was intentional or just something that was Jace. She pushed herself forward and dropped a loving and chaste kiss on his lips but before she could pull back, he was drowning her in a more passionate one.

They broke apart and her eyes sparked at the sheer exuberance she found on his face. "I thought you wanted to know what was bothering me?" Jace lifted a brow at this. "You know if you start something it will be..." Millicent gestured with her head to the window in the large room, insinuating something being thrown out.

Jace sat up and held onto the air of seriousness that filtered through.

"Do you remember what happened in chapter 22 and 23 of part two of Anna Karenina?" She saw his brows scrunch together in focus.

"That's very specific, baby. But Anna had started the affair with Vronsky then." He saw her impressed look and suppressed a smug grin but she shook her head and that feeling evaporated.

"What else can you remember?"

"Baby, you never said we were going to have a pop quiz on your bedtime story." Millicent giggled when he whined about this.

"Well, if you don't want to answer, I may as well take my reward away." Her mouth stretched a pinch when his eyes caught a gleam and he sat up higher.

"A reward." Jace said in bubbling curiosity before proceeding to think about the story.

"Wait, wasn't that when she found out that she was pregnant?" He watched with an expectant look but his wife never responded. She sat back on her knees before holding his shoulders as leverage and leaning forward so her face was beside him as she spoke slowly into his ear that was next to her.

"If you were Vronsky at that moment, what would you do?" Jace blinked in surprise as a cloud of confusion settled on him.

"What do you... You're saying... What?" Millicent chuckled at his dumbfounded expression as she brought out the test kit she had grabbed and showed it to him.

Jace's trembling hands reached out to take the kit and he stared in amazement at the two lines. His gaping eyes and mouth struggled to focus on anything as Millicent gathered him into her hands for she had been anxious concerning because she feared how he would react. He was still staring in disbelief at the kit he was holding.

"You are pregnant? I'm going to be a father?" Millicent's eyes glistened with tears as she tightened her hold on him and nodded into the crook of his neck needing no words to convey how excited she felt about the journey ahead. Her neck was now in a gentle hold in the embrace as Jace pulled her back. She saw everything in his eyes - the excitement coupled with disbelief and his awe - as his meteor blue gray eyes traveled down to her stomach.

Jace placed a warm hand there and then lifted his head so she could see the broad grin plastered on his face and contagiously she mirrored that.

"Gosh I love you!" Jace announced as his eyes traced her face. "I'm going to love you and protect every family we make together." His hand that still was behind her neck dragged her forward as he captured her awaiting lips in hers. The kiss held no doubt but all the love the couple shared.

Just as they were drowning deeper, their doorbell went off. They both leaned away with questioning eyes.

"Isn't the flight late at night?" Millicent grumbled.

"I'm going to kill them if it's either Sean or Elle or Tamara." Millicent chuckled under her breath when she remembered events from the previous day. Jace held her up as she climbed off the bed.

"Did you see Tammy dance yesterday? She was having a blast." Millicent's intrigued voice spoke as he wrapped an arm almost protectively around her.

"I did. I'm glad they easily blended into the culture and enjoyed it." Millicent hummed in agreement.

When they opened the door, they were met with the face of a smiling Anthony.

"Dad?"

"Hello kids. I'm sorry to interrupt your very first official morning together. I just needed to have a word with you." Anthony spoke as they walked him into the house that Millicent had yet to fully see. This was as much of a surprise to her as it had been to her family who knew that she was going to be moving into the new, bigger house with her husband.

"What's going on uncle Anthony?" Millicent swallowed at the sharp glare she received at the name before she sheepishly smiled and corrected herself in a small voice. "Er, dad." A little smile of contentment settled on Anthony's face at that and a pleased Jace watched the interaction also wondering why his father had come around.

Anthony sat up and the air took a serious turn. "I'm sure you noticed that something did not seem right yesterday and I don't want to keep you in the dark. I didn't tell you yesterday because it was supposed to be filled with happiness." Anthony stopped and looked at the young ones who now sat a little stiffly in their seats. He saw their hands linked together and a small smile graced his lips.

"You were almost attacked by people sent by the Dumas. I sent my men with you so that was dissolved." He quickly added when Jace rushed to speak. "We have them in custody."

Jace released a breath and wrapped his arm around Millicent's shoulders. "The Dumas?"

"As you know, his kids are in jail. Their father was the orchestrator of this and has also been arrested but since there was no harm I doubt he'll be held there. This was also just to scare him."

Jace grinned an acknowledging appreciation to his father. The man does not take any threat to his family lightly. "Thank you dad."

"Thank you." Millicent knew that the situation could have a wrong turn if Anthony did not have his foresight into situations.

"You're family honey. We Elrods protect our family till our last breath. And don't worry, Dumas cannot do anything. He's a businessman who is always scared of offending and this he knows was just a warning.

"Especially after that drop in his stock market." Anthony spoke undertone so they did not hear him. He looked at Jace and Millicent and found them lost in some eye contest. Anthony cleared his throat with an amused tone and they slipped out of it.

"I'm not going to take more of your time. I just wanted to assuage any worries you might have had." As he stood up, Millicent walked to him and embraced him as did Jace.

"See you at eight." Anthony greeted before entering his awaiting car.

"You!" Millicent attacked her husband when they were all alone.

"Me?" Jace playfully questioned as she caught him and trapped him between herself and a wall. He smiled at the height difference. Millicent's head tilted back slightly to catch his face.

"Yes, you. How does everyone know where we are going when I, your wife, has no idea where my honeymoon is going to be?" Jace just grinned at her. She was so bad with surprises. His thoughts got locked when her lips were suddenly at the base of his neck. She traced it around never really attaching to his skin as he had been awaiting.

"Little M." Jace's voice strained out but Millicent took a step back with a smile. He tried to reach out but she escaped his hold.

"Please tell me." She asked in a sweet voice which tormented him as he watched her twinkling orbs.

"Urgh, little M, this was supposed to be a surprise." He groaned in exasperation and humor at the woman that had him wrapped around her finger.

"What if you ship me off somewhere?"

"Ha! You should trust me to lead you to greener pastures, baby." Millicent brightened when she recognized the word from their devotion in the early morning.

"Oh!" His face was amused at her expense and he stretched out his hand asking her to follow him.

"No way! Switzerland? You remembered." Of course he did. Jace recognized and put everything she said to heart, always eager to make sure she was happy. Millicent was rarely discomposed and it pleased him that he had been able to surprise her like this. He was delightfully tackled into a hug and before long they were wrapped in themselves.

"I can't believe my feet are touching the land of Switzerland. It's even more beautiful than I've seen." Jace just focused on the shining skin and demeanor of his wife as they sat in the classy train.

"It looks almost fake."

"You remember we were in a fake relationship before we saw reality." She turned her eyes from the scenery and cheekily grinned.

"To think that you were using me as much as I was using you."

"I think I was intrigued with you from the very first time which is why I agreed to your proposition." His hand cupped her face. "You were such a horrible actress, baby. No offense."

"Is that so?" She found herself lost while she was enraptured by his handsome look that had incarcerated her from the very beginning. Jace hummed leaning forward. He felt his heart tastefully squeeze at her beauty, disbelieving that he had such a woman in his life to spend eternity with.

"I love you." Millicent grinned at the confession that she currently heard every minute or so. Her heart was full as she stared at the token of their real union on her finger. The ring was beautiful.

"I love you."

"What's going to be our next bedtime story, darling?" But Jace ignored the question and sent her to bliss as he captured her in an embrace of love.

The dowry had now been fully paid and they could spend the years without worries.

Epilogue

Regina emerged from her room draped in multiple layers of clothing and yet she appeared to still be shivering. She heard a laugh which caused her to raise her head to catch her daughter's shoulders shaking in mirth.

"Herh, Aba, this coldness is not a joke."

"Ma, you should have told me, Jace would have turned the heater on today. The temperatures have weirdly dropped." Her mother frowned at the suggestion.

"Eh, take a picture of me in the broni's clothes." Millicent chuckled and picked up her phone, taking a picture of her mother.

"Jace Kwaku Asante Elrod!" Anthony, who sat next to Millicent and was chatting with her, startled at his wife's voice. "I told you that it was for Millicent. Now put it down and send it to her."

Millicent hid a smile knowing that the fight was over food.

"He always gets into trouble with food and you would think he would learn better." Anthony muttered to which Millicent snickered. She supported her protruded tummy by securing her hand at her back before walking to her mother who was slightly shivering to set her jacket right and an additional layer of fur cover over her. It was a little early in March and the temperatures had dropped considerably in New York where they had stopped by to spend the past month at a villa the family owned. It was different from the warmth that California provided them. They had held her grandmother's funeral before she had worked on the transfer to work in the US with Jace.

"Okay, stand this way." Millicent smiled in humor when her mother did a completely different pose than she had been told. "No the other way."

"Oh leave me and let me do my thing. You think you young people are the only ones that have swag. Give me my two." Regina lifted two fingers to complement the pose as she had seen a lot of the younger generation do.

Millicent choked on a laugh and she heard Anthony let out a breathy laugh. Behind her he was correcting Regina to lift her index finger instead of her middle finger being paired with her ring finger. Millicent peeked back when her mother seemed to fidget while trying to follow the instructions of someone else and she turned to see Anthony's fingers wiggling. Unable to control her amusement, she slightly bent over and doubled in laughter.

"I hear laughter." She heard Jace's slightly amused voice but that took a noticeable turn when he saw his wife standing instead of relaxing.

"Little M, why are you standing? You are supposed to be resting which is why we are in this getaway villa." He could feel the frown before it started to form. Her dark brows contoured on her face and they made it look like her eyes had pushed up beyond their bounds. Her eyes blazed and Anthony shook his head with a smile while rising to go find his own wife.

"I am perfectly fine Jace. I've been resting for the past month and that is boring. I love your massage though." His face flashed with a smile when she added the last sentence after a moment of thought. He normally wouldn't tell her what to do but she would be due any moment.

"Ah love is sweet but my dear Jace, a mother is the strongest person in the world." Regina reminded him. She would have been worried but it was true that Millicent had been in bed for a good amount of the previous month and she needed to work her muscles a little now that she would be delivering any day from the present.

Millicent's face scrunched up as the sudden pain that had been hitting her since morning increased in intensity. Jace who was watching her rushed to her side at the look on her face and gently grabbed onto her.

"What's wrong, love?" She tried to speak but a sharper wave of pain hit her and this time she did scream. Footsteps rushed from all around her and multiple worried looks were in her face though the two mothers seemed calmer than the men.

"Little M?" Jace asked worriedly and she scrunched her face again at the discomfort that settled at her lower abdomen.

"I've been having some pains but they were so light at the beginning that I thought it was nothing. They are getting sharper now." She lightly flinched when she saw the disappointing look on Jace. He always wanted to know if there was anything wrong with her but she had been distracted with the fun during the day.

Millicent felt a wetness pool under her and her eyes widened in alarm.

"What?" Her mother questioned carefully. Their hauntingly similar faces with unique expressions of concern and horror were visible.

"I think my water broke." Everyone was stunned into silence and no one moved. Anthony sucked a breath and turned to see his son's ashened face with worry.

Josephine snapped out of her daze first and slapped her son on the back.

"Hurry and go get the car!" He shook his head and stepped around to find the stuff still in his confounded state. He didn't think that it was going to happen so soon - that the head of a baby was going to make the love of his love scream in pain. His father had filled him in on the horror stories he faced when his mother was birthing him. Jace shuddered as he picked the car keys. He loved his baby but he met his woman first. I'll protect both of them.

"Auntie Regi, I'll grab the bag after you. The way the contractions started earlier in the day, I don't think it will be long before we hear the new cry so let's hurry." Josephine said to Regina who nodded in agreement and hurried along.

"Is it scary?" Millicent whispered to her mom.

"Very but your scare at harming your baby by not pushing is the most prevalent so it's going to be okay." She nodded.

Two hours later she was pushing out her child while Jace whispered sweet words in her ears. When the doctor said she saw the head of the baby, Jace stood up even more confused at what was happening in the delivery room. He held the extremely warm hands of his wife and looked at her concentrated face in wonder.

Her light brown eyes caught his eyes in question as he tilted his head analyzing her.

"What is it, Kwaku?" There it was. She always used this name when she was displeased about something. But he was still at sea nonetheless.

"Why aren't you screaming?" Millicent closed her eyes in disbelief and squeezed his hand in pain as the nurses and doctor laughed at his question. She found herself laughing too.

"What, you want me to curse you and your generation out? In as much as your seed fertilized mine, I consented and cursing you would be cursing our child." She concentrated and pushed again after her words came out in short pants. "Plus, I need that energy to give birth rather than waste it screaming insults on you."

"Your wife is a strong woman." Jace's blue-gray eyes twinkled with pride as he finally moved closer to kiss her as she pushed once again and then wiped her sweat with the cleaner the nurse handed him.

"I know." As soon as he said that, Millicent slumped and smiled with relief. Before he could analyze the action further, his body was alerted with the sound of cries in the room. He stood and turned to where Millicent was watching in awe as a nurse walked forward with a tiny baby which was placed on Millicent.

She felt her baby and both she and her child instantly calmed. The feeling of being a mother.

"Congratulations, you have a beautiful baby girl." The tears pressed down her face when the child blinked open her eyes which made both Millicent and Jace gasp. She had her father's eyes without a doubt. The stormy blue eyes stared at her and moved to Jace as her little squeak filled the room.

"I think we should call our second girl Zara. She fits..." Millicent said. Jace completed the second name they had debated if their child was a girl as they had not bothered to find out the sex of the baby.

"Sienna Ewuradjoa Elrod." He felt the tears in his eyes as he spoke adoringly looking at the tiny baby.

And suddenly, Jace saw a pretty light skinned child running in an open field with skin that reflected the bronze of Millicent running to him with a toothy grin. Her curly pigtails bouncing off their hold cutely with arms wide open as her white dress twirled with the wind and he saw her mouth open as she screamed a word looking back to see Millicent playfully chase her.

"Daddy!" Instant happiness blossomed and though this seemed like a limbo of a dream, he heard that soothing childlike voice scream in the hospital room like a vision.

"Daddy!" It was the perfect ending for him as he watched his new family in tears.